ADVANCE PRAISE FOR *Lady Lazarus* OF *LADY LAZARUS*

"Intriguing, beautiful, and impossible to put down."

—Meljean Brook, *USA Today* bestselling author
of The Guardians series

"Lyrical, haunting, and full of a dark, sublime beauty, *Lady Lazarus* is simply stunning."

—Nalini Singh, *New York Times* bestselling author
of *Blaze of Memory*

"Michele Lang's *Lady Lazarus* is a beautifully written tale set in a complex, alternate Nazi Europe. The characters are dark and well developed, and the author is a talented storyteller."

—Faith Hunter, author of the Rogue Mage series

"*Lady Lazarus* is brilliantly original and delicious to read. It's the sort of book that keeps you up all night and leaves you wanting more."

—Diana Pharaoh Francis, author of *Bitter Night*

"A fascinating story and concept—a daughter of the Lazarus bloodline capable of rising from the dead. Filled with adventure, imbued with history, and beautifully told. Wish I had thought of it."

—Sunny, bestselling author of *Lucinda, Dangerously*

BOOKS BY MICHELE LANG

Netherwood

Lady Lazarus*
Dark Victory* (coming in 2011)

*A TOR BOOK

Lady Lazarus

Michele Lang

TOR®

A TOM DOHERTY ASSOCIATES BOOK
NEW YORK

LADY LAZARUS

Copyright © 2010 by Michele Lang

Edited by James Frenkel

A Tor Book
Published by Tom Doherty Associates, LLC
175 Fifth Avenue
New York, NY 10010

www.tor-forge.com

Tor® is a registered trademark of Tom Doherty Associates, LLC.

ISBN 978-0-7653-2317-0

First Edition: September 2010

Printed in the United States of America

0 9 8 7 6 5 4 3 2 1

In loving memory of my grandmother, Irene Weber

"Did we not throw three men, bound, into the midst of the fire?" They answered and said unto the King, " 'Surely, O King.' He answered and said, 'Lo, I see four men loose walking in the midst of the fire, and they have no hurt; and the form of the fourth is like an angel.' "

—Daniel 3:24–25

ACKNOWLEDGMENTS

I am grateful for the advice and encouragement of Juliet Blackett, Amy Lau, Bianca D'Arc, Chris Keeslar, Monika Lahiri, Michelle Rowen, Jackie Kessler, Charlene Teglia, Jill Myles, Megan Crane, and many more friends and readers who encouraged me along the way. Needless to say, I am solely responsible for all historical inaccuracies and unintentional blasphemies.

My deepest gratitude to my grandparents, those who survived the Holocaust and those who didn't. Love and thanks to my mother and father, Judith and Michael Lang, who survived the unspeakable and gave me life. Thank you to my brother, Henry, and to my sister-in-law, Lana, who encouraged me, supported me, and dared me to write this book.

My love and thanks to my mother- and father-in-law, Gerald and Seena Palter, for their beautiful outlook on life, their unwavering love and support, and their superb grandchild-watching skills.

I have been very fortunate for the help and skill of my wonderful agent, Lucienne Diver, who believed in me and this book and never gave up on either of us. She found the perfect editor for this book, James Frenkel—many thanks for being this book's champion. Thanks also to my sharp-eyed copyeditor, Christina MacDonald, who caught and corrected various factual and continuity errors.

Last and foremost, my husband, Steven Palter, has endured my obsession with Magda Lazarus and her many incarnations since at least 1994, and he has been a loving husband, a discerning, careful first reader, and a constant inspiration. For this and for so much more, I am grateful beyond my ability to express. To you, and to our sons, Joshua, Gabriel, and Sam—together, you are my greatest teachers. Thank you for everything.

Lady Lazarus

✳ Prologue ✳

I damned my soul in the summer of 1939. I did it for the noblest reasons, the best ones—to save the people I loved; to make a terrible wrong turn right. But still I am tormented by the thought that my sins overwhelmed my intentions and turned my noble sacrifices to dust even as I made them. Only time will tell if my desperate measures, in the end, were justified.

In my mind, that final summer is saturated with golden sunlight. My beloved home—gilded Budapest, the Paris on the Danube—glittered brilliantly in the sun, even blighted as it was by the stain of fascism. The cafés still buzzed with energy, the city still throbbed at night. My Budapest still lived.

And I felt at home there like no other place I have lived before or since. To me, a girl of only twenty, Budapest was the culmination of a life's dream of freedom. My family, originally from the northern mountain town of Tokaj, was drawn to Budapest's brilliant light at the end of the nineteenth century, and my father, a wine trader, eventually made his fortune.

Not even the depredations of Béla Kun's Bolshevik regime in 1919, followed by the genial fascist toad, that hypocrite Regent Horthy, not even an army of their small-minded followers could destroy the restless creativity of the city. I knew it was dangerous to be a Jew. But I had one secret advantage, and I clung to it for dear life.

I was a Lazarus. And the eldest daughter of an eldest daughter.

The city teemed with magical folk, living alongside the pure mortals. Vampires, dryads, dwarves; other, hidden, immortal beings—and the adepts, the sorcerers, necromancers, and witches. As for me, I am a Lazarus witch. My power is passed from mother to daughter, and has been so conveyed since time out of mind.

My mother, bless her vanished soul, tried her best to teach me the Lazarus creed and how to use the power I inherited, and the dangers such a power brings, but I was born rebellious. And when she died suddenly, my training was still unfinished. I preferred to haunt the cafés, debate Communism and literary theory with half-starved poets living on weak tea and rumballs, indulge in mad affairs of the mind and heart that in the end led absolutely nowhere. In short, I was a young fool, but a happy one.

The trouble crept up on all of us, a shadow that lengthened

over everything we knew. Horthy's regime was dreadful, but after the disaster of Béla Kun, we all believed we could survive the regent. So we, the Jews, kept our heads down and worked. And we, the witches, kept to our creed, respected the destructive potential of our powers and invoked them rarely. We told ourselves useful lies, that the trouble would soon pass. And a fragile balance held.

Such a state, balanced on lies, could not sustain itself for long. Despite this, when the end came, none of us were ready.

And now I hold my breath, my pen hovers over the paper before I write. How can I explain to you, a stranger, what has happened to me? At this pause in my earthly trials, I do not know which is better: to press forward and leave the past to die, or to commit my strange tale to paper.

Well do I know the power of words. In many instances, I am the only witness, the only one still living who knows of the great-hearted sacrifices of those who are now gone, the only one who can now remember. So: I write this story not to glorify the living, but to honor the dead.

The summer of '39 is seared into my mind, and lives on forever unchanged in my memory. Hitler had not yet invaded Poland, war had not yet exploded the world I had known into irredeemable shards. I was still a girl, the future still lay before me, indefinable, infinite with possibility.

I was still kissing-close to the people I loved most in the entire world. And simple love matters more than magic, treasure, or even the promise of eternal life. It is for love that I now set this strange tale into words.

Remember this as you read on, for though my story has its

triumphs, in the end it has always come back to two fundamental questions:

Who do you love?
Do you seek the darkness or the light?

✳ *I* ✳

The world I had known ended on a steamy Tuesday night in Budapest. It was so late that only the poets and vampires still remained at the café, and my employer and I sat at our usual table as the stranger from the east told his dreadful tale. I was surrounded by Art Nouveau stained glass and by giant brass hookahs imported from the Orient, but all I could see and taste was blood.

"You say that the Americans . . ." Bathory's voice trailed off, and for once he seemed completely at a loss. I watched him light an unfiltered cigarette with his absurd jewel-encrusted Zippo lighter; it was a clear sign that we were all in trouble, for Bathory only smoked in times of deepest strain.

I took refuge from the stranger's words in our familiar

surroundings. The Café Istanbul wrapped me in beloved, Levantine luxury. Inside the Ring Road, in the center of Budapest, the café catered to vampires, musicians, and wine merchants, an unlikely but nonetheless harmonious combination. It made for fruitful and prosperous encounters.

The man's voice shuddered in the mirrored, high-ceilinged room; fear rose from him in a stink. He stood before us in supplication, his hat in his hands, and the very chandeliers trembled as he spoke.

His words came in German, but haltingly, as if he had to translate the words in his head from another language before he formed them aloud. "Yes, the Americans. They have uncovered a weapon. A doomsday weapon. Whoever can claim it first will have the upper hand in the war that is to come. My people must have this weapon, or Stalin will kill us all. You must help us."

The stranger sounded like a madman. Bathory and I had entertained any number of desperate callers at our permanent table on the mezzanine of the café, and we heard many a tale of woe in that terrible year, 1939, but nothing yet as grim as this. As I replaced my demitasse, the delicate porcelain chattered a little too loudly against the saucer.

A glance at my beloved employer didn't help to calm my nerves. The count's piercing gaze pinned me to my seat. He expected me to do what I had always done for him: draw the truth out of this supplicant, as I had from every other mortal that sought his favors. My job was to lull them into doing my master's bidding, encourage them to do business with Bathory so that he could line his pockets and keep me in rumballs and off the streets. I was still innocent enough to believe the truth protected both the supplicants and me.

But the truth I now sensed in this strange, foreign man was volatile, unstable. If I brought his truth into the light, all of us could die in the explosion.

In 1939, I made my living as a servant of one who preyed on human fear in its many permutations. And though more frightful creatures existed in Budapest, Bathory was nightmare enough for most of our mortal visitors. As I now considered this man from the east, the stranger's fear tasted of bitterness. It was cloying and metallic on my tongue.

The man's fears did not originate with the sight of my employer, that much I could readily sense. Bathory scared me more than anything else in Budapest. But this stranger knew things that made Bathory seem tame.

I took another slow sip of Turkish coffee. As the warm liquid burned a pathway along the inside of my throat, I sent my witch's caress into the stranger's mind, and coaxed him into mastering his fear so he would stay.

The man sank into a cane-backed chair. He held his hat in his hands and balanced it on one knee. His whispers rose into the stuffy air above our heads like smoke, vanished into the early morning mist swirling outside on the terrace.

"Please help me," the stranger said in German. His diction was formal, his expression anguished.

Bathory leaned forward, his narrow, pale face reflecting the Istanbul's electric light like a trapped moon. "But of course. I am here to help. For a price." He caressed the bone china plate at the table's center. "May I offer you some refreshment? A rumball?"

The man cleared his throat, trembled. "No, thank you. No rumballs." He dragged his gaze away from my employer, and Bathory let him go. With wide eyes, the stranger stared at the gaunt young composer sleeping alone at the corner booth, his artist's plate of cold cuts all but untouched on the table next to him.

I riffled through the stranger's mind as gently as I could, leaving him to the café's pretty distractions as I worked. Flickering images, like an old silent movie—a pumping oil well, a black stallion trotting along a cobblestone street—moved through my mind and floated away.

"I didn't catch your name, sir," I said, my voice as silky and gentle as I could make it.

"Ziyad. Ziyad Juhuri."

"And you come from Stalin's land."

"Yes. At great danger to my people, I come."

He did not want to reveal his story; he wanted our help without too much exposure. But this Ziyad's secret was too dangerous to us to allow him to hide his origins. How could we know his mission would not endanger us?

"And how can my master assist you, sir?"

"Sir . . ." He addressed Bathory, not me. "I—I know what you are."

Bathory's spidery fingers crept along the cravat knotted at his bony throat. As he considered the stranger's words, Bathory's lips parted in a wide smile, revealing the rows of long, needlelike teeth. The man paled and clutched the edge of the table. I hummed under my breath, tightening the cord of the stranger's fear like a golden leash around his neck. He gasped in surprise, but I held fast. His heart surged like an engine, and then steadied as a thick despair spread through his veins.

Despair was an improvement. Ziyad straightened his tie, and I felt him relax, as he accepted the knowledge he spoke with a vampire, and that such encounters usually end badly for the human supplicant.

Now he and Count Bathory could do business. Bathory's face grew serene. "Yes, I am a Drinker, my friend." He let his statement linger like the smoke in the air between us as he took a long, languorous sip of his milky coffee. "But what will that do for you?"

The man watched in fascination as Bathory's long fingers dabbed at the corners of his mouth with a linen napkin. "I need help, from you and your . . . kind."

"All of us are in grave danger in these wretched days. In fact, those like my little assistant Magda who thrive in trouble are in a small minority." Bathory favored me with a fond little smile.

And how I treasured the old vampire's sincere approbation. Bathory had lived long, dapper in his antique silks and velvets, and many human assistants had served him faithfully and lived out their mortal days untouched by his fangs. He had once told me that I was his favorite protégée, and it pleased me mightily to believe him.

The stranger rallied his courage. "I am here to make arrangements to procure this superweapon immediately. My sources have revealed that an American has it."

This earned a raised eyebrow from Bathory. "Your sources? Call upon the American ambassador. You describe a matter for diplomacy, not for private profit, yes?"

The stranger shook his head. "No, my lord. Your guild

stretches around the world, Count Bathory, you are the only ambassador I need. I must move through, shall I say . . ."

"Unorthodox channels."

"Yes. And I would pay in prayer rugs or ready cash, pay a premium to succeed."

Bathory made a dismissive wave of the hand, though I caught the acquisitive sparkle in his narrow eyes. "My dear Magda here, the daughter of a brilliant businessman, can help you should you wish to engage in trade, sir. But that is no special favor."

The man's face clouded over, and he stroked his drooping mustache and scowled. "I do not come for fortune, or for trade."

I caressed the man's mind as he spoke, and I looked for his true desire. I saw blood, blood, children and women slaughtered in a mountainous place. Their deaths called to me as well as to him, and they demanded revenge. The stranger did not lie. He needed to reach the Americans, find the hidden magic, and kill his enemies before they killed him.

I tasted the metal of blood in my mouth, and I shuddered as I chewed on a lump of sugar to dull the bitterness of it. "Ah, I understand. You are only a messenger," I muttered, only realizing I had spoken aloud when the man turned and of his own volition met my gaze.

"We are all messengers," he said, and for the first time, the stranger smiled.

I took a deep breath and allowed myself the luxury of doing what I had learned never to do: speak honestly. "You may not live to see your message delivered."

His lips trembled with emotion as he played with the brim of his hat. "That is no matter. What matters is only that the message is received. Ah, you are a holy messenger to me, indeed, miss."

"Do not fear . . . we will help you, sir. We will."

Bathory interrupted our interchange with a low hiss, and I saw that I had exhausted his patience. He spoke in Hungarian, to hide the import of his rebuke from our supplicant. "You are *my* messenger, Magdalena Lazarus," he said, baring his fangs to make his point. "But you are only my messenger. Remember your place!"

I had learned to tolerate his periodic rages, understanding them for the symptoms of panic they were. Bathory, now landless nobility, desperately missed his portion of earth, swallowed up by Romania and the Treaty of Trianon in 1920. Without the comfort of his native soil, my poor count could not cope with the massive dislocations of history.

As for me, such chaos was my native state. That is why he relied on me, and why, no matter how much I angered him with my naïveté and rebelliousness, he kept me in his service. But we both knew I did not belong to him, no matter how much we both wished it were so. "I do not know my place, dear count. And that is why you love me."

With an effort, Count Bathory recovered himself, reverting to speaking German for the benefit of our visitor. "Magdalena Lazarus. You are stuffed like a goose with romantic notions and sentimental paradox. When you know what you are willing to die for, you will know what to live for. It is that simple."

Bathory's thin shoulders knotted together and he slouched, staring sullenly into the middle distance. "And unless you figure *that* out, Magda, your nonsense will get us all killed someday."

My face burned like fire. Given the fact that Bathory hovered in the undead shadows of a vampire's existence, his comment shouldn't have cut as deeply as it did. But what can I say? Twenty was young to carry the burdens I bore, but Bathory had no way of knowing my age or my burdens—I worked too hard to hide the secrets of my life from him.

I cleared my throat, smoothed my periwinkle silk skirt against the tops of my thighs. "Well, I haven't failed you yet, have I?"

I looked him full in the eye, and defied the hooded menace of his ancient gaze. He pursed his lips, studied me coolly as if I were a brood mare or a blood slave. "This man, unwillingly or not, brings war to our doorstep, make no mistake," he said. "Ready or not, I am afraid you will soon receive an education on how to die."

"So be it," I said. Part of me wanted to die: after all, to die and return was my heritage as a Lazarus witch. I wanted to choose the time and place of my death, too, but who gets to decree one's end like that? Even the most illustrious citizens of Budapest had to accept the mystery of death.

The man surprised us both by interrupting. "Forgive me for entangling you in my affairs. In the end, they will be yours, too, alas."

"It is too late already, dear sir," Bathory said. "We are here caught between Hitler and Stalin, a precarious passage indeed."

I inclined my head in deference to our visitor and dared a smile. "You bring us adventure as well as danger, Mr. Ziyad Juhuri. And that is good business for us, and good life experience for me."

I expected Bathory to jump on me again for opening my big mouth, but instead he looked past me. His eyebrows shot up, and he half stood and bowed to a shadow in the corner behind me, near the archway that led to the staircase. I blinked hard, shocked. Who could arrest Bathory's attention so and bring him to his feet?

A distracted smile played along his thin, curved lips. "My. Oh, my. Is that your sister in the archway, Magda? Why, she is lovely. No wonder you have kept her hidden away from me."

My heart pounded, and the knowledge that Bathory could hear the syncopated rhythm of my distress made it even harder to disguise. I stood up so fast I knocked my chair over, for at this time of night my sister was in mortal danger at the Café Istanbul.

But when I turned and saw the figure framed in the archway near Bathory's customary table, I realized matters were even worse than if my sister had come. No, it wasn't my sister. At least my sister Gisele was also a witch and had her own magic to protect her.

I licked my suddenly dry lips and forced myself to speak the truth. "Ah, no. That is my best friend, Count Bathory, from my girlhood days in Tokaj. Her name is Eva Farkas, and she is a silly and reckless girl, without even a drop of magic in her."

A girl with a talent for waltzing into danger with a smile dimpling her rounded cheeks and sparkling in her powder blue eyes. If I got her out of this alive, I was going to kill her.

Ziyad sighed. "Such beautiful girls, wandering alone by night. Both of you hurt the eyes to see."

Bathory laughed, the sound a dry, husky rustle of dead leaves. "Budapest is full of beautiful girls, sir. But beware, my friend . . . they are dangerous. Every last one."

I marched out of the café with my head high, but I was trembling so badly I stumbled on the cobblestones. Eva trailed behind me like a shadow. The mist from the Danube had risen in the night, and it obscured our feet as I stalked to the tram stop around the corner from the opera house on Adrássy Street.

We stopped beneath a streetlamp, the mist-wreathed lamplight glowing like a huge, hovering firefly. I caught my breath with some difficulty, my fear and anger still gathered around me like a second, darker mist.

Eva smiled her infuriatingly unflappable smile. "It took skill to get us out of there alive, Magduska. Seriously. We should be deader than ducks right this minute."

"Eva, the danger was only to you. I'm under Bathory's protection, while you are an unknown, mortal woman. No magic."

She made a face and crossed her arms. "And what of it? You say 'no magic' as if I am the odd one! This is a 'no magic' world, Magduska."

"It doesn't matter about the world, darling. You wandered alone into a nest of vampires at three A.M." My voice caught in my throat and I swallowed hard to get past the fury and the guilt choking me.

I kept my voice low, even outside. Vampires have excellent hearing, as sharp as bats, and even all the way down Andrássy Street I feared Bathory could overhear us if he were determined to do so. "I love you, darling. I don't want Bathory to eat you up alive, turn you into something dreadful. Better no magic than that."

She shrugged and rolled her eyes at me. "Ah, Magda, don't be so stupid. You work for a blessed vampire, my dear. What do you think? It's a nunnery in there? How many times have I told you it is madness to work for such a creature? But do you listen?"

She gave me a pointed look, a sign that she herself was on the verge of losing her composure. Her lips trembled as she adjusted her unfashionable yet inexplicably adorable gray cloche on her head. "I came running so fast I almost lost my hat in the gutter. And this is the thanks!"

Words rumbled out of me, low and heavy, like thunder rolling off Lake Balaton before a spring storm. "I can handle myself. You don't understand. Bathory looks so harmless, like your uncle Lazlo after three glasses of Tokaj wine. But you have no protection against him! And if I lost you to him, it would be my fault. I couldn't bear it."

Eva's features grew soft in the filtered light of the streetlamp.

"I don't have your magic, it is true. My wits and my smile will have to do."

I cleared my throat, and when I spoke again, my voice was low, soft, a half-apologetic caress. "If I didn't work for Bathory, the three of us would be starving in the street. Gisele makes a pauper's wage sewing, and the florist pays you in flowers, for pity's sake."

I couldn't bear the thought of endangering my girls through my very efforts to keep a roof over their heads. All this talk of poverty and danger sent a sudden spike of hunger shooting through my stomach. My head spun, and I covered my face with my hands. When Bathory worked late like this, I cheated and ate rumballs for dinner while he held court. The Istanbul rumballs were the best in Budapest, but they did not make for a fortifying meal.

"What's the matter with you?" Eva asked, not unkindly. She stood close to me and rubbed my back. "Please don't be sick. I couldn't bear it, not both of you sisters knocked flat. Come home and I will bake you a potato."

The import of her words sank in slowly. "Both? Is that why you came charging in there? By the Witch of Ein Dor, it's Gisele, isn't it. She's that bad."

When I looked into her face, I saw the flash of tears in her eyes, and knew it was even worse than I feared. "I know you told me never to disturb you at work. This Bathory—he's deadly to regular girls. I know. But Gisi's never been worse . . . I couldn't wait any longer for you to come home, so I ran nearly all the way."

I started walking, then half running down Andrássy Street; the knowledge that Gisele suffered alone, vulnerable, in our apartment on Dohány Street forced my trembling, aching legs to move. The run across the Seventh District seemed unbearably long.

Eva clattered after me, even as she tucked her wayward blond curls behind her ears. "Slow down, Magda! You know I wouldn't leave her alone unless she was all right."

A sob stuck in my throat, and I smacked Eva in the shoulder, my patience all but at an end. "She might have started up again for all we know. And here we dawdle, just talking."

Eva slowed down, her sides heaving. "We're not dawdling, idiot, I can't keep up with you. Will you listen for once?"

I slowed to a fast walk, and Eva struggled to keep up with my longer legs. "Gisele's the one who insisted I fetch you home right away. But she told me to tell you, 'Don't hurry, and don't worry.' "

I imagined my little Gisi crumpled on the floor, eaten alive with fever, her hand to her forehead as she proclaimed herself just fine. My sweet little martyr.

My footfalls grew gentle on the pavement; Eva was right, I needed to save my strength. Every breath I took burned in my chest. "What's wrong with her? I can't stand these fits any longer! Maybe the doctor . . ." My voice trailed off. We both knew no doctor could cure Gisele of what ailed her.

Eva caught up, gave me a one-armed hard little hug, and she reached up high to smooth the damp tendrils of hair that had gotten into my eyes. "If any soul can help your sister it's you, Magduska. And you know it better than I do."

We stood facing each other in the mist, Andrássy Street magically silent in the night. I tried to apologize, but that was not one of my gifts. "The man in there with Bathory scared the soul out of me," I said instead. "And what do you know, he has no magic either."

"Ridiculous," Eva said, but she still spat to avert the evil eye. "The whole world's getting ready for another great war, and you blame some wretched stranger. You don't need a Tarot deck to see it!"

She relented when she saw the expression on my face. "But you can see us through anything, you know."

"You give me more powers than I have, Eva girl."

"Do I? What about the bullies on the bridge? Remember?"

It was summer in Tokaj, the northern town where Eva's family and mine came from. We were nine. A group of little toughs had cornered us on the bridge planning, I guess, to throw us over the side, into the Tisza river.

Eva finished my thought for me. "There were five of them, only three of us. And their leader was the size of a bear. We should have been the ones in the river, but you threw them over one by one."

She paused for emphasis, as if she were telling the tale to a stranger. "And you didn't even use your hands to fling them over the side. They threw rocks and called you a Jew witch, but they couldn't touch you."

I unclasped my handbag and took out one of the pink handkerchiefs that Gisele had embroidered for me. I swiped at my nose and shook my head. "This is different. Worse."

"Well, you'll just have to get a bigger magic wand, that's all." That was Eva's way, to make a fine joke out of everything. "You're the eldest, and you swore an oath on your head when your mother died, to look after us."

That oath hung over my head like a sword. My beautiful

Eva . . . how bitter to reflect back upon that oath I swore so long ago, to know how badly I failed you. But on that night, my anger felt righteous and it emboldened me. "I will see you two through everything, you know that."

But I recalled the terrible scenes overrunning Ziyad Juhuri's mind, and my conviction wavered. "I just don't know how."

Eva took my right hand in her left, and we walked along like schoolgirls in the night. "You don't need to figure out everything in advance. Not when you are an expert in making magic out of nothing."

"But Gisele . . ."

"You'll figure something out. The witchy things you do can cure her better than any pills or medicines could. And that's a good thing, because your witchy stuff is free."

I sent my witch's sight down the long curve of the street, searching for the Horthyite thugs that sometimes roamed late at night, looking for Jews or Communists to rough up. Nothing. My footfalls sped up again, and Eva ran to keep up with me.

Eva's laughter pealed like a bell in the gloom, and I could feel how cold her fingers were, even through her thin cotton gloves. I squeezed her chubby fingers, caressed her little hand with both of mine. "You're a silly, reckless girl . . . and I love you with all my heart."

Eva laughed again, but her mirth sounded brittle and false. "That's your bad luck, girl. Easier to love nobody and only have your own skin to save."

I stopped walking to consider her words. "I wish I could do as you say. But I can't help loving you, or Gisele, either."

She smoothed her blond curls back behind her ears, her eyes

sparkling again with tears. "Ah, you are always so earnest. I was joking, joking!"

With the encroaching dawn, the mist grew luminous, and that meant no matter what else the stranger had told Bathory after my departure, my boss had gone off to his rooms to avoid the sun and to sleep. The knowledge we had survived the night gave me a surge of strength.

"We have to get out of Budapest, Evuska," I said.

"But go where, my darling? War is coming everywhere."

I sighed, knowing she was right. We were foxes hunted by hounds. "Paris, maybe. Let's set Gisele to rights, and then we'll see."

⚭

We finally arrived at the little flat where the three of us lived, on the third floor of our apartment building on Dohány Street, near the Great Synagogue. I had visions of finding Gisele sprawled across the kitchen floor dead, but no. Instead, my little sister Gisele rocked on my dead mother's favorite chair, sewing away at her mending as if her life depended on it.

My gifts do not include foreknowing, seeing a flicker of the future played out before its time. But something dark in my Gisele's unusually serene expression sent a chill into my flesh.

The girl loved almond horns. She loved pickles. Gisele's dearest joy was sunning herself in the front window of our flat on Dohány Street. A rosy-cheeked child like her, no more than sixteen. To see such an evil overshadow those beloved features meant something precious had died. Been murdered.

I made no sound, yet she started and looked at me and Eva, eyes unseeing. Gisele looked through me, to the hot darkness in the landing behind me, as I stood in the doorway, stupefied.

The darkness overspread her face like water closing over her head. Her gaze finally connected with mine, and tears began coursing down her cheeks, faster and faster.

"Little star," I whispered, though it seemed she couldn't hear me. "It's Magda. You are all right. Hush, my sweetheart, hush." And I ran to her side and pulled her down to the floor next to me, held her close.

She trembled in my arms like a little trapped bird. I stroked the long, tumbling black hair, and I muttered fierce, sweet endearments into her ear, listening to my own words as if another person were speaking them.

Finally my voice trailed away, I held her close and we rocked together on the floor; I was no longer sure who was comforting whom, for my heart was filled with a melancholy so huge it threatened to bury me. We Hungarians are renowned for a romantic malaise that makes the world so achingly beautiful and so ineffably sad we immerse ourselves in its unbearable beauty— before we jump off the roof or swallow the cyanide.

"The ovens," she said. And the eerie calmness of her voice frightened me worse than the chills and the tears had before. There was a certainty in her tone, a matter-of-fact, mechanical tension. As if she was automatically reciting the story of the world's demise, a thousand years after the last living mortal had been slaughtered.

She began to explain the future, as mildly and precisely as a businessman dictating a memo to a stenographer. The lightning strikes of Hitler's army. The bloodthirstiness of the werewolves and demons, unleashed by the Nazis on helpless human mortals in violation of every cosmic law.

The factories of death. Systematic murder: of children, mothers, old men, innocent people. Warehouses filled with confiscated shoes. Dolls. Human hair.

The tidal wave of blood overwhelming the continent of Europe; indeed, the entire world. "It's the Final Solution," she whispered. "Our existence is the problem."

In the end I could not bear it. My beloved little sister was in a trance, and she didn't understand all the horror she transmitted from a far-off vantage point. I knew she didn't know. I shook her by the shoulders so hard that her teeth rattled and her head whipped backward, I slapped at her cheeks until she stopped her recitation and suddenly burst into a blessedly ordinary storm of bitter tears.

And I cried too. Because every horrible word she had spoken prophesied our own doom. She and I hugged each other against the world she had spoken into life, the world that waited to swallow us up.

"You believe me," Gisele kept saying. "I don't want to believe it all myself, but you . . ."

I hugged her tighter against her tears, covered her hair with tiny kisses. "Yes, darling, hush, hush, say no more of it. I cannot take any more."

She sighed, fell completely silent in my arms, and I tensed for another fit of prophecy to overtake her. And my mind raced, frantic, looking for some escape, some technicality to avert our terrible collective fate.

"We'll run away," I whispered into the curling glory of her

hair. "We'll run so far away that the Nazis can't catch us. Paris, or Australia. Maybe even Zanzibar."

I refused to consider the state of our finances and our ability to marshal our resources to flee. We were leagues ahead of the Jews in Germany—our government had not yet confiscated everything from us. But in our case, three orphan girls hanging by a thin thread over the pit of disaster, we had nothing much for anyone to take. Nothing, that is, except for our lives.

"I'm sorry," Gisele whispered, her shoulders hunched in her misery. "I know you'll think of something, you always do. But, oh! When I open up my mind's eye, I . . ." and the poor thing started crying again.

She smelled of honey and dandelions, my poor little girl, my doomed little sister. I swiped at her tears with the soggy wreckage of the hankie in my purse. "I swear I'll see you through. I swear it, you will not be murdered, no matter what happens to this world."

Eva's voice sounded far away and scared. "Um, what about . . . me?"

Eva was harder to fool. I turned my head and flashed my most expansive, confident smile. "You! Golden swan, you'll outlast us all!"

Grief made Eva shy, but she joined us on the floor, and we drew her into our hug. She is as much of a sister to me as Gisele, really, though we're no more related than I was to Eleanor Roosevelt. We had been friends since we had started in school together at the age of seven. Her quick, sometimes savage wit and her vitality had indelibly marked my childhood memories with incandescent light.

"You two witches better quit your fuss," Eva warned, a

strange, contained smile lighting up her eyes, seemingly against her will. "I'll have none of it. I'll pack my bags and light out for Tokaj, I will. My uncle Lazlo still lives there."

"Girls, we can't stay crumpled up on the floor like dishrags," I said, pretending at a resolve I didn't feel. "Disaster is around the corner. So what will we do about it?"

Gisele shuddered in my arms, and then she rose onto shaky feet. "Magduska, I will tell you one thing. We can't run away."

I refused to look at her as I slowly got up, my joints complaining like I was two hundred years old instead of twenty. "Yes, we can. We don't need money. War is not yet. We can walk out of Hungary if we have to, and we already know how to get by on nothing."

I watched Gisele pace, her hands pressed against her rounded sides. "We can't just run. You know visions are a gift given. We can't run out on a prophecy. We have to proclaim it, to act."

My heart started pounding against my chest. "If by act you mean me putting my soul in danger, conjuring spirits, then no thank you."

Gisele stopped pacing, and she swiped at the tear tracks on her chubby cheeks, as if wiping them away would lend strength to her side of the argument. "Magda, you know what you are! Mama was right—to throw your gift away is to act the fool."

My heart turned to ice. "Don't throw Mama at me. Don't you dare."

"I'll dare anything, just to get you to wake up. Don't you believe me like you said you did? It's worse than any words I can find to describe it."

Cold despair settled over my heart. Gisele had never spoken

to me like this, the way my mother had spoken to me once, not long before her death. I stormed away from her to our grotty little kitchen and I banged around, starting water for tea. "You know I believe you. But that doesn't mean I have the right to wreck my soul."

Eva rescued me from the teapot before I burned my fingers lighting the stove. Of the three of us, only Eva remained dry-eyed. "Gisele's fit was quite the horror, you have to admit that, Magduska darling. Can even a witch run away from something like that?"

"*This* little witch just wants to live," Gisele murmured, casting a baleful glare in my general direction. "Unlike the Bride of Death over there, content to die and return from the dead as she pleases."

Eva colored a bit but said nothing in reply. She knew as well as we did that the Lazarus girls were born witches, who could curse and bless, and visit with the citizens of the next world. But she was too polite to insist we manifest our powers in public. Like our religion, our witchery was something for private, and it was only for emergencies.

I wrestled the grubby teapot back from Eva, and poured myself a cup of weak tea though the water was barely warm. "Don't talk about me like I can't hear you, Gisele," I muttered in reply. "I'm not about to go to Gehenna for a lost cause. It's one thing to see visions that come to you, even such a one as this. But it's another thing to force the dead to appear in your front parlor—force those souls to come to us here, in the living world, where we flaunt our youth and breath in their faces—like warm bread under the nose of a starving man."

Eva blinked hard, played with her left earring as she tilted her head. "So, what are you fighting about, exactly? Gehenna, starving. Sounds pretty bad to me."

"Gisele won't come out and say it—she knows I'm not allowed to summon our ancestors. Gisele wants to do something about the end of the world. But I think the future is foreordained. Anything we do to try to change it will only make everything worse."

Eva's lips moved, but she made no sound. Her wide blue eyes made me want to laugh and cry at the same time. "The end of the world," she finally said. "That sounds pretty bad, Magdalena. Maybe you can't change the future, but you could save my neck, maybe. And I for one would be most appreciative."

She wrinkled her nose, and I had to laugh. She made life-and-death matters sound like a light comic farce and not the darkening storm that they were. Gisele graced her with a grateful, watery smile, and I felt suddenly empty inside. Gisele had been having the waking horrors for some time now. And she had confided them to Eva first.

My fear for them came out in grumpiness. "Fine, try to force my hand." My darling, maddening girls—they didn't understand the dangers.

"Call Mama," Gisele said, almost reluctantly. She folded her tiny white hands together over her heart, as if in supplication. "She will help us. She has to! Or it will be too late, the hammer will fall, and we will die. Not the first to go, but it will be hard. So terribly hard." Another tear escaped over her pale, round cheek, and I suppressed a groan.

I took a slug of the tea like it was whiskey. "Mama could come back any time she wants to." Grief roughened my voice still more, made me sound angry. "But she doesn't want to. For whatever reason, she stays on in the next world with Papa."

"He must need her help in the next world more than you need her help here in Budapest." Eva's eyes were dreamy, far away. "He has no magic, nothing. Just her. And there is the matter of love, you know."

Eva didn't have to say it for me to know. My parents were crazy about each other, like newlyweds until the day my father died. He succumbed to pleurisy when I was only nine, and the best part of my mother died with him. She carried on, a melancholy specter with one foot in the next world. When the last of our money finally ran out, seven years later, she faded all away. Love like that can be cruel.

Gisele sank back into her beloved rocking chair, as if the splintery wood held my mother's soul within it. Her voice was soft, but it withheld all mercy. "If Mama would only come back, she could help us. And you could make her, Magda."

Eva and I looked at each other as Gisele closed her eyes against her misery. I adored my girl, could eat her like marzipan; but I couldn't do what she asked of me. I could summon spirits from the dead, true. But my creed and the most basic tenets of my education dictated that I not compel souls against their will. Forcing my mother to appear would be a desecration of her memory and a misuse of our training.

When Gisele opened her eyes, she was crying again. "Do it, Magda. Call up the dead, summon who you will. We need help! If you don't . . ."

I put my empty teacup on the rickety kitchen table. Eva and I waited in the silence. "You'll what?" I finally said.

Gisele's features grew calm, and I recognized the serene

despair the Eastern revolutionary had displayed before at the Istanbul. "I'll go to Count Bathory. Throw myself on his tender mercies. I may be a witch, but I'm still a young girl, and for my blood he'll do what he can to save me. And you and Eva too."

My pulse pounded in my temples, and I felt sick. "You can't, little star. You wouldn't." I respected the count, my employer. Though he was a vampire, his word was his bond. But even he could not resist a willing supplicant, one willing to sacrifice her innocence for his patronage and connections.

I dared to look my mild little sister in the eye. She had turned into a creature of iron. "Watch me do it, Magda! Either you protect me, as you swore to Mama you would do, or I must protect myself, the task must fall to me. You know my vision is true. I can't stand by and do nothing, as the world goes up in flames all around us."

I swallowed hard, the sensation painful in the back of my throat. The silence crushed me like an implacable weight; Gisele was right.

"I'll do it." The words scratched at my throat like thorns.

Gisele smiled and Eva applauded me with a little bow, but I stuck the pin into the rising balloon of their spirits with a single glare. "But I'm not calling Mama back. Oh no. When she died, I swore to protect you myself, and I swore I'd never look to her again. Mama can stay buried. If the matter is as grave as you say, my little Gisele, I am summoning no one less illustrious than the Witch of Ein Dor, our ancient great-great-grandmama herself."

Gisele's smile fell from her face as if I'd slapped it away. She understood the insanity of what I'd just said, but Eva looked from me to her, unknowing.

I answered Eva's unspoken question, my voice low. "The Witch of Ein Dor is our ancestor, the original eldest daughter. She summoned the shade of the prophet Samuel at the command of King Saul."

"Oh, *that* Witch of Ein Dor." Eva's laugh was a little too merry. "Of course."

I sat myself down at the kitchen table, took off my shoes, and I unhooked my garters, slipping off my stockings one at a time with a sigh of relief. "The witch foretold the doom of Saul, summoned demons and prophets at her will. She taught King Solomon how to chain demons with magic, got them to build the First Temple at his command. They say the angels themselves knew her as a friend. She warned Solomon to humility but Solomon fell. Like all the kings did. And the Temple crumbled too, in the end."

"And you think this shy, gentle creature will meekly appear at your command."

I chewed on the inside of my cheek, and played with the cracked and glued cover of the Herend sugar bowl, a gilded remnant of our vanished opulence. "Oh, yes. The witch has no choice, once I summon her. But she knows as well as I do what a serious transgression I commit."

"Well, in that case, can't you call somebody who does not have an inkling? Some jolly king or something, who would maybe let us off the hook? After all, isn't this just some glorified séance?"

She had a point—in the Budapest of my youth, families still mourning their dead in the Great War conducted séances every week, in an attempt to resurrect the loved ones they had lost. But no. "We aren't speaking of a séance at all, Eva. A séance is a connecting, an invitation. This is a summons, a declaration of war. Trust me, the spirit summoned does not welcome the disruption. It is a disturbance of the natural order."

As I spoke, my own words reverberated inside my ears. I had the unsettling sensation of watching a drama of the past, a golden fleck of history destined to be forgotten even by the participants. Upon such random, throwaway moments does history sometimes turn.

Gisele hugged me, knowing I had chosen her path rather than my own salvation. She well knew the magnitude of the wrong I was about to commit in the name of love. "I knew you would do it, Magduska. I knew it. You would never just stand apart."

✳ 3 ✳

At midmorning, Eva left for her job at the florist's, and Gisele, exhausted, slept. I dragged myself to the narrow cot I shared with Eva in the back room. I collapsed onto the bed, then rolled over and stared at the ceiling while I rested, fully dressed, on top of the blanket, on my back with my arms folded over my chest like a corpse.

Random words from Gisele's vision assaulted my mind: tattoo, firing squad, children, crematorium. Images born of the words marched in the muted morning shadows playing over our fine arched ceiling, the only evidence that once our hovel had been an elegant residence in a thriving city.

I blinked hard, willed the tears to come; but I could not weep, I could not scream. Gisele spoke the truth in all. A prophecy given, of such a magnitude, demanded a more courageous response than to simply save your own skin.

With a groan, I roused myself from the unquiet grave of my bed. Ten o'clock. Daily life went on outside our window, leaving us both behind.

I rubbed the sleep out of my eyes and forced myself to get up, to move. Pace, pace, ten paces one way, ten paces back. Ten paces again, and I paused at the only window in the tiny room I shared with Eva, looked down three stories to the courtyard of our building. A pack of little children on school holiday swooped through the courtyard like starlings, their laughter and cries of joy rising like a reproach to my gloomy little mausoleum on the third floor.

But Almighty in Heaven, I still lived! And I wanted to stay in this world, lusted for life fiercely, with the energy and selfishness of youth.

The rational part of my brain sought to tidy these unpleasant revelations all away. Surely Miss Fragile Flower was exaggerating, surely things could not get as dire as all of that. Those screaming, bratty children knocking over the wrought-iron chairs in the courtyard downstairs, nobody would waste the time to do them any harm. Mass murder, so boring and illogical . . .

But my heart knew the truth.

I would have to conduct that "séance" as Eva so quaintly called it, despite the obvious dangers. The calamity hurtling toward us took up the entire sky, a storm the likes of which I could never have concocted or imagined.

I rested my forehead against the cool panes of glass above the open window, and I knew that at midnight that very night

I would gamble with our lives and summon the fell Witch of Ein Dor. Only she, a demon-hunting witch and unquiet spirit, could surrender a spell strong enough to avert the harsh decree.

I had at least one faint consolation: if I failed to keep the witch in check, the three of us would be spared the grief of seeing Gisele's vision coming true.

6

The rest of that wretched day passed in a long, slow, disjointed haze. Gisele and I stumbled through our ordinary chores, and she lunged for her piecework like a drowning man clings to driftwood.

All day, the secret knowledge of our destruction ate away at me, until I itched all over and could no longer sit still and wait like a lamb for my fate. Instead, I washed my hair, curled it, and put on my finest clothes and sorted the few others I had left as I counted the hours until night fell.

6

As it turned out, the "séance" went far too well. As we started, I chewed on my lower lip and risked a peek at my companions around the little lace-covered round table in the sitting room. Gisele, pale but resolute, sat to my right, holding on to the edge of the table in an obvious effort not to run. On my left, Eva had her arms crossed in front of her, as if she could protect herself with her lack of magic.

My heart skittered in my chest like a crab in a trap. The girls didn't understand how essential they were to the success of this dangerous operation. I took a deep breath, and as I considered my little sister's round, tense face, my eyes finally filled with stinging tears.

"I need you to help me, girls. Courage!"

"You know it's as bad as can be, an emergency!" Gisele shot back, her voice quavering. "I don't have visions of destruction every day."

Doomed. The three of us, walking dead. I forced myself to smile, to lie. "Nonsense, or else why would I bother with the summoning?" I directed my bravado at Gisele, and she put her despair away, at least for the moment.

Once I saw I had her with me, I could reveal a bit of uncertainty. "But I don't quite know what I'm doing. Mama never taught me what to do in the event of the Apocalypse." I allowed myself a little sigh.

I glanced over at Eva, and saw she had her chin down, with her famous stubborn look on her face. "Stop browbeating her, Magduska! What do you want from her?" Eva said. She was always defending Gisele's melodramatic vapors. "It's not her fault the world is about to end."

I fought to keep my voice level. "She's the one who demanded I do something." Ah, the famous Lazarus fury . . . Gisele seemed to have escaped inheriting it, but I was cursed with a double dose.

I calmed myself by contemplating the hideous flowered curtains that adorned the alcove overlooking the courtyard. I hummed a gypsy love song my father used to play on the violin, until I could trust myself to speak civilly.

"I need your help to call up the spirits. This bickering is making it impossible to maintain a connection."

Gisele's delicate rosebud lips started trembling. She brushed away her tears with the tips of her shaking fingers. "I'm sorry," she whispered. "I can't get the pictures out of my mind. It makes me want to put my head in the oven."

"Don't say that!" Eva and I both said.

I cleared my throat, waited until I had the other two girls' full attention before I spoke. "I'm the oldest here. Since Mama and Papa died, I'm all you've got. If everything is truly as bad as you say, we need help. I'm willing to do whatever I have to do to protect you, the both of you. But you, Gisele, can't hang from my neck and drag me down with you."

I spoke with all the authority of my twenty years, even as my heart weighed heavy with the knowledge. Magda Lazarus, orphan and untrained witch: I was a thin protection against disaster; we all knew it. No matter how much Gisele pretended that I could save them all from any misfortune, I was realistic enough to know our lives were all but forfeit.

Eva drummed her stubby fingers against the surface of the table, her huge eyes dreamy. "We know we're nothing but trouble, Magda! I can't speak for Gisele, but I'll try to be a good girl." Her lips crooked in an ironic smile, and I couldn't help laughing. We both knew Eva's brand of wickedness couldn't be restrained for long, and I for one was glad of it.

"Good, then," I said, my anger smoothed back, out of sight. I rubbed my hands together to raise the spirit energy, molded it with my palms like an invisible snowball. The power strengthened between my fingers, and the pull of the spirit world waxed heavy, a huge, silent tide drawing me away. "Hold steady, girls, and strengthen me. Once the Witch of Ein Dor appears, there's no going back."

Dead silence was their only response, but in this altered state, I sensed them on either side of me, augmenting my strength. My palms burned. I opened my hands and released the quivering sphere of light above the table, where it hovered, a crystal ball made out of ether. It spun, brightened, and grew, and I whispered a prayer under my breath, the Twenty-ninth Psalm. And then I prayed that the evil spirits attracted to the light would leave the three of us alone long enough for me to receive the help we urgently sought.

"I summon the Witch of Ein Dor," I said, my voice matter-of-fact. I didn't know how to conduct a séance in the grand, old-fashioned way, I didn't have the spirit trumpets, planchettes, and other tools of the trade. So I did the job the only way I could, by simply calling on the soul I compelled, directly. I knew it could not resist my command, however unembroidered I made it.

The flickering immediately strengthened into the figure of a bent, ancient crone, dressed in a long robe, her ghostly hair floating unbound and free. The spirit regarded each of us in turn before resting her gaze on me.

It spoke in a furious gabble in a language incomprehensible to us. "Speak in Hungarian," I said, and the rush of words halted.

The witch smiled, and that dark merriment frightened me worse than anything I had seen in my life.

"What place be you?" The apparition's words, finally whispered, held a heavy accent but we could comprehend her speech.

"Budapest. Hungary."

"And when?"

I swallowed, my mouth completely dry. "It is 1939. In Christian years."

"Who be the Christ?" The crone cackled, knowing the answer to her own question. "You know I come from a time long before the carpenter walked in my city."

I nodded, held on to the citrus scent of the melting candle I had used to center myself. Otherwise, I was in danger of slipping away from the conscious, everyday world altogether. "We need your help, Grandmama of Ein Dor."

The crone's smile widened, but this time my fear stayed under control. "You know your lineage, little one. Or do you?"

"Oh, yes, my mother was not remiss in teaching me who I am."

"One of the Lazarii."

The word sent a shiver up the back of my spine. Before I could answer, Eva piped up—not even the sight of an ancient, undead sorceress could silence her. "I'm not a Lazarus. I'm an ordinary girl, Grandmama. But I need your help even more."

My body shook with shock, and I smacked Eva hard enough in the shoulder to make her gasp. Such rudeness from the young was tolerated less by the spirits than the most formal, stiff older mortal who still walked the earth. We needed the witch's help too desperately to risk aggravating her.

But the Witch of Ein Dor ignored Eva's nervous chatter, kept her merciless gaze fixed directly on me—the young, untried witch who had managed to summon her. "Why did you not call your earthly mother to help you, child? You have less to fear from her than from me, and you know it. She would not curse you. And I may well give you my curse—you wish it on your head, no?" A cold breeze began to blow, though all of the windows were shut tight.

My jaw clenched, and I balled up my fists in my lap, where the witch couldn't see them. I looked directly into the witch's eyes, suddenly not afraid to meet her gaze. "I left her in the cemetery. If my mother wanted to come back, she could. We don't need her, not anymore. If she doesn't want to come back, well, she can keep sleeping in the dirt."

The witch's smile quieted on her thin, luminescent lips. "So. She chose your father, a man of no magic who reposes in death, over you and your sister, alive and in need."

A bolt of pure fury shot through my body, but I held my peace, although with difficulty. After a moment of silence, punctuated by Gisele's all but silent weeping, the witch inclined her head. "Hold on to your anger, child. It is not of Heaven born. And it will never desert you."

This coaxed a smile onto my own lips. "That is certainly easy to believe." I couldn't keep a note of dry sarcasm out of my voice, though I meant what I had said with all due respect. "But we need your help for something much more immediate. My sister, Gisele, has had a vision. We need to know if it is true, and if so what we can do to avert it."

"What will you do for me?"

The question shocked me into silence, so much so that Gisele's reply sailed by me, unchallenged. "Nagymama, we will do whatever you say," Gisele whispered, her voice quavering and throaty, almost a sob. "Whatever you want, we will do."

The witch's gaze finally shifted away, and I leaned against the table, all but exhausted. The witch's form wavered, and then strengthened as I fought to keep focus. "Youngest daughter of the Lazarii, you have been granted the gift of prophecy. You know as well as I that your vision is true. War is coming for you, for your people. This is no secret. By the end of this year, 1939 in Christian years, the Jews . . ." The witch made a dismissive motion with her fingers, like she was brushing cobwebs away from her face.

"How can we stop it?" Eva was too brave, or too foolish, to avert her eyes, to keep out of a conversation that was going far above her head.

"You can't," the witch snapped. "You, impertinent human child, can do nothing to change this fate. September the first, all goes into the fire."

"No," Gisele said, her voice growing stronger. "We have to do something. You don't understand! I saw trains, factories of death. Millions of people, children, murdered. We have to do something. Hide them away, stop their killers, something. Or else we might as well jump out the window and be done with it now."

"That would be the easiest, little Lazarus. Follow your mother into the afterworld."

I surprised myself with a little laugh. "That would be too easy, Witch of Ein Dor. You would never have accepted the easy way, yourself. That is why we dared to call upon you, our ancestor."

"What do you know of my ways?" The witch's voice held no rancor in it now, no bitterness.

"I know that you called upon the prophet Samuel on the day of King Saul's doom. That you bequeathed your magic to King Solomon, and that he built the First Temple in Jerusalem with the intercession of your power. And that you warned him, the way you warned Saul, but the kings wouldn't listen . . ."

"As you children will not listen to me."

"Still, as your wayward children, certainly we merit some special dispensations."

"Perhaps." She squinted and leaned forward, coming so close to my face her ethereal form almost passed through me. Her aura scratched like rough fabric against my skin.

"You have no idea," she whispered, "what you ask of me. Saul himself didn't have the gall to do it."

My voice emerged as a hoarse croak. "We are desperate, probably even worse than Saul. He was a king, we are just girls."

The witch snorted. "Just girls. You have no idea who you are, then."

My sister drew closer to me, and her soft shoulder brushed against mine. "Ah, Nagymama, perhaps we called upon the wrong spirit. We should have prayed for our angels to come."

The witch wheeled on poor Gisele and blasted her with the force of her spectral fury. "You do not dare. Creature of dust, daughter of the fallen ones, you have no right to command the celestial host."

I remembered my mother's half-whispered tales of the witch's enslaved demon army, but I held my tongue, only held Gisele steady with one arm. I felt her crumple under the force of the witch's attack and my fear turned dark and ugly inside of me.

"Isn't that the angels' job, to watch over us?" I asked.

I had intended to distract her from going after Gisele, and I succeeded. The witch returned her attentions to me. She hissed,

"Maybe, maybe not. It is for the Almighty to will, not for you to say."

"What other choice do we have, Nagymama? We have the right to live."

The witch sighed. "You will not like my answer, child. If you insist on living, despite what the Almighty may will, you must retrieve the Book."

A chill of unease slicked down my spine like an ice cube. "The . . . Book?"

"Yes, our book. You know of it, yes? *The Book of the Angel Raziel.*"

I took a slow breath, but the oxygen in the room had been gobbled up by a huge, invisible fire. My mother had told us about a book of the Angel Raziel, but it was a bedtime story, a cautionary tale. Not the stuff of real life, let alone our temporal salvation.

"I thought the Book was a legend, nothing more."

"Am *I* a legend? That book was mine, those words. How do you think Solomon could command the demons who built the Temple? It was the power inherent in the Book, little star. You are doomed, destined to join me in the afterworld. Your only hope to avert your sisters' vision is to get that book, translate it from the angelic language, and make the Book's power your own. But that way is full of danger. You may well join me sooner following the pathway of *The Book of Raziel.*"

I studied the Witch's ghostly features, my living heart pounding painfully in my chest. I refused to die. I was certainly a fool, but my life had not yet properly begun, and I refused to be cheated. Even if the price for that refusal was unbearably high.

I roused my daring. "Where is the Book?"

The witch closed her eyes, flickered in the candlelight like a shadow. She opened them slowly, and for a moment I caught a faint echo of the living woman the witch had once been, a young woman who looked like me.

"Let us say . . . Amsterdam," the witch whispered. "And how an impoverished Jewish girl like you can get from here to there in the summer of 1939 is something beyond my ability to foretell."

"But I must try."

"Try you may, but you seek to avert your foretold destiny."

I was touched by a faint spark of inspiration. "If Raziel wrote our book, he certainly must be our angel, then. At least a friend of the family. I will summon him, and he will save Gisele at the least."

"NO!" The witch's fury blasted me. My body trembled as Gisele's had, but it was not for fear but a bodily reaction to the witch's ferocity.

Her rage rose like a storm. I had to break her rising wrath, but I knew no spells. I would have to improvise. I swallowed hard and muttered a singsong under my breath, a nonsense fairy tale from my earliest days. "An elephant's nephew defeats the entire Turkish army . . ."

The Witch of Ein Dor gasped and turned to flee. I settled into my chair, felt the wood vibrating with the trapped soul's power. I wove the ancient fairy tale like a braid, into a spell, used the words to wrap her soul and hold her tight. "An ancient baba turns a bottlecap into a hermit's castle . . ."

She pulled against my whispered words, started sneezing

with the effort, slowly at first but harder and harder each time. After a dozen hard ones, she held up a hand for mercy.

I allowed myself the tiniest of smiles. "Shall we speak civilly, my venerable nagymama?"

The last sneeze shook her body so hard she almost vanished. To break the spell, I whispered, "And so the prince found the enchanted kingdom, and they lived to a great age, in immense happiness, ever after . . ." and the Witch of Ein Dor went still and sneezeless again.

"I spoke of angels," I said. "I mean to call the angel to my side. An angel came to the aid of the English at Mons, no?"

"That was the Angel of all England who came. And she did nothing but burn a hole in the sky when she revealed herself— the soldiers, inspired, did all the work."

"But—"

"But nothing. Summon and bind an angel of the Almighty, and damn your soul to Gehenna forever. That is no curse of mine . . . it is the first tenet of the Witches' Creed! 'Summon no unwilling soul!' And you have already violated it!"

Though the Witches' Creed certainly existed, my education was so deficient I could not recite even one of its verses. But I would cut off my nose before admitting it to the Witch of Ein Dor. "Of course, of course. But how do you know the Angel Raziel would be unwilling?"

The crone threw her smoky head back and laughed hard enough to set herself to wheezing. The hairs stood up all along my forearms, and Eva half bolted for the front door before she grabbed the crook of my arm to steady herself.

The ancient witch narrowed her eyes, and her nostrils flared.

"I had thought to curse you, when you dared to force me here. But no. Your destiny and willfulness is curse enough. You, girl, hold to your fury—you will need it. I have no more to tell. Will you now release me, child?"

I nodded my assent, quivering like a leaf in a storm. The wind in the room grew stronger, and I shivered in the icy breeze. "Thank you, great nagymama, for your patience. Go in peace."

"I have never gone in peace, but ridden the wind. As now I do—so!" And the wind blasted through the room, redolent with the scent of cinnamon. The citrus candle blew out, and Eva screamed in the sudden darkness.

✳ 4 ✳

I didn't want to go to Amsterdam; to my mind, survival depended upon the three of us staying together in Budapest, or fleeing somewhere safer. Gisele tormented me with her saintly insistence that she join me in my fool's crusade, and that all but convinced me not to go at all.

It was lucky for me that Eva realized Gisele was insane, and that she convinced Gisele that I had to go alone, leave the girls safe in a place that they knew.

So, defeated, Gisele settled down to her sewing.

Everyone has a worldly gift, some talent they need no magic to perform. So far I haven't found mine, and I muddle along in search of it. But Gisele's gift, to sew things together, matched her housewifely and practical nature. Within a day she had unearthed a bolt of dove gray cotton from some mysterious hideaway, and she raised the humpbacked Singer sewing machine from its hidden perch underneath the sewing table. When it came time for buttonholes she took her thimbles and her sewing basket upstairs, and hid away in the communal attic among the tubs where the washerwomen scrubbed clothes. She emerged holding a gray suit that fit me perfectly and looked like it was sewn for the Queen of Romania.

I slipped into the slender, feather-light creation, buttoned the jacket up to the base of my throat, and wished silently for a matching hat. I had only a white one, and I swear, as I pinned it on my head with my trembling fingers to complete the ensemble, I came close to abandoning our desperate plan altogether.

As I stood before the long mirror in the corner of the sitting room, I adjusted and readjusted the little Eugenie hat on my head, the pins sticking straight into my skull.

I spoke to my reflection. "I look like a retarded sailor. This isn't going to work."

"No, no, it looks fantastic. Gisele is a genius." Eva reached up from behind me and with a little tug got the hat on the perfect angle along the back of my head. "With your reddish hair, the hat stands out beautifully. And the gray of the suit makes your eyes look green."

Gisele said nothing, just inspected her handiwork with too-bright eyes. Her gaze met mine in the mirror, and I saw her eyes getting bigger and bigger, threatening to overspill with tears again.

"The suit is perfect," I exclaimed in an unseemly rush, and I pasted a crooked smile on my face. "It's this stupid hat."

"I could cover it with the gray, I still have a remnant," Gisele said, as her hands rummaged in the pockets of her housecoat for a hankie.

"No, forget it, my darling, it will have to do. Bathory is expecting me, you know. I owe him at least an explanation for why I skipped work the night of the séance and where I've been since. And why I have to leave."

I glared at my reflection in the glass, willing myself not to say anything else peevish and thoughtless. The suit was perfect; I was the one straining at the seams.

6

At dusk, I ate a piece of sausage the girls had saved for me and I left for Café Istanbul as if I were late for my own execution by firing squad. I dragged my feet down Dohány Street, promising myself I could walk instead of taking the tram and postpone my encounter with Bathory even longer.

By the time I arrived full night had covered Budapest, and I walked along in shadows and mist, my feet pinched in my pretty shoes. The moon rose overhead, a splinter of sharp silver.

The café was all but empty this night; people with only a few pengös in their pocket will spend it on a husk of bread, not a cup of coffee or a rumball. At least sane people, respectable citizens of society, not people like me.

At the top of the stairs, near Bathory's customary table, I looked over the balcony and nodded to Imre, Bathory's factotum, at his familiar perch at the bar near the door downstairs. He saluted me and smiled his silent, melancholy greeting with closed lips.

Imre looked like the meaty, scarred prizefighter he'd once been, with a thickened nose knocked askew and small puffy eyes like a rat terrier's. But the creature spent his spare time translating the poems of Yeats into Hungarian, and many a night he cried into his Turkish coffee, remembering the young lover who had committed suicide when he had discovered Imre was turned vampire.

As you might infer from Imre's example, despite its name Café Istanbul was a most Hungarian place.

Bathory perched in his accustomed corner of the mezzanine as always, his small, bent body surrounded by the corpses of newspapers from all over Europe, mounted like hunting trophies on long bamboo rods.

I admired the ancient lace cravat knotted at his bony throat, but hid my fond smile. Bathory had come of age in the 1600s, and like most people he remained moored in the aesthetics of his early youth. But unlike Imre, Bathory was vampire born, a princeling of the fanged nobility. He hailed from the mountains of Transylvania, the native lands of the tribe of Drakul.

Cigarette smoke curled decoratively all around him like gray filigree, and I warmed to the rich, redolent scent of the cup of Turkish coffee that rested on the table.

"Magdalena, your dove gray suit is most enchanting," he murmured, hardly looking up from the *Pesti Hirlap*. His bony fingers clamped a lit cigarette, and he took a long, deep breath of smoke.

My pulse pounded, with pleasure or fear I'm not sure. "I thank you, my uncle Gabor."

I let his pretty manners enfold me like a cloak, and accepted that our farewells would take some time to conclude. So be it, as long as I could contrive to keep secret my true motives for leaving. No easy task, while dealing with an undead who could scent my emotions like perfume and who had encountered nearly everything in his centuries of vampiric existence.

I pulled a cane-back chair close to his tiny round table and sat down on his left, with a rustle of the newspapers. His thin lips twitched in a smile, and he slid the Turkish coffee at me. I admired the enameled blue espresso cup as it moved along the surface of the round marble table.

I removed my gloves, wrapped my fingers around the cup, and let the Turkish coffee warm them. I studied the square red saucer, the hand-painted detailing along the rim of the cup, and took a long, slow sip of sweet, muddy coffee.

"Forgive my absence, count. I've been called away by a family emergency." The best lies contain a core of truth.

His left hand darted out and captured my right hand around the wrist. The tips of his long fingernails scratched along my skin like claws. When I looked at him, our gazes locked and I swallowed hard, willed my pupils to somehow not enlarge with fear.

"Do you understand what is happening?" Bathory asked, his voice affable and mild. "The Poles are in London as we speak, ensuring that England will fight in the impending war with Germany."

"The war," I replied, my voice faint and far away even to my own ears. "So, it's worse than Ziyad said. War comes to us all, then. The way it has already come to him."

"Yes, war, and soon. How I detest war. You have not seen its ravages yet, but do not worry. It will be hard, but you are young, beautiful, and resourceful. You will survive it, my dear."

For perhaps the first time, I knew more than my employer. I placed my left hand over his and gently squeezed. "I wish I shared your optimism, dear Count Bathory."

He released my wrist one finger at a time, and I rubbed my bruised skin and reached again for my coffee. With studied indifference, he returned to his reading, muttering under his breath at the headlines and graciously ignoring me until I regained my bearings.

I took a long slug of coffee. Bliss: warm, bitter, sludgy, sweet. No matter what the war brought to Budapest, I hoped with all of my heart that the Café Istanbul would remain open for business, with my boss installed in his corner and a steady stream of perfect coffee waiting for anyone who could afford the price.

I cradled the still-warm, empty espresso cup in my bare hands as if it were a baby bird. "I quit. Sir."

The count snuffled over his cigarette and slid the Hungarian newspaper away with a great crackle of newsprint. "Quit? But my dear, you have your little nunnery to support."

Not long before, his comment would not have rankled. But now, in the world of Gisele's vision, Hitler had already set his plans into motion, and Horthy and a good percentage of my countrymen had already done plenty to the Jews beforehand. And with that knowledge, a secret, invisible barrier had gone up between my beloved, frightening Bathory and me.

I rolled the empty cup between my fingers. "Ah, so you understand I am the man of the family now." I shot him a half smile, to let him in on the droll joke of my circumstances. How amusing, the young pretty girl the head of her little family of girls. How charming. How . . . plucky.

I sighed and continued. "But, to take care of my little nuns, I must travel abroad. Without delay."

I looked at Bathory to see how he was taking the news. His eyes narrowed as his gaze rose again to capture mine. "A . . . trip. Nothing like a pleasure cruise off the edge of the world, eh, Magdalena? Where the sea monsters await?"

My demure smile felt tight, like an imperfectly applied plaster. I plucked at my nice white gloves. All around us, the Café Istanbul hummed with the warm, intimate sounds of conversation, the clink of coffee cups, and the metallic clatter of silverware. No place in the world was as comforting and civilized as a café in Budapest; no place in the world was so irretrievably lost to me.

I slid the espresso cup back onto its saucer, where it belonged. "Do you have any family left alive, Count Bathory?"

His paper-white face went a little green. "Er, I am not sure. Ruthenia is now Hungarian again, and we hope for Transylvania next, but my estates were well scattered after the wretched conclusion of the Great War and the difficulties that followed. And, regrettably, I do not know if my ancestors remain undisturbed."

Bathory meant that the villagers, left to their own devices, most likely dug up and staked his defenseless old relatives once the Hungarian *gendarmerie* in their employ had gone. The peasants, both Magyar and Romanian, had always, understandably, hated the children of Drakul.

We sat together, the truth a silent presence. Until this moment, I had been his first assistant, in the sinful city of Budapest, the closest creature he had to family. And yet barriers—between mortal and vampire; Jew and Christian;

guttersnipe and nobleman—kept us apart, separated by an un-acknowledged chasm.

"You are alone and unencumbered, dear sir. I still have a little family. They need me now."

"But don't they need your salary to eat?"

He wasn't being funny, my courtly vampire count. He, who had never known material want, could only guess at my life outside working hours.

I found his wealthy innocence rather endearing. "Of course, we all need to eat, yes? But we three also need to stay alive. And if I don't take this action now, all three of us are dead."

The war, the deepest chasm of all, interposed itself between us. He folded up the newspaper like fine linen and set the bamboo rod alongside his table. A waiter ran to gather up all of the papers now that the count evidently had finished with them.

He leaned toward me, took my hand in both of his. "But my dear, I will simply send the three of you away, then. To America, or perhaps South Africa. I have excellent prospects in Istanbul also, as you well know from our trading contracts."

How he tempted me, so unintentionally and so cruelly, little knowing what exquisite agonies he inflicted. I wanted to agree, send at least the girls away to safety so that I could grapple with the witch's backhanded blessing alone. But they would never agree, never, no matter what I did or how I tried to trick them into it. I also knew that Bathory, no matter how courtly and generous he appeared on the surface, would extract an exorbitant price for his generous act of mercy. From them, as well as from me.

No matter how much I wished it were not so, vampires are not human beings. Bathory's offer was not motivated by the spirit of self-sacrifice; he saw our salvation as a good investment, nothing more. The girls were a great prize, turned or not.

"It is certainly an enticing offer, sir. But Budapest is my home. Our home." The count was such a patriot in his undead bones he accepted my explanation at face value, even though we both knew I spoke nothing more than a fervent lie.

His expression never altered, and I could not tell if I had offended, bored, or amused him. As usual, he charmed me and threw me off balance at the same time. He smoothed his whiskers with a linen napkin. "Where, then, Magda?"

"Sir?"

"Your trip. Where is your destination?"

"Amsterdam."

At the city's name, Bathory's face lit up with a rare, enormous, and sincere smile. His yellowed fangs flashed his pleasure at me, and I involuntarily drew back: like a dragon's wings unfurled, they were impressive and frightening to behold. "Ah, my dear, one of my closest contacts resides in Amsterdam. An American, but cultured and discerning. What brings you to Amsterdam? An emergency, you said."

I took a deep breath and squeezed his cold fingers. I determined to keep my tone of voice casual, at all costs. "An old relative. She's asked me to look after some family business that needs urgent attention."

The count's smile turned shrewd, and he let my fingers go free. Ah, he knew too much, too much . . . I had little hope of hiding my errand from those knowing, old eyes. "Lazarus business, eh. Then the matter is settled. You must go, and immediately."

Surprise flooded through my body in a warm rush before I could make sense of his words. "I don't mean to abandon my position so quickly, sir. I came to offer you two weeks' notice."

"Nonsense. You are a Lazarus witch, and the eldest, no less."

I felt the blush rising into my cheeks, and I pressed my lips together hard against my teeth to force myself to stay quiet.

The vampire's eyes twinkled as he leaned back in his chair and watched me squirm. "I am old, my dear, but your line runs older. Your service is useful to me, but tut, tut! You are meant for greater things than this."

"No, I am not."

The words came out too quickly, and Bathory leaned his head back and crowed with laughter, thin high blasts like a rooster's over Tokaj in spring. "Now, you are worth infinitely more to me should you learn how to properly wield your power. War is coming, I am old enough to recognize the obvious signs. Go, run your little errand, and come back to me alive. I will pay your way, and you will owe me favors."

I shook my head against his generosity, and he drummed his fingers against the marble tabletop, the sound a staccato tattoo. "You are wasted by my side, your mother was right."

My blush deepened, grew painful. I had no idea how he knew about my final battles with my late departed mother. My cheeks burned as if gasoline had set them aflame. "I don't intend to waste your time or your money, Count Bathory."

"Nonsense. I have a packet of letters for you to deliver to my contact, Knox, and you will go on Ziyad's business as well. Ziyad needs me to inquire into his mysterious doomsday device, and Knox will know better than most if the Americans are working on one or have one. So. Go on my business as well as your own, and travel with my resources in hand. I suspect that your business is more important than all of mine totaled together."

The breath caught in my throat. I had not wanted to entangle him in my family's disaster, for a myriad of reasons; I kept forgetting our little doom was knotted up in the world's great affairs. And I desperately needed money to speed the journey.

"Thank you," I whispered, but Bathory pretended not to hear me. His attention returned to the newspapers now perching on the metal frame against the far wall, and he rose to his feet as he waved his fingers vaguely in my direction. "Imre will make your travel arrangements and prepare the necessary documents. Take the Orient Express—nothing less for my personal ambassador."

As I rose on rubbery legs to go, he shot me a final stare, half hidden by the clouds of cigarette smoke rising like incense all around us. "You seek *The Book of Raziel*, yes?"

My stomach did a backflip, and I held on to the back of the chair to keep my knees from buckling. "Ah, but what is *The Book of Raziel*?"

Before I could speak any additional foolishness, he laughed again, this time with a good strong dose of menace in it. "Good question, my little protégé. Bring it back, give me my rightful share of it, and I will make your fortune."

ᕲ

I woke late the following morning, the day of my departure. Eva took the day off to stay with me, and Gisele's sewing lay untouched in her woven basket by the rocking chair.

We sat quietly at the kitchen table before our meager midday meal. I forced myself to eat some bread and cheese, to drink a cup of weak, tepid coffee.

I looked across the table at Gisele's face. She smiled at me, even as her eyes shone with unshed tears. "When will you come back to us?" she asked.

I swallowed hard; there was no answer. Instead, I nodded at her, forced my lips to smile as I rose from the splintery table. "Soon, my darling," I lied.

"Can you believe our Magduska is going to Paris?" Eva cut in, her tone of voice carefully bright. "She'll fit right in with that new suit, Gisi."

Eva brushed the crumbs from her lap and joined me where I stood, and she hugged me so hard the air was pressed out of my lungs. "Come back to us, my darling," she whispered in my ear, her breath a soft tickle against my neck.

"I will, I will," I managed to say. I smoothed Eva's brilliant blond hair back, rubbed the smudged mascara from her cheeks.

It was time. We walked to the station, took the far way to Keleti so that we could stay together as long as possible. Eva insisted on carrying my valise; I held my satchel with my precious papers in one hand, held Gisele's hand with the other.

The platform was crowded with families making grand farewells, a grand fuss as their grand suitcases were lugged by the porters onto the royal blue cars of the Orient Express.

Time for farewell. My girls hugged and kissed me once more, Eva straightened the white hat on my head for the last time.

"Stay safe, girls," I said, my voice trembling. "Beware of Count Bathory. He looks like a charming old rake, but he drinks blood. Don't let him drink yours."

Gisele clung to me, weeping. "Don't worry about us. Just do what you must, Magdalena. But swear you will come back to me!"

"By the Witch of Ein Dor, I will." Even if I had to return as a ghost.

Eva handed me the valise. "Bless you, Magda. Keep your wits about you, magic or no magic."

I wanted to tell her, "You don't need magic, Eva . . ." but a long, harsh whistle interrupted our farewells. With a final kiss, I untangled myself from their embraces, turned, and dragged myself up the steps and entered my car. A porter took my bags and led me to my opulent compartment; I lifted the blinds, opened the window, and leaned out.

There they stood, together, the two girls I loved beyond all measure. An unintelligible announcement rent the air, and a huge puff of steam escaped the engine as the train began to move, slowly, then faster and faster.

I watched them grow smaller and smaller as the train pulled away. I did not know if I would ever see them again.

✳ 5 ✳

Vienna was a city hatched from my worst nightmares—gilded and cold and filled with hatred for me and my kind. I was grateful that I didn't have Gisele's talent for envisioning the future or the past. Plenty of dreadful events had already transpired here, and I didn't want to know what new travesties waited for me now.

Until Gisele's screaming horrors, I hadn't considered my Jewish ancestry much of anything to remark upon. I was Magda first, a Lazarus witch second, Hungarian third, and only then, as an afterthought, did I consider my Jewish descent as part of my identity.

But the world, and Austria in particular, begged to differ with me. Here, I was *jude*, beginning, middle, and end, and my humanity never factored into Vienna's calculations at all.

By some small, mysterious miracle, the false papers Bathory's factotum Imre had arranged satisfied the armed guards in black uniforms at the border of the Reich. They surmised no Jew would be insane enough to voluntarily enter Hitler's living room . . . so without too much further scrutiny they assumed my papers, proclaiming me a provincial Catholic and an ethnic German no less, were all in order. I had been prepared to bribe them, but it hadn't been necessary to test whether their greed outweighed their loyalty to the Fatherland.

But, immediately afterward, I had heard the furious whispers in the hallway outside my compartment. And once we arrived in Vienna station another first-class traveler, with a gentleman's clothes and a fine face pinched with fear, was made to vanish off the platform. After I witnessed through the window blinds his quiet, futile struggle, I could not sit still; could scarcely breathe.

According to the timetable tucked away among my papers, the train was scheduled to depart from Vienna's West Bahnhof station after a short stop, only thirteen minutes. I hoped to get some fresh night air on the platform and calm my nerves before the whistle blew and I could get out of this cursed place, Vienna.

I sat on a wrought-iron bench, and watched the steam rising from the engine at the head of the royal blue Wagon-Lits sleeping cars. All the souls inside reposed in peace, while I took the air on the platform and fretted. With any luck, the whistle would shriek and the westbound train would depart on time . . . that is what the Germans were famous for, after all.

To distract myself, I unfolded and read again the letter of

introduction that Count Gabor Bathory had written on my behalf:

Ulysses Knox, Bookseller
Spuistraat 334, Het Spui
Amsterdam, Netherlands

Dearest Ulysses [Bathory wrote in French]:
A pleasure to know you still remain in Amsterdam, my old, beloved friend. I send to you my lovely, and quite mortal, young assistant—she is not a Drinker, so have no fear of her by night. As she will explain more fully, her name is Magdalena Lazarus, and she comes to you on urgent personal and professional business.

As you are the most informed connoisseur of the written word that I know, I have commended you to my dear Miss Lazarus, and ask that you afford her the benefit of your breathtaking expertise in this regard.

Miss Lazarus seeks an ancient volume belonging to her family. It is long lost, but certain signs point to its return into the stream of mortal time. I suspect that you, with your fine discernment and perspicacity, may know more than I of this legendary book's true history and present location.

She also brings to you information concerning a client of mine who requires your assistance as well. Miss Lazarus will supply this additional information as it becomes salutary to do so.

When you and she are done with the present projects, I will make it worth your while to visit me in

Budapest—I seek a family Bible of great antiquity. Needless to say I require your assistance, since, as you may be aware, I may not touch such a volume due to my family's congenital . . . infirmity.

May God in his infinite mercy bless you, my friend, and may we meet on the Ring Road before this year is done.

Salut

(Signed) Bathory

I could not restrain a smile as I regarded the archaic flourishes and Byzantine turns of phrase which unwound line by line. How like the count himself, slender and bent, clad in velvet and silk dressing gowns in the daytime, surrounded by dusty, hidden opulence in his rooms on Rose Hill in the heart of old Buda. The count, despite his many flaws, still adored the scratch of pen on paper, and I loved him for that, and for a thousand other little reasons.

A low growl snapped my attention up from the page. I shot a quick glance along the platform.

I was alone. Completely, utterly alone.

"I smell a little Jew," a voice growled, and I saw a wolf the color of dirty dishwater emerging from a clot of shadows clustered around the curved stairway.

This beast was immediately joined by a pack of others emerging from the rising steam of a locomotive at rest beside the platform; I saw to my horror that I was surrounded by a pack of werewolves of the German Schutzstaffel (SS).

They circled me, snarling, and it was all I could do to maintain my composure, to stand my ground and not run away screaming. Still I faced them, with at least an outward pretense of calm.

Because I was a Lazarus, you see. I knew I had the ability to, however painfully and laboriously, summon my own soul back from the dead, reanimate my body to pick up my life where it had stopped before. So I feared the werewolves' great slashing teeth, their blood hunger—I feared the terrible pain of their attack, the pain of my death. But I could withstand the death they came to inflict on me. The knowledge was cold, but comforting—a bitter, clarifying winter wind.

"Leave me alone," I said, with all the authority I could muster, as I clutched my satchel in my hands. I glanced up at my train across the platform, suddenly so very far away.

I rose from the bench and began inching toward the steps leading up to safety. The dogs snuffled and whined, and the echoes of their ravening laughter slithered along the platform and snaked around my ankles.

"We've been waiting for you," the leader of the wolves growled, his yellow teeth and gray, dingy gums flecked with foam. "Our master comes."

"Your master?" I kept my voice steady, but my heart sank. I thought this mangy cur was the worst of my present troubles.

I took a deep breath, felt the tingle of magic burning painfully in my palms. My mother had taught me the rudiments of energy manipulation, showed me how to use my natural talent of summoning to channel that energy. I lamented my lack of spellcraft, felt it like a sharp pain as the wolves circled closer and their growls rose menacingly all around me. But my anger rose in me like spring sap—and I tried to convince myself that my raw fury would be enough.

"I have the power to summon the souls of the dead," I warned, loud enough for my voice to cut through the cacophony of the circling pack. My mind raced as I tried to think how to stop them before their fangs sank into my flesh.

I didn't know their names, but I knew he who they served, and I hurled my fury against them. "Creatures of Hitler, back!" I could feel the wall of energy pushing against them as they slid backward, their long claws scraping against the spotless cement platform. But without their names to lend power to my command, I could not keep them away.

The leader lunged for me, snarling and ripping through the barrier. I swung my heavy satchel in his face—a lucky blow, for I hit him in the eye before his jaws could close over my ankle. I shoved hard against his big skull, and sent his ugly, evil soul hurtling off the platform and onto the sharp metal tracks, his yelps and whimpers rising from the pit to infect the others with his fear.

I dropped my bag, held my palms out, felt the fury rising in me like an electric blue inferno. Perhaps if I pretended that magic, and not a satchel full of papers and books, had stopped their leader, I could somehow still prevail against them.

"Well then, Nazi dogs! Who shall I punish next?" Howling, they shied away, as if I had hit them all across their snouts with a rolled-up newspaper.

I took another deep breath and grounded myself, when I felt an onrush of an ancient and profound malevolence close upon me on the platform. I couldn't see it but knew it was huge, uncontainable, repulsive, and evil. And it had come for me. Evidently, I was about to make my acquaintance with these Nazi curs' master.

I summoned forth the spirit, invited him to materialize—not that the materialization could help me in my fight with him. It simply felt a little more comfortable to confront my nemesis face-to-face, even if I was destined to lose.

His features were blunt, unyielding, hideous, lined with wrinkles, wizened and yet also hardened. But his eyes. His yellow eyes retained a quick knowingness that froze my blood. I didn't recognize this man—not that he was any ordinary kind of man. But his face split open in a sickening smile, a smile of delighted recognition.

"Ah. The Lazarus. Beautiful." He bowed slightly as he addressed me in clipped, formal German. His pointed teeth glinted in the yellow lights marking the end of the train platform. A train whistle screamed in the distance. The desolate sound only underscored my sense of abandonment, of isolation.

"Call me Magda." And I forced my lips into a smile. Any creature of magic could make foul use of my true name, but the fact he knew of me meant I couldn't keep my name hidden for long. Better to show him that, recklessly or not, I had no fear of him.

His smile widened and I realized I was lying to myself as well as to him. I was terrified of this man, of what this creature in the form of a man was capable of doing to me.

"I know about your book. Raziel HaMalach."

He named the angel in Hebrew, the holy language, and it then became apparent that I had acquired a foe of the first magnitude. For he spoke the sacred words without even a flicker of pain.

"Yes. My book. My inheritance."

"I want it for myself. And I am happy to kill you for it, Magda the Lazarus."

I smiled; the effort of clenching my jaw so tightly sent a dull knife edge of pain sliding along the side of my temple. "You know me, sir. And so, you know you cannot relegate me to the next world. I will return."

"Ah. But you do not know me. Your mama, your ancient grandmama, have all been remiss in their teaching, *hein*? I am a wizard of great renown, my dear. The Staff, I am called; I vanquished the Witch of Ein Dor even in King Solomon's time. Unlike her, I live still. And she could have told you that I know how to deal with your kind, as I once dealt with her."

"But aren't you Jewish yourself then?" The question, so stupid, slipped out before I could stop myself.

He surprised me with the heartiness of his laugh. It almost sounded wholesome, genuinely amused. "Herr Hitler would be appalled if he believed that to be true, for I serve him and his cause. But alas for you, no, I was a priest of the Lord Baal. I left my old master in the past to fade away into the darkness. Time has passed, and I now walk in a different age, with different gods and devils."

"All that is quite interesting, Herr Staff. But my train is due to depart in another six minutes, if my wristwatch still speaks true . . . so, if you will excuse me." And I made as if to go, knowing all the while that I could not shake this ancient enemy without invoking a power far beyond my reach.

"Not so, my dear. I have come to claim your soul for mine. You, the descendant of the line that could summon the power of the Angel Raziel, to serve kings for the glory of God." He spat out these last words like they tasted foul to him. I backed away, and he advanced upon me, long bony fingers reaching out with long, yellowing nails curling at their tips.

"I will desecrate you, little girl child. Take your soul and drink it like blood. And then the power of the Book will be mine. You think you can return from death. But this kind of death—the death and pillage of your immortal soul—no. You will die again and again, and your death will serve me and my master."

He smiled again, my pulse pounded behind my eyes, and a cold sweat crawled over my skin. I had to do something, stop the headlong assault of this ancient creature's words. My journey westward had only just begun; I could not let this wizard defeat me so soon.

I gathered my belongings around me and drew myself up to my full height. "This isn't about me, or my soul. I have nothing whatsoever to do with the matter," I managed to sputter from behind my clenched teeth.

"Yes, more's the pity or I'd linger to savor your death for longer. It's all about that book. Your old book. Once I have your soul, the Book will be mine."

"And why are you telling all of this to me?" Tears began spilling down the bridge of my nose, tears of anger.

He brushed against Gisele's gray suit, against the tips of my nipples with the very ends of his yellow nails, and I leaped back in revulsion. "It is simple. I want you to suffer," he said, and he shrugged.

I called up a huge rush of energy—anger and terror, remorse and disgust all rose up in me, implacable and huge, a surge of emotion ready to work my will. Magic works through the manipulation of energy, and life force I still possessed in abundance. But I did not have the knowledge to channel that force into a weapon I could wield against such a formidable foe.

I could not fight him magic to magic—my spellcraft, puny and untutored, was no match for this ancient and terrible wizard.

I had but one choice, hard as it was to make. It violated every rule I had been raised to honor. But this Staff had to be broken.

"I call upon and summon the Angel Raziel."

And before the Staff could crush my soul between his horrible fingers, there came a sudden, furious beating of huge, invisible wings. My desperate prayer had been answered.

✳ 6 ✳

I shut my eyes, dazzled by a brilliant, multicolored radiance, and didn't see the blow before it came. Something hard connected with my chest and threw me backward. But instead of falling down, I fell *up,* into that divine, coruscating light.

When I opened my eyes again, I was flat on my back, my skull aching where it had connected with the platform. I saw a living tapestry of luminosity, heard a cacophony of little bells, smelled a heavenly scent. My senses were scrambled. Suddenly, the ordinary world seemed dull and feeble.

After another moment of celestial confusion, I realized I was still in the Vienna station; the Angel Raziel stood over me, golden beams of light streaming from around his shoulders. After another moment, he looked not like a heavenly being, but like a man—an exquisite, chiseled, Grecian statue of a man. A man dressed in ordinary street clothes, a man who held a sword, streaming with silver shafts of light, over my head.

And I realized, finally, that he raised this weapon of righteousness, his fabled sword, against me. Before he could smite me, I sat up, my muscles sore, my knees still shaking.

I rose to my feet, smoothed my hair, and did my best to compose myself. "Help," I said. My Hebrew was far too rudimentary to use in a magical battle to the death, so I spoke in Hungarian, hoping an angel of the Lord would surely understand. The Lazarus family spellcraft is based in the use of the holy words of the Hebrew Bible, but my ignorance of the family spells was just one of the gaps in my training.

He frowned. "You broke the Law." I risked a look into his eyes, squinted against the unearthly godlight his face still generated. Raziel was glorious. Terrifying. And truly, cosmically furious at me. "I should strike you down where you stand." His voice rumbled all along the platform.

I heard a low cackle behind me, felt a hideous whisper of a touch along the tops of my shoulders. I shrugged my shoulders away from the Staff's fingers, rose slowly despite a prickle of pain through my entire body. "Don't do the wizard's work for him. Please, give me a chance to explain myself."

The deep brown eyes narrowed, then relaxed as he registered the implications of this encounter. "Fear not, Lazarus." He spoke Hungarian, and the words, soft and familiar, soothed me. Almost imperceptibly, he nodded, shifted his attention to the werewolves clustered around me.

"*Baruch Atah . . .*" Raziel's voice was no louder than a whisper, but the platform under our feet began to tremble violently. The light along the edge of his sword blazed brighter as he stepped forward. Almost too late, I stumbled out of the angel's way.

He stopped a few inches from the Staff's face. To give the wizard credit, he didn't budge. And I, at least temporarily the beneficiary of Raziel's righteous wrath, had to fight to keep from bolting.

The wizard's face split into a leering smile. "Ah, the author."

"No. Merely the scribe."

The wizard's smile widened, like a rot overspreading an overripe fruit. "Tut, tut. False modesty. How long since last you walked the Earth, eh? Much has changed since then. Join us, Raziel. Join me and your brother celestials. We can rule the mortal ones, rid the world of useless creatures, and claim the entertaining ones, like Magdalena here, for our own amusement and pleasure." He spoke Hungarian too, to taunt me with his words.

Raziel's laugh, soft and even, sent a cascade of warmth melting through my limbs. "You seek to tempt me, yet again. I have heard this all before, wizard."

"I merely offer you an attractive proposition."

"It is not my place to choose."

The wizard sneered, scratched at one hairy nostril with his long, curving pinkie finger. "Ah, yes . . . the Almighty has deprived you and all celestial beings of the power of free will, instead bestowed it upon girls like Magda, who are more than happy to order you about!" The wizard shook his head, scraped at his stubble with his horrible fingernails. "Ah, mysterious is the way of your God. He gives you intelligence and discernment, and yet forbids you to use it."

I tried to speak, though my voice was so hoarse I had to

clear my throat before I could choke out my words. "Raziel. Destroy me if you must, but get him first. That's all I ask."

Raziel ignored me, spoke to the wizard. "That argument is as old as the Fallen Ones and their first kin. I have been offered temptations since time out of mind."

"Ah, yes—your beloved Asmodel has told me so."

The angel's face stiffened. "Speak not that name to me."

The wizard leered. "But he is so special and dear to you, beloved Raziel."

"Begone, wizard." He lifted his sword above his head, and the werewolves flinched, widening their circle. Their low growls rose to a collective howl.

But the wolves froze in place, quivering with arrested energy. The wizard shoved me aside to stand in the middle of the circle, and he pointed his fingers down toward the ground, muttering an incantation I didn't understand, but which, nevertheless, made my skin crawl. Despite their obvious pain and desperation, the werewolves closed the circle, drew it inward. With yelps and foam-flecked moans, they attacked the angel, one by one.

And each wolf lunged to its death. As soon as their claws or teeth made contact with Raziel's body, each wolf gave a final scream and died in a writhing mass of melting flesh and hair. The light streaming from his face and sword grew blindingly bright. I cried out in fear mingled with gratitude. Out of the corner of my eye, I saw a porter poke his head out of a half-opened door to peek out onto the platform, then quickly pull back and slam the door, an absurdly polite expression pasted imperfectly on his face.

The last wolf met his gruesome end, and lay smoking at the

angel's feet. I looked at the wizard, saw the unholy glee on his face, and realized that he relished the angel's display of wrath.

As for me, I stood rooted to the spot, knowing I was next to die unless something fundamental changed in this encounter. I wasn't used to being the object of righteous—even if justified— scorn, and the knowledge burned. Despite the danger, I could not tear my gaze away from the sight of him, filled with a luminescent rage.

The angel turned to me, eyes wild. The sword he held above my head loomed huge; I wondered how I could possibly return from a death inflicted by an angel of the Almighty.

I thought of Gisele, and Eva, and held my ground, though I trembled so badly that I sunk onto the pavement. Behind me, I heard the wizard close in as if to grab me away from Raziel's judgment.

In that moment, the angel's attention flicked from me to the Staff. "She is not yours to take, wizard."

I glanced over my shoulder and gasped. The wizard hovered over me, his hands reaching for my throat—he'd meant to choke me where I knelt.

Revulsion poured through my body. With a quick shove upward, I elbowed my way behind the angel as the two faced off. I hid behind Raziel, knowing he fought in the Almighty's Name, not mine. But I sheltered behind his brilliant, light-filled wings all the same.

The angel's voice boomed over the platform, as if it had issued from an independent source. "Judgment is mine. You have committed no wrong upon this child, wizard—not yet. Leave now."

To my astonishment, the wizard made a long, formal bow,

and smiled again. "How satisfying to witness you completing the task that I had begun, Raziel. Thank you for upholding the Divine Plan, and have a pleasant evening. I will see you soon—with many challenging questions concerning your book. Good night." And with a flourish, he whirled and vanished into the steam of a train departing across the platform.

My body went numb with the realization that I had survived my first encounter with the Staff. For I sensed to the marrow that the wizard would hunt me until he got what he wanted out of me. But now, the angel loomed over the furry, smoking bodies of the dead werewolves, and the stink of their singed hairs rose to my nostrils.

Before Raziel could swing his sword and chop me in half like a melon, I backed up quickly, to the very edge of the platform. I was ready to jump, if it came to that. "Divine Plan! So how could you let that monster just disappear?"

He hesitated, and the fierce expression on his face softened. "You do not understand, Magda. Free will matters far more to the evil-inclined than to the good."

I rubbed at my arms, trying to banish the chill in my bones. "Free will? A Nazi murderer like him walks away after a few pleasantries and a girl like me—his intended victim, you know full well—now gets hacked to pieces by your sword?"

I was too furious to remember my fear. I confronted him the way I berated my own cowardice in the night, the part of me that longed to flee to the ends of the earth. "What about my sister and Eva—who are both depending on me to survive? How could you enforce judgment on me and not that wizard, when Gisele needs me? She's completely innocent. I am riddled with flaws, but reveal to me one of hers. One!"

Raziel's face broke into a smile. It was like the sun coming out from behind a thunderhead. "She snores."

His answer dumbfounded me. I sputtered, "But snoring isn't a sin!"

He started to laugh, and I remembered to breathe, forced myself to smile back. "How do you know that about my Gisele? Was that a vision or a guess?"

He shook his head, laughed harder, lowered his sword, and I began to think that perhaps I could survive this encounter with an angel, one who had a good case against me.

He wiped at his eyes with a marble-smooth hand before replying. "The witch did not tell you? I am your family's guardian angel. I have watched over the Lazarii since ancient times."

"I know. But I had no idea you hung around enough to know Gisele's snoring could wake the very dead at night."

I half heard the train's warning whistle, heard the faint calls of the conductor from far, far away. I took a deep breath and tried to clear my mind and senses. "So you understand why I must go to Amsterdam. And you know what is coming."

"No."

"No?"

"I do not have your sister's gift of foreknowledge. I know a horrible conflagration is coming, the entire world can sense that. But the particulars, no. Gisele is a far better judge of that than I."

"But you know our hearts, yes?"

He hesitated, then sheathed his sword. The great gilded scabbard shimmered and disappeared, and the angel somehow transformed into a preternaturally tall man in a chalk-striped suit, no wings, only surrounded by an ineffable cloud of the glory of the Almighty. "No one can know the truth of the human heart. I know you seek an ancient book, my book. I know you seek my intercession." Again his face grew stern. "And I know you have twisted Divine law in order to achieve that which you seek. Compelling a celestial being to perform your will is forbidden."

I kept my many objections to myself. "I don't care. As long as I save Gisele and Eva too, I don't care what happens to me."

"The world does. God does."

I gathered my satchel, which I had left sitting on the cold cement, and, on shaky legs, began to walk along the platform. Other people, mortal and magical, began straggling out from the waiting area onto the platform and onto the westbound train. The porters began to pass the heavy luggage through open windows rather than drag the trunks up the steep stairs to the sleeping cars that loomed high over the platform.

Raziel drew closer to me, and the people around us drew back so he could join me on the platform. A few of the passengers sweeping onto the coach gave Raziel a long, assessing glance before hurrying a little faster up the stairs and past the conductor. Otherwise, no surprise or reaction. The good people of Vienna had witnessed much more mortifying sights in recent days, in broad daylight, on their bustling, modern thoroughfares.

I dropped my bag, grabbed it again, dragged myself along. Raziel followed. "I am going to Amsterdam."

"I forbid you."

"I thought I retained free will, angel. I cannot stay in Vienna, that's for certain. That wizard will snuff out my soul, all of my lives, the moment you disappear, and you know it."

I hesitated at the foot of the stairs, the last passenger still standing on the platform, and I turned to face my disapproving angel, standing a small distance away. Despite my obnoxiousness, Raziel still sought to complete his own mission—to guard me and Gisele in this dangerous, pitiless world. A thankless task, no doubt.

I climbed the stairs, looked back one last time at Raziel. "Come on, then," I said, as the train whistle all but drowned out my voice. "Please. If you could let that dreadful wizard go unscathed, you must come with me, try to mend my impious ways."

Raziel stiffened and shook his head. "So you compel me, even now, against the will of the Almighty. Beware, Magda Lazarus."

I tried to look meek. "I'm not compelling, Mr. Raziel. Only asking."

His eyebrows bunched together and he frowned. But the angel followed me up the stairs and into my private compartment. A moment later the train I'd been sure I would not live to ride began rolling out of the station.

✳ 7 ✳

I insisted on the berth by the window, and like a child I strained to watch the lights of the station from behind the blinds as we fled Vienna in the night. The lights grew smaller, disappeared, and my angel and I traveled through the darkness on my fool's mission.

I, the fool, looked through chipped and smoky glass and caught my own reflection, superimposed on the sleeping city slipping away. What was I doing? I stole a glance at my companion, who sat upright and silent next to me in the darkened compartment.

His even, beatific features were dappled in shadows as we rocked along the tracks with the other sleeping passengers, tucked away in their own private places. This otherworldly being had saved me from the wizard and his minions, but now the train rushed into the depths of my living hell. Hitler's Germany.

The warmth of Raziel's love radiated through his eyes as our gazes met; his tiny smile, half exasperated as it was, told me that he knew me, in all of my weakness and fear, and somehow loved me still. This creature from another level of reality loved me more than anyone in the entire province of Ostmark, in what was once the free republic of Austria, and now a part of the Third Reich. In the middle of danger, he waited for me now to come to my senses.

How could I explain that I agreed with him? "Thank you for saving my life," I began.

"I don't want your thanks. I want you to get off this train and get out of the Reich immediately. It is almost too late. Don't you understand the dangers?"

I did, and he knew I did. I folded my hands in my lap, did my best to impersonate a tired, ordinary girl. A girl who had the right to exist. "It is a two-hour-and-fifty-five-minute ride to Linz. Enough time to get a bit of rest."

But I could not rest, not with such an extraordinary companion, not in such surroundings. And not in the midst of such danger.

We rocked along in the gold and blue sleeping cars of the grand Orient Express, which originated in Istanbul and ran all the way to Brussels. Bathory, with his usual grand excess, had insisted I travel first class, in a red-velvet-papered and wood-paneled compartment, the finest accommodations offered by the Compagnie Internationale des Wagons-Lits. Two beds in my lonely compartment, no other passengers, and no unanswerable or dangerous questions asked.

How Eva would have appreciated the journey, even as dangerous as it was. As for me, my nerves were worn to nothing. I consoled myself with the thought that such opulence should not be wasted in sleep, though the bed was turned down and the bedding soft and luxurious.

I washed my face with rose-scented soap at the washbasin in the corner, dried my hands and cheeks with the deep-plush wash towel that hung alongside. Unlike my fellow travelers hidden away in their berths, asleep, I had to keep watch to pretend I belonged here. I somehow had to pass muster.

Raziel leaned closer, whispered into my ear. "Get off the train. Now. Sneak off, jump. By the time we get to Linz, the Staff will have the SS after you."

My heart turned into a hard little stone. I searched the angel's face for mercy, found none. Yet even in the midst of my worry, his beauty arrested me. It also disturbed me.

I held on to my mission like a talisman against his beauty and my fear. "You are an archangel, aren't you? With you here, who can touch me?" I thought of the wizard on the train platform in Vienna, his cold hatred, and I settled into my downy white berth, reveled in the knowledge I still lived to travel in such luxury.

"Angels have their limits."

Raziel's breath brushed warm against my ear, and I leaned toward him, suddenly exhausted from my brush with evil.

It was easier to listen to him without looking at him. I closed my eyes and focused on his words. "I am an angel of the Lord, but He allows human will full rein in this world. There is only so much I am permitted to do."

I kept my eyes closed, swallowed hard. "Does the Almighty permit you to come along with me on my errand?"

He would not answer me. I pulled away, sat up straighter, and looked into his eyes. "I have to get to Amsterdam. And you will help me to get there alive."

A half smile played along his lips. Perhaps he thought I was joking. "No. Go home. And we will find some way to save you and the girls. I can promise you I will try."

I wanted to obey him more than I have ever wanted anything in this life. I wanted to trust his words and pretend he was right. He had so much authority, my angel. I wanted so much to relinquish Gisele's vision, to let him think for me, lead me to safety.

But in my heart of hearts, I knew nobody could save me but myself. "I can't. You can't protect me against what's coming. I believe you want to, that you'd do your best. But destiny is something only mortals have the power to challenge, yes? If I go home now, nothing will alter Gisele's prophecy, and all of us are dead. I can't have that."

"There are worse things than death."

I tasted tears in the back of my throat, swallowed them away. "I need to get that book. And I will do anything to get it."

"Poor girl. It's not your job to save the world, you know. Don't you think you should go home, love the people you love, and do what you can in a place where you are wanted?"

I steeled myself against his sympathy, resisted the urge to rest my head on his shoulder. The Staff was right about one thing— how could a celestial creature like Raziel live condemned to merely execute the Almighty's will? Raziel's soothing words distracted me from the truth even as they warmed me.

I considered his admonitions, admired them like gemstones sparkling in the sunlight. But I could not surrender to his commands, no matter how much I wished I could.

He mistook my silence for a weakening resolve. "My imperative is only to save you from evil. Go home while you can, before they catch you."

The train was picking up speed as we left the city limits, and its rhythm and hum pulled at me, lured me in the direction of acquiescence. Somehow I had to resist.

I shook my head impatiently, like a horse on a too-tight rein. "I can't go home. I have to get that Book."

I kept my voice quiet and calm, but the muscles all along my back tightened into a knot. His slow dismay washed through me, a coldness that set into my aching muscles like a chill.

His whispered voice vibrated with urgency. "Forget the Book. Please. Go home."

I took a deep breath, and prepared to argue Raziel into submission. But a rap on the door of the compartment interrupted us mid-battle. I slid the door ajar, and two railway men stood swaying in the dim, carpeted hallway. The first one, the important-looking one, looked down his nose at the male passenger in the single lady's private compartment, crossed his arms against his chest and somehow kept his balance as the train banked deeply into a curve.

"Ahem. Miss, your papers, please," the man said.

6

The two men loomed huge in the doorway of my first-class compartment. One tall; one short. One man dressed all in white, an obsequious porter who respected all of the money it had cost to secure my superior accommodations; the other squat and heavy, with dark braid overspreading his double-breasted uniform like climbing vines. His brass buttons gleamed like ghoulish eyes in the dim light, and the man in white interrupted, with an apologetic whisper. "Forgive the intrusion, miss. But there is a report of undesirable persons on the train to Paris."

I cursed my desperation, my need to trust in Bathory's forgeries. These men had no special reason to detain me, or so I hoped, but the papers Bathory had obtained to hide my identity as a Jew exposed me to special scrutiny if anyone official questioned them.

"Miss, your papers." The second man's voice was ice, his face a passive mask. "And who is this, in your compartment, this gentleman? He certainly is not assigned to this compartment." The man's eyes narrowed, his long, disturbing eyebrows waggled in the breeze of his huffy breath. An edge of something—malice, fear—crept into his voice.

My heart shuddered, for that edge of something told me I was walking dead. Stupid, stupid! I cursed myself silently for my arrogance, for pretending I was indestructible. I smiled into one face, then the other; the smiles were not returned. I took the false papers out of my satchel, whispered a little prayer over them in my mind as I held them out.

The second man's eyes glared down at the papers; this one had a scent of magic around him. Perhaps he was of goblin stock, or maybe was a warlock of some kind. The scent of the forest clung around his shoulders.

He sensed my magic too. I could see it in the tightness of his fist, bunched around my sheaf of papers. "Come with me, the both of you," he muttered, his Tyrolean accent heavy and mossy. "We are nearly to Linz. Come."

I forced my feet to walk, though my ears roared with the sound of my surging pulse. I had the presence of mind to clutch my satchel close to me, and we followed him down the gently rolling aisle, the compartment doors closed tight against our passage, stretching forever down the hallway as in a nightmare.

We reached the end of the sleeping car, and I braced my feet and held on to the leather strap near the exit door. The second man looked over my shoulder and nodded at the tremulous porter, who bobbed his head and turned to stagger away.

"Are you crazy?" he snapped, so quietly I thought at first I was imagining the words. I startled, gripped the leather strap above my head, felt the blood pumping through my muscles, urging me to run away.

"Your papers are shit. Utter shit."

He emphasized his coarse words with a crackle of magical energy that ran up my arm like a mouse. "You will never make it through Germany." He acknowledged my angelic companion with a curt jut of his pendulous chin. "I don't care if you travel with the Almighty Himself, your only hope now is to jump."

I had to blink hard and shake my head to get the words to make any sense. His rudeness to Raziel's face stupefied me. I studied his craggy, gray face—the heavy, iron-hewn features, the saggy jowls. The lowering eyes, filled with a darkness I didn't want to absorb.

He shook his head, the tufted bristles along his beefy chin

pointing in all directions; in my heightened state of alertness, it seemed as if I could count each one. His voice came out in a low, rough growl. "If you jump, I will say you slipped away and escaped." He clutched my precious, worthless papers in his fist. "These will have to stay with me."

He slid the door open with his other hand, and the night screamed outside, rushing by in a thunderous blur. "You must not reach Linz! Do it. Now."

The night, my freedom, rushed past our feet, fast and dangerous. I shot a glance at Raziel; he nodded once, his face alight with hope.

I jumped.

6

I clutched my satchel to my chest and I rolled, over and over again down the side of the embankment, the gravel tearing at my forearms and my face. Gisele's gray suit was in a sorry state by the time I reached the bottom. My forearms were pocked with gravel to the elbows, and I had lost a shoe somewhere in my tumble.

I sprawled on the ground, the breath knocked clean out of me. Out of the corner of my eye, I could see the stars whirling wildly overhead, and the tops of the trees swaying in the wind. I waited for the shout, for the gunshot, for rough hands to grab at me.

Instead the wind whistled through the branches, the train tooted mournfully as it disappeared into the night. I was alone.

Alone. My eyes narrowed and I whispered, "Raziel."

Silence.

I sat up with a groan. "Raziel!" I tried to keep the panic out of my voice, but I failed.

Like a sunrise, the angel manifested slowly before me. He came against his will, but still I warmed myself in his light. "Stay with me, please. Don't leave me alone here."

Raziel cracked his knuckles. "Do not fear, Magdalena. I am always with you."

I groaned again and started picking pieces of gravel out of my arms. "Are you? Poor angel."

His laughter surprised me. "You certainly make my assignment more challenging."

I managed a rueful smile, even as the night whirled faster around me. "You sound like my mother when you say it that way."

His hands held me steady, and only after he kneeled to me did I realize how close I had come to fainting. "Peace," he whispered, and a warm current of energy flowed through my bedraggled body. I breathed in his healing, accepted it. After a few moments, I could see again, though gray splotches still moved across my line of vision.

"What now?" His words were whispered so softly I first mistook them for my own unvoiced thoughts.

I looked up at the embankment, saw my shoe perched halfway down from the tracks. Avoiding his gaze and question both, I rose unsteadily to my feet and untangled myself from his hands.

"First I get my shoe," I muttered, and the gravel slid under my feet as I clambered up the slope. I reached hard overhead, grabbed the shoe, and slid down as gracefully as I could.

Two shoes on my feet. Progress. I looked up at the sky, edged with predawn pink. "I'll have to cast," I said. "Find somebody who will help me, some coven of witches, maybe a hidden enclave of Jews."

"Those poor souls are hard-pressed to help themselves. And you know it."

I bit my lower lip, chewed at it as I willed myself to think through the sting of my banged-up arms. "They don't have to do much. Help me clean up, hide me before I go. To Amsterdam."

"Amsterdam." His voice vibrated with disbelief.

"Of course, Amsterdam! I will have to walk across the borders now that I have no papers at all. Perhaps I can find a boat to ride up the Danube."

I sounded ridiculous, a petulant child, but my wounded outrage was my only bulwark against Raziel's kindness.

"Forget finding safe haven in Austria. The land itself is against you."

Raziel did not say it: that he could not rise up against the land itself to protect me.

So evil, in this particular case, prevailed. *Why?* My unspoken question tasted like cigarette ashes in my mouth. Raziel's presence was a comfort, but nothing more.

The cinders poked at the soles of my shoes as I shifted my weight. "I'll just start walking then. Hide in the woods and cast by day, see what I can find."

"You will not like what you find in these parts." His sadness was tinged with a fury that drove deep into my bones.

Bountiful or evil land, I had to keep moving regardless. I shrugged and took up my satchel. Knew the tracks pointed north, so I turned due west, away from the rising sun. "I will walk to the Swiss border, try to reach Amsterdam the long way."

He shook his head in apparent disbelief, opened his mouth to speak and closed it again when I turned away from him and started walking. He unwillingly trailed behind me as I moved into a copse of fir trees, while the dawn broke in pink and golden glory over our heads. We walked together in silence for a few minutes, and when I admitted to myself I was being stubborn and wayward I slowed, then stopped. Raziel closed the gap between us and stood next to me, waited for me to make up my mind.

I studied his face, those hooded, deep brown eyes, the aquiline nose, sculpted features serene even despite his disapproval of me. I couldn't stand the hurt in his expression; I needed his blessing to go ahead.

I unclenched my fists and clasped my hands together, my fingers shaking. "Why did you write it?" If you had told me a week before that I would have the temerity to ask the Angel Raziel such a question to his face, I would have laughed in yours.

But danger made me reckless. "What possessed you to endow a book with such power?"

He stood and stared at me, and for a moment I thought he would not answer. But a slow, sad smile caught at his lips, and he shrugged.

"Why did I write *The Book of Raziel*?" he finally said. "The world was young. I felt sorry for humanity." His laugh was sharp yet not unkind. "The Almighty had granted me His dispensation, but I learned quickly that my sympathies were misplaced. Humankind can take care of itself. Better than the celestials, I found out soon enough."

His smile faded away. "I was wrong to write it. Leave the book alone."

"We both know it's too late, now."

"Too late?"

"The Staff seeks the Book now. It is my suspicion that a group of Azeri rebels, represented in Budapest by one Ziyad Juhuri, seeks that book too. My own boss wants it for his profit. Honestly, Raziel, if I don't claim my book, somebody else will. It might as well be me."

A bird chattered somewhere above our heads, and I cleared my throat. "I better sit down now, before I fall down," I said. I came to rest on a bed of fir needles.

Raziel loomed over me, and then slowly, with a swan's grace, he came to rest by my side. His wings unfurled behind him where he sat cross-legged, an ever-expanding radiance, a peacock's tail made of golden godlight. "Let the Book go. Let its curse fall upon their heads, not yours."

His talk of curses sounded quaint to my ears. "Raziel. The witch of Ein Dor said my life was curse enough. The entire Reich wants me dead, wants my sweet little sister dead. At some point, curses are redundant, don't you think so?"

Raziel half groaned, half laughed as he reclined on the blanket of fir needles under our bodies, and rested his head in the cup of his left hand. "Let me convince you why the Book must remain hidden, Magda."

I considered my predicament. Undoubtedly, the Staff waited for my train at Linz; by now, he must have discovered I had escaped before the train ever pulled into the station. Certainly he and his minions still hunted me. I could not outrun him, could not shake him. And the land would not hide me.

"If I stay here in the woods, hiding, I am surely doomed. That book is my only faint hope now."

"You are my human ward. If you only listen and understand, I may yet save your life. Stay here with me; I promise you they will not find you in these woods if I hide you."

I inclined my head, said nothing. The fir needles smelled clean and wild under my body. And I let him think my silence meant my assent.

His wings became a diffuse light that shielded us from all of Austria. "Now, listen, Lazarus mine, to what I have to tell you."

✳ 8 ✳

The Angel Raziel spoke, his voice a low murmur. His words echoed through past and future, seemed to erase time itself as we hid away among the fir trees.

"Here is all that I will tell of *The Book of Raziel*, the book I wrote when the world was young.

"My book was not the first book. Before Adam was raised from the mud by the hand of the Almighty, the Torah contained the world within it. The very angels demanded to keep it, and when our prayers were denied and the Torah granted to the children of men, the seeds of discord grew among our ranks.

"I saw the grief of Adam and his children, felt their exile as mine. I came upon the children of Adam as they toiled, as Eve's daughters bore their young in agony. And I watched death stalk the children of Earth, imagined the pain of death, and walked two steps behind these mortal ones in their stumbling path.

"The sages say I bequeathed the Book to Adam himself, to ease the grief of his exile from the Garden. But that is not true. It was to Eve I gave *The Book of Raziel*; and I entrusted it to her and her daughters because of the demonesses who from the beginning sought to destroy her and her kind.

"The world is woven through with holy speech, in the angelic tongue Eve and her daughters spoke. I wrote the words in her language and mine; the Torah, written in the Lord's own speech, Hebrew, undergirds all I gave to Eve. Her people waited endless generations for the Torah to come to the world of men; *The Book of Raziel* stood Eve's children in its stead in its early days. And instead of the Father tongue, it was written in the Mother's.

"Eve bequeathed the jewel of Raziel through her lineage; in each age did the Book assume a form that could speak to her children. But Lilith, Adam's first wife, escaped to become the Queen of Demons, along with her innumerable daughters. Ever did the daughters of Lilith seek to steal the Book and cast the children of Earth into utter darkness.

"In the days before the Great Flood, the daughters of Eve tempted the angelic host to fall from grace. And so they fell, Asmodel, Semyaza, and their host, my brothers, and they loved the daughters of women, and taught them the arts of adornment, of witchcraft, of transcribing speech into written words.

"In the devastation of the Flood, the jewel of Raziel was lost in the deeps of the water. My brother Raphael, moved as I by human grief, retrieved my book from the depths of the sea and returned it to the children of Shem. And the women kept it, the daughters of the watchers, the daughters of Eve.

"The Book became lost again, found again, ages of blindness, ages of sight. The daughters kept the Book in the days of Judges, the days of Saul, the days of the Kings.

"The Witch of Ein Dor, the most illustrious of your kin, kept the Book well and made her fame with feats of generative sorcery. She put the Book into papyrus, the court rolls of King Solomon. She devised the amulets, the numerology, the metaphor of the Book you now seek in your world. In her age of Solomonic wisdom, the Book spoke clear.

"Ever the Witch of Ein Dor battled the daughters of Lilith; taught King Solomon how to bind Lilith's children, Obizuth, Onoskelis, and Enepsigos, in service to the Lord. And Solomon himself learned to compel the most ancient of demons to manifest the will of God, to lift the Temple's very cornerstone into place.

"But within temptation, destruction. Solomon, tempted by woman as the angels themselves fell by women in the days of the Flood, abandoned the way of the Lord and his dominion fell into ruin and death. And your forebear of Ein Dor, abandoned to her fate by the king, battled long and valiantly against the ascension of Lilith, before she lost the fight.

"*The Book of Raziel* disappeared with the destruction of the First Temple; prophets, in the long exile in Babylon, recalled remnants of it. The Second Temple, bereft of the Book, was doomed to fall into ruin, the demons trapped within the temple stone finally freed to roam the earth and feast upon men during the long Exile.

"Ever have I loved the daughters who honored my book

and kept it faithfully. Ever have I watched over them in their turn.

"In every age, the Book calls to the daughters of Lazarus, ready to protect them and their children from the plagues of Lilith: fire, death in childbirth, the smothering of infants in their sleep. The amulets your grandmother of Ein Dor made are still invoked to protect her daughters in their times of need.

"Your blood now calls the Book to light. Turn away and it may slumber once more. Do you not see? Hitler and his demonic horde remember the Book's scourge, and seek its power for their own. Better the Book stays hidden."

𖧷

The wind whispered in the fir boughs for a long time when the Angel Raziel had finished. His words stirred me strangely, but not even an angel of the Lord could stop me from my determination to save my girls from their horrible fate. "That is quite a story. What is its moral? Do I go home, let Eva and Gisele die? You know the time is short, that Hitler is mad enough to believe the world is his by right."

I rubbed my eyes, forced my voice to steady. "The world is at the edge of the abyss, and one young witch with nothing to her name isn't going to change anything. But—"

"What?"

"Gisele." My voice caught, but I steadied myself by looking into the sky, speaking to the new dawn unfolding over our heads. "And Eva. Who will save them if I don't try?"

"You don't understand. I fear your success, not your failure.

You are more qualified than you know to reclaim the Book and bring it back to light. But I don't know what you will become."

I smiled up at the sky's blind face, shook my head against the angel, against the Germans, against every thing and every living creature arrayed against my little apartment on Dohány Street and its beloved denizens. "By now, I don't care what happens to me."

Our gazes met; Raziel's face had turned to chiseled stone. His voice stayed soft, but it froze me to the bone. "Who are you to put the world in peril to save three girls from a fate greater than any of you can even understand? You presume, Magda. So did Asmodel, before he fell. So did Ephippas, so did Rath, so did Beelzeboul."

His face was pale with fury. How I hated to disappoint him, my family angel, but I could not abandon Gisele to her fate. He sighed, hunched his impressive shoulders with his frustration. "Now I understand why celestial hosts with more sense than I stay far away from their human charges, stay quiet and distant no matter how they suffer."

I reached out, daringly took his hand in mine. The grief in his gaze pierced me, threw me into deeper confusion than any of his words had managed to inspire. "I'm the one who forced you to come here. Heaped sin on my head, using you as the instrument. I will make a bargain with you, my guardian angel."

"I do not strike bargains."

I brushed at the fir needles caught in the skirt of my ruined suit. "I have the power to call the terms, so let us not call it a bargain, then. Teach me the witches' art. How to cast spells, how to vanquish evil ones like the Staff. And then in exchange I will gladly let you go."

Raziel shook his head and laughed, truly laughed for the first time since I had encountered him. His laughter boomed and echoed among the trees, startled the birds overhead out of their birdsong. "Did you not hear anything I told you? I am not a witch, nor Fallen. Those arts are beyond my ken."

He smiled, held his hands open, helpless. "Keeping me won't get you my book. Only you can find it—it belongs to you and your clan, not to me. If I had a choice in the matter, I would keep the Book hidden. You may do more harm than good if you succeed."

I considered his words. They sunk in slowly, their implications burning like hellfire. "But—I thought you were the author. That the Book was in fact yours."

"No. As I told the Staff, I am only the scribe. A messenger. The jewel of Raziel is yours, not mine. I gave it away, a gift long ago, with only the best of intentions."

Ah, good intentions. My battered satchel suddenly felt too heavy to hold. "It really is up to me, then. But I'll never be able to do it by myself, never."

"So let it go. Come home, with me."

The choice tore me apart. All roads seemed to lead to death. "No." But I wavered, and Raziel knew it.

He hugged me close, whispered in my ear. "Love drives you forward. Do what you know is right, come home with me."

The tears flowed freely now, and I made no effort to restrain them. "I have to try. I swore I would, I have to . . ."

He stroked my hair and kept silent. We both knew that words could no longer tip the balance one way or the other. I listened to the songbirds trilling overhead, and I thought of Gisele, her squeaky little laugh, her chubby cheeks, and my promise to protect her to the edge of death and beyond.

I hugged Raziel tighter to me. The heat of him burned against my skin, and his wings wrapped around us, hid us inside a holy fire.

"You did your very best to save me, angel. But I must have your book. I know very little of Hebrew, but I know your name means 'secrets of God.' My mother taught me that much, at least. I need your secrets, or Gisele will die."

One of his hands stroked my hair, slowly, like my mother used to do when I was little and had sustained some real or imaginary hurt. But his voice was rough where it caught on his words. "Gisele will die one way or the other, little star. You choose a dangerous path."

"The Witch of Ein Dor told me as much—but I have chosen. I swear not to call upon you again. I know I mustn't. One mortal sin is enough, no? Farewell, Raziel."

The pressure of his fingers receded, faded into a caressing breeze. I closed my eyes against his passing.

I opened my eyes, took a deep, alpine breath, and saw that the world was still the same. I watched a crow fly over the tracks to reach a cluster of his brethren waiting on the other side. But I was all alone.

✳ 9 ✳

My lips itched to whisper Raziel's name, to force him to return. But I had insisted on retaking what was originally his, what he had wanted to keep hidden. And I had sworn to go forward without the divine protection any ordinary human being could call upon Heaven to send.

I wished I could take back my solemn oath.

The sun rose higher into the sky, making my search for a safe haven all the more urgent. Austria was closed to me, cold and hostile. I would cast to find hidden witches or Jews; either population would welcome me as one of their own, a sister member of a hated minority in need of shelter.

Time was my enemy. I had to get to Amsterdam. Undoubtedly the wizard would get there first, but if I didn't get there soon, I needn't bother getting there at all. I took a grounding breath, centered my feet on the spongy moss, and tentatively sent my inner senses through the fragrant fir trees, toward the small villages nestled in the countryside.

I sensed a clot of human misery, thick and horrible, to the east. No, this land was not safe; hidden away among the perfect little villages and magnificent stands of evergreens grew dreadful, hidden secrets, multiplying like a cancer. A cloak of invisibility hid the place in plain sight, unnoticed by the folk living their ordinary lives. No magic necessary to hide it—the people simply didn't want to see it. A name whispered into my mind: *Mauthausen.*

I turned my inner eye away, sending a prayer to those enchained souls but nothing more; I had nothing more to give them. Narrowing my focus, I surveyed the forest with my second sight, and sensed the air around me thick with spirits, most of them born of the forest, rivers, and stones. Benign, ancient, indifferent at most to human affairs.

But in the air, wafting among the branches . . .

I saw them with my eyes before I could sense them with my witch's sendings; they wanted the advantage of surprise. The three sailed through the branches, like wraiths, ordinary human ghosts. But in full daylight.

I wasn't fooled. I squinted hard, saw three old babas of the forest, ancient demons, coming for me. And there was nowhere I could run to escape them, so I stood my ground instead.

"Lazarus," the one in the center crooned. Without squinting, I saw through their disguises: three beautiful women, each one what we Hungarians would call a *vadleany,* a forest spirit, innocent and seductive. They knew as well as I their charms were wasted on me, for when I homed in with my witch's sight, I saw their scaly skin, their long curved claws, their fangs.

Daughters of Lilith.

"I have no quarrel with you, sisters," I said. And I meant it. Such demonesses hunted men and newborn babies, not young, childless women. They were not my natural enemies. But, alas, we all were trapped in unnatural times.

"No quarrel indeed," the crone to my left agreed. She came close, caressed my cheek with one long, scaly hand. "Little sister, you know something of a thing we seek. In the name of Adolf Hitler, we seek it."

I stifled a groan. It seemed half the supernatural world wanted my book. "I know nothing except that I hunt for what is mine." The crone stroked my cheek a little harder, but I kept my gaze steady, didn't flinch under her probing fingers.

"The Book," the third demoness whispered.

"Yes. *The Book of Raziel.*" My breath took on the golden light of my angel's name, and the three demonesses drew back, hissing.

I licked my lips, thought of him. Refused to call upon him, even now. "I can't let you have my book," I said. Raziel at least stood in solidarity with me behind that statement. I'd keep faith with him, even in his absence, for as long as I could.

"You will, little sister. You will. Blood calls to blood. You will call the Book for us, or we will have your blood from you and call the Book ourselves."

"No. I can't let you do that." I thought of what Raziel had said. The Book was dangerous enough in human hands, let alone in the clutches of demons.

They moved closer, and the crone's fingers entwined in my hair. A whisper of fear blew its soft breath along my spine, but only a whisper. Fear was too much of a luxury for me to indulge in at that moment. I looked the crone in the face. "No. That book is not meant for you."

All at once, the three of them were upon me. I let them pin me to the ground, the gravel gouging new holes in the back of my arms. "Give us the Book, or you die!" the young one screamed.

"I don't have the Book," I tried to explain, though their voices rose together in an unholy cacophany. Their false beauty began to slip away, their eyes glowing red in the rising light.

Only the crone fought to keep control of her rage, and it was to her that I appealed. "If you kill me, you gain nothing."

"If you live, we gain nothing," the third demoness hissed. Her hatred was so hot and pure it all but stood and stalked me in the clearing. Pale sunlight filtered overhead through the trees, but unlike vampires and even werewolves, these dread creatures did not fear the light of day.

I twisted out of their grasp and grabbed for my satchel. My sister had insisted I bring her book of Psalms with me, and it was this book I reached for and drew out like a pistol. I held it before me. Tiny and fat, its gilded pages caught the morning light.

The Psalms were in Hungarian translation, not their original Hebrew, but even that vestige of their original power held the demonesses at bay. I held the book between us, and I frantically riffled through the pages in search of Psalm 91:

Because Thou hast made the LORD, which is thy
refuge, even the most HIGH, thy habitation;

And there shall no evil befall thee, neither shall any
plague come nigh thy dwelling. For HE shall give
His angels charge over thee, to keep thee in all thy
ways.

I read aloud, and I stumbled over the archaic, strange words,
their sounds thick and heavy in my mouth.

"That is not the book we want," the young demoness said,
and she laughed. That hard sound cut through my armor of
self-control, and I began to tremble.

The crone shielded her eyes against the light reflecting from
the little book's pages. "These are words, just words. Written by
human hand, no more."

She was right. The Psalms, written by mortals, had the power
to inspire prayer and magic in the human heart. No small
thing. But the book itself held no inherent power.

My magic was rooted in the power of words. I could work
spells, but only ones based in the power of the Hebrew language, the language in which the Bible had originally been
written. Unlike the Book of the Angel Raziel, my little book
of Psalms in Hungarian translation was written in human
tongue, not the language of the Bible. If I had spoken the
Psalms in Hebrew, I might have had a chance. But Hungarian
held no elemental magic for me that I could wield with my
native power.

I had just played my last hand and had come out the loser. I didn't have the power to withstand them. "This is the only book you will get from me," I replied.

My poor mother. She left this world, insisted on following my father into the grave, even as she knew I was not prepared to face its dangers. She knew I resisted the lessons she was able to teach, so she left me to learn those lessons for myself the hard way.

Dying hurts as much for me as for any hapless human being caught in the trap of life. I wanted to live—I fought them hard, fought them hand to hand. But I could not prevail against three. By the time full sunlight shone upon the face of Austria, I was dead.

But not for long.

✳ IO ✳

Being dead has its advantages. The first time I died, at the hands of the daughters of Lilith, I left my failures and worries behind like a heavy package full of junk.

The physical shock of death—a jump into a numbingly cold lake too early in spring—slapped my worries clear out of mind. I recovered consciousness in bits and pieces, disjointed and disconnected, as broken as my dead body.

My first conscious thoughts in the beyond—of course of Gisele, and then of Eva—burned me with the knowledge of separation. I'd thought I was alone in the fields after my angel had left me. But I'd had no idea how agonizingly alone a human spirit could be.

That isolation, my profound sense of disconnection, drew my awareness to the fact that "I" existed, an entity separate from the cold, wide world. I blinked hard—then realized to my shock that I, in fact, could blink while dead.

My confusion spun into a huge snarl when I raised my hands to my eyes and saw—*saw*—my fingertips, the long, straight lines of my somehow unbroken arm.

"You are in the second Heaven, Magda. In my home domain," a by-now familiar voice said.

The sound reverberated through me, a concussive bomb that shook me so hard my form began to unravel. "I thought I had set you free, Raziel," I said, to cover my shock at finding another being I recognized in the hereafter. For I had believed Gehenna was my destination.

"Free," Raziel muttered, a little too quickly.

I gathered my form together and forced myself to look where he stood in the swirling, endless gray mist that surrounded us.

There he was, in all his golden glory. Just seeing him, his wings unfurled, bathed in celestial mist and godlight, Raziel sounded in me a strange cacophony of mixed emotions.

"You are free, and yet you are here, Raziel. And where is here?"

"As I said, the second Heaven, the place of transit for souls in the balance. This emanation is where I come to rest and contemplate the Glory. Here, Magda, you too may rest."

I resisted the temptation of Raziel's comfort. "I don't have time to rest. I have to get back. Now."

"Do you, really? Are you sure it really matters?"

Raziel's soothing voice threatened me, threw the floodgates of doubt wide open. "I don't have time to consider the cosmic implications, dear angel. I don't suspect Hitler sits around and thinks about whether he matters or not."

I distracted myself with an astral hangnail. "How curious, though, to have a body in this alternate place. What do I do with it? Can it get hurt?"

"Your astral body reflects the physical, a prism through the many planes of existence. Magda, you are of the same essence, whether in body or spirit, at every level of emanation."

I nibbled at my astral thumb, and had to laugh. "Even Gisele's suit survived the trip to the next world! Shouldn't I be wrapped in a shroud, or . . ." Naked, I wanted to say. But my astral cheeks burned as I sneaked a glance at my companion. I blushed not because Raziel was an angel. But because he was a "he."

When I looked back at him, Raziel was smiling. He drew a little closer to me, but kept a respectable distance, as if he understood how profoundly his presence confounded me. "You don't have to go back, you know."

I pulled back, testing my ability to function on this new, dreamlike level of existence. "No. I *must* get back. For all I know, it may be already too late, but I have to try."

A shadow caressed the edge of Raziel's jaw, its darkness dimming the extraordinary light in his enormous eyes. "But do you know the way? If you don't, and you refuse to pass into the afterworld, I fear you will become lost between the emanations, and wander this intermediate plane as a ghost. Lost to the world, and to yourself."

I squinted hard, encouraged myself to get mad at him, anything to stop me from agreeing with him and giving in to his decency and reasonableness. "So help me descend, then! You are my guardian. I'm not forcing you, not ever again, but please, protect me, lead me back. It's my choice; you are absolved of it."

He opened his hands in mock helplessness, and suddenly my anger was no mere affectation. How could Raziel pretend he had no power to help me—he was an angel of the Lord, for goodness' sake!

"I am a messenger, not an earthly actor," Raziel said, the smile on his face clashing with the real grief in his voice. "I convey, I do not lead. That is not my portion in this world."

"That's a bunch of piffle! What's your sword for, then?"

A flash of anger passed over his features like lightning. "My function is to render the judgment of the Almighty, not my own. How can I explain it to you? Ah . . . remember Madame Rodinsky?"

His question, such a non sequitur, made me blink. The name brought back a lost world of Chopin, satin pointe shoes, and a long-vanished, innocent opulence. "Madame? Of course, she was my ballet teacher. But—"

"But nothing. She was the fiercest ballet master in all Budapest, correct?"

My lips twitched at the memory of her hard, square, tiny body, the white-haired bun yanked into place at the very top of her hard, square, tiny head. May Madame rest in eternal peace for a blessing. "She was a fury sent straight from Bolshoi Hell to torment every baby ballerina in Budapest."

"So. Did Madame lift your legs for you? Pull you up onto pointe? Did she toss you into the air every time you jumped?"

"No, but . . ." I crossed my arms against his Socratic argument. The fact he was right only made our exercise more tiresome. I remained all too aware of time's passage: Lazarus lore held that I only had three days to return to my dead body.

I had to change his mind somehow, or come up with a better

plan. "Madame did force my turnout with her stick, smacked my behind too if I got lazy in class or too mossyheaded. Madame had a clear opinion on what I was supposed to do, and she used whatever she had to make me do it."

The silence hung suspended between us. His fingers brushed along my shoulder, feather light but full of voltage. "I only encouraged you to leap," he whispered, his voice choked with some emotion I fought not to recognize. "I urged you to jump! Jump! You did the jumping, you made your pirouettes and leaps."

"But now, you do not urge me to leap? To return?"

He withdrew his hand, rubbed at his eyes with the tips of his fingers. "I want your salvation, want you to arise, not descend."

The absurdity of my situation—arguing in the second Heaven with an angel about my right to reinhabit my corpse—made me hesitate. I thought I was an expert in disaster. Little did I know, then, the complexities that disaster generates.

I tried to keep focused on practicalities; that way, I could avoid thinking about the fact that my own guardian angel opposed my plan. Which way back to Earth? I began to move down in what I thought was the right direction, but Raziel blocked my path.

"Your time is done." He spoke into my mind, in the universal tongue of the angels. And his voice roughened with regret.

"No."

His features sharpened, creased into a smile, one with no mirth. "No? But here you still are, Magdalena. Dead."

Could disembodied souls cry tears? I did not intend to hang around long enough to find out for sure. "So you double as the Angel of Death, dear Raziel? You know my task is not done, I must go back. Please, please, don't get in my way."

He crossed his arms, flexed the muscles in his shoulders. Raziel was visibly annoyed with me. "Your poor mother—did you never learn the meaning of no? The silver cord is cut. There is a peace in death, if you will only embrace it."

Panic rose in me. "But I am a Lazarus . . ." My words trailed off; it was useless to plead.

He hesitated; awaiting, I imagined, an expertly wielded litany of spells to force him to return me from this swirling night of souls. We hovered together, I ensnared by fear, his face shadowed with frustration.

When I kept silent and no spells were forthcoming, he sighed, shrugged, and moved forward. "Alas, Magda, there's nothing for it. Come with me, and I will speak for you in the place of judgment."

"No, no, never!" And despite myself, I laughed. I had inadvertently parroted the official Hungarian protest against the outcome of the Great War.

Raziel's laughter mingled with mine. "So you protest the Treaty of Trianon in the great beyond. A true Hungarian patriot!"

Our shared amusement gave me a way to reach him, and only strengthened my resolve. "My poor Raziel. If you cannot help me, then farewell. I will find the way back myself."

A sly expression flashed over his features, and I could see I amused him. Good. Anything to win him over as an ally, anything to coax him to join in my mad crusade.

He leaned forward, arms still crossed. "How will you find the way if you don't know it?"

We looked at each other for a long moment. Only one being

in the wide world had the knowledge I needed, the spiritual map back to my body. I gathered myself up for the inevitable battle, consolidated my energy, prepared to lose to a more formidable foe.

"I summon my mother. Tekla the Lazarus, daughter of Rachel."

The smile died on Raziel's lips, but before he could stop me, my mother's shade interrupted him. I watched my mother arrange herself before us, and the depth of the gray intensified all around. I had desperately wished to see my mother, ask her forgiveness. But not like this.

We gazed into each other's ethereal eyes, hovered less than a handsbreadth away from each other, and yet she seemed more inaccessible to me than ever. Her beautiful, familiar face was closed to me.

"Mama," I whispered, my voice choked into nothingness.

She floated in the silence, her eyes speaking eloquently of grievances and bitter regrets. I heard the angel impatiently clearing his throat as he hovered beside us, but I dared not glance away, lest I break my connection and allow my mother to escape.

I drew as close to her as I dared. "I was wrong. I am so sorry."

"And well you should be." Her lips folded into the thin, straight line of disapproval that had haunted me in my imagination since her death. I had failed her in my willfulness, but that didn't give her the right to abandon Gisele and me to our terrible fate.

Fury in me rose up huge, a demon willing to strike at even my own mother, and the weight of it began to drag me lower, out of the second Heaven altogether. I counted forward and backward, and did long division in my mind until I calmed myself.

"Mama. I am desperate, and I call to you in the hour of my greatest need."

"You know not to."

She was relentless, but so was I. We faced off against each other, and I am sure to Raziel we looked like mirror images. "I do not know that I should not call upon you. Mama, you never taught me! And Gisele needs me to come back."

Her eyes softened at the mention of her favorite, my mild little sister, nobody's enemy except Hitler's. "My poor girl. Soon her sufferings will be over, and she will be swept away, to join me."

"No. I need your spell to go back and save her."

"No. Let my little girl come to me."

No. That was all I let my mother teach me, the power of the negative. Fury rose in me again, implacable. "No, mother. The family spell. I compel you."

She laughed at me then, but it was a sick, frightened echo of a living soul's honest amusement.

"No." I pulled on the word like a chain, drew us still closer together. She tried to draw away, but I held her fast. "Teach me, now. Before I am dead too long."

Her eyes narrowed and we stared each other down, will to will. "I never taught you, child, because you were not ready to learn. Are still not! You are too willful, too naïve, too lost. You don't know what you are, the damage you could cause. The knowledge will turn you into an evil creature. Don't you understand, even yet?"

"I don't care. You owe me this knowledge, Mother. You owe it to me. You don't have the right to hoard it, not when I need it so badly!"

We both knew I could not force her to say the actual words of the spell. Without training, all I could do was compel her to stay.

My mother yanked against my compulsion once more, grew still when she could not break our connection. She turned to our angel, her smile hard. "See, angel, how my own daughter mistreats me so."

To my surprise, Raziel did not immediately take my mother's part. "I have seen worse, Tekla. Worse by an infinite magnitude. To her credit, Magda's heart is true and she seeks the good, misguided as she is."

Emboldened by Raziel's gentle words, I drew closer to my mother, and we stood nose to astral nose. "Give. Me. My. *Spell.*"

"Do not defile my memory, Magda."

I steeled myself against the beloved cadences of her voice. "I'll do what I must."

"You don't understand what you are asking of me."

We stood together in the silence. Her features wavered and broke as she realized I would not relent. "I cannot fulfill my destiny in the afterworld when you hold me this way. The two of us will sink down into the lower emanations, where demons reside, if you do not stop it. Only the angel's protection keeps us here at all."

"So be it."

Her face went blank, iridescent and fine as the surface of a soap bubble. Her features contorted with grief, and the pain of her anger and disappointment cut through me like a strike of the angel's sword. Well I remembered that pain from my misguided youth, and that familiarity helped me to withstand it now.

For a moment she held her arms out to me, then she lowered them, slowly. And my mother's spirit looked away. "Your father, Magda. You say Gisele needs you—you have no idea how much your father needs me. He is a mere mortal, assailed by demons for his sin of consorting with me. You forced me from my soul mate."

That was the unkindest cut of all; she knew all too well how much I adored that man. But still I held fast. "Give me the spell and you can return to Papa in time. Give it to me for Gisele's sake, if not for mine."

We stared each other down, a contest of wills. My mother broke first. "You stubborn wretch, you get my spell, but it comes with my curse."

"I'll take it any way I can get it," I said, even as I winced at her words. But I would not relent.

She rubbed at her face with her hands, as if she could wash herself clean of what she was about to do to me. "I will give you the key to return, Magdalena. But if you dare to use it you will lose your humanity, one degree of your soul at a time, *nefesh, ruach, neshamah.* Piece by piece, you will become what you resist. Every time you go back from death, you leave a piece of your soul here with me."

I had to smile. Without her blessing, I was broken-souled anyway. "How about this, Mama? Don't leave me, then. Just haunt me until your shade is satisfied."

Her thin lips twisted into a sardonic smile. "In that case, Magdalena, my shade would haunt you until the end of time."

Raziel cleared his astral throat and both of us turned. "Do

you accept your mother's curse?" He looked every inch the warrior, with his muscular shape and brutal sword. But it was the compassion in Raziel's voice that almost broke me.

I fought to keep my voice steady. "For Gisele's sake, yes."

Our eyes met, and in that moment the angel and I made our peace, one with the other. He could not yet understand why I preferred cursed life to the serenity of death, but he respected my right to choose. And this acceptance gave me the courage to shoulder the burden of my choice.

My mother began intoning our family spell, in Hebrew but filtered in this place into a universal language that I could understand.

I turned to her, tried to touch her face, and she wavered like a shadow at midday. "Farewell, Mama, thank you, thank you. I kiss your hands, will kiss Gisele for you."

She turned away and closed her eyes in concentration, murmuring her spell all the while. Now I knew: astral spirits could shed tears. My attention strayed to Raziel, and I whispered again, to both of them, "Farewell . . ."

My astral body trembled like a tumbling leaf in a winter wind, and my being coalesced into an infinite number of tiny globules of pure light. I reached for the angel, stroked his bare shoulder, my fingertips rolling over and around him like a shower of ball bearings. "Bless you, Raziel. I will try my best to set you at your leisure."

His smile widened as I caught his gaze, and for the first time in that gray, indeterminate place, his eyes twinkled. "You are lying . . ."

His words trailed off after me as my mother's spell shot me back to earth, threaded through a needle of light.

⊚

I came back to myself with a hideous groan so guttural I thought at first it emanated from a beast in the forest. But no, it was my own throat, raw and choked.

The spell had healed the fatal wounds inflicted by the demonesses, enough to allow me to live again—but that didn't mean that my every scratch had vanished. Oh, no. The flies rose in a furious cloud as I sat up and rearranged my blood-matted hair, wiped the dirt out of my eyes.

I was alive again. Altogether, being dead seemed easier, considering the circumstances in which I found myself. And yet, my life was an inexpressibly precious gift, for it was a weapon that allowed my fight to continue.

My lovely suit was shredded into useless bloody rags, and I was wounded and filthy, vulnerable to my enemies. Who was to say that the demonesses wouldn't come to kill me again? I considered their absence—anything to distract myself from the physical pain of the long slashes they had sliced into my skin. They knew what I was. Why didn't they stick around to make sure I stayed dead for good?

A cool, mossy voice interrupted the tangled train of my thoughts, and the first spoken syllable shot a bolt of fear through my brain like a bullet.

"They won't bother with you anymore, Lazarus. The three already got what they wanted."

✻ II ✻

I forced my bloodshot, stinging eyes to focus on the source of the voice—I was too weak to hide myself or to run away. Still, when I discovered the creature who spoke, I scrabbled backward as best as I could, my bottom prickled by fir needles, my battered heart pounding hard enough to burst.

The demon crouched in the shadows, not even a meter's distance away. Only the flash of his white, blunted fangs betrayed his location to my blurry vision. His smile was like a pearl in the shifting face, animated like iron filings in the presence of a magnet.

I bit back a curse as I watched him watching me. He rocked back and forth on his haunches and folded his long fingers over his knobby knees. I rubbed my eyes to behold him more clearly, and when he didn't lunge for my throat, I slowly began to calm myself. "What are you?" I finally asked, as the heat of the waxing day grew.

He laughed then, and the sound pierced me with a strange pain of recognition. The long fingers rubbed at the corners of his jewel-like eyes. "You can't make me tell you." His singsong voice poked at my bad temper.

"Don't tease me, whatever you are." I tried to keep the pain and impatience out of my voice, and I failed, of course. Not even breakfast time yet, and I had already leaped out of a train, defied a messenger of the Almighty, been murdered by demons, and absorbed my own mother's curse to return from the dead.

I stood up, forgetting my modesty in my determination to stand up against this unnatural creature and protect myself any way I could. A snail clambered across my left breastbone, and I gently reached up and plucked it off my skin as if it were a gray, sticky pearl.

My clothes hung off my limbs in filthy tatters. Ah, Gisele . . . such a waste of a gifted seamstress's talents. The gray suit she'd made for me was a blood-soaked ruin.

"I have a new dress for you. It's blue, your favorite color," the creature of the shadows muttered.

His familiarity with my preferences gave me pause. I crossed my arms over my breasts and saw, folded neatly at his feet, the dress he described. "I look better in green, don't you think?"

He chuckled, an almost pleasing, throaty sound, the sound I imagine a dragonfly's laugh would make. That laugh gave me joy, I don't know why.

I smiled, and the warmth of simple amusement brought me a little more out of the grave. "Blue will suit me fine, of course.

But you didn't mention the price." I waited for the trick, the temptation. Surely, all he wanted was my soul. That's all he was supposed to want.

The little imp covered his face with his long fingers and giggled. "You shouldn't look a gift dress askance, for I do mean it as a gift, a love offering, if you must know. When a forest spirit gives you a present, you should welcome it with open arms. Ever your doubt and despair are your worst enemies, Magdalena."

My hand paused in midair, mere centimeters from the dress. "How do you know me so well, since we are only now first acquainted?"

He shrugged and scuttled sideways, clutching the dress now against his bare, hairless chest. "Now that you question me, I must demand a fair price for the dress. A shame, really. But you don't have a choice. You can't fight your battles wearing a shroud, dearie."

I tensed against his words. "What do you want?"

"A name. Give me a name, lovely witchling. Any name will do."

His request caught me by surprise. I licked my lips, looked for the danger in it, found none. "You don't have a name? Nobody ever named you? How sad." And despite the utter strangeness of the setting and circumstance, my heart swelled with protective instincts toward this mysterious stranger.

He shrugged but said no more. For a moment we stared at each other, and I was overcome simultaneously with a powerful thirst and a revulsion for the dirt that covered me. I motioned for him to stay, and I went in search of a stream or some standing water, anything I could drink and wash with.

I limped deeper into the trees, my bare soles tickled and scratched by the fir needles and broken twigs underfoot, wondering whether I would find a place of safety by the end of this unholy day.

"The nearest river is too far for you to walk," the creature said from behind me. He had followed me through the trees at some small distance, as if he were afraid of me.

"Leopold."

"Excuse me?"

"Your name. You asked me for one."

He sat back on his haunches, smacked his lips together as if he was tasting it, to see if the name was to his liking. The heavy eyelids narrowed. "Why Leopold?"

"I don't know." I was telling the truth . . . his name sprung into my mind, spoke itself through my lips unbidden by me.

He tilted his round little head. "Leopold." He rolled the name over his tongue like wine, a low, trilling sound, and he repeated it again and again. With every repetition, he grew a bit in size. He stopped, and nodded. Now he was the size of a twelve-year-old boy.

Our eyes met, and he smiled. "Handsome." He bowed, clicked his heels together smartly like a hussar on parade. Bending from the waist, he presented me with his offering, the dress that hung loosely in his hands.

I sighed and accepted the pretty cotton dress; I could now see it had pearl buttons and an embroidered collar. Covered in dirt and blood, I looked like what I was—a murder victim. But if I could only cover myself properly and get washed before encountering a living mortal . . .

I shucked off the rags that hung from my body, absurdly

wished for a silk slip so the skirt would hang perfectly from my hips. "So, the demonesses got what they wanted from me, Leopold? What do you mean?" I asked him to distract myself from my appalling physical condition, not because I believed he actually knew the answer.

"You know quite well. Your blood, Lazarus."

As soon as the words had escaped his lips, I realized that they were true. My spirits sank within me. "My blood. Why?"

"They seek your holy book. Your blood speaks to the Book, and that is all they need to hunt it down for themselves."

"My blood." I sounded stupid to my own ears, weak and stupid and slow. I buttoned the pearl buttons, my fingertips shaking with vexation. Leopold chuckled again. I looked up to see that his smile had widened, huge and inviting, and terrifyingly intimate.

"Blood, you know, is an inherently magical substance. It contains the essence of life. They'll trick your book, they will. Like Jacob stealing Esau's blessing by dressing in disguise as his hairy big brother."

Vague memories of Sunday school flickered in my mind. A picture from a child's book of stories, a trickster swathed in goat skins, a ruse he had learned at his mother's knee.

I remembered asking my own mother about that story . . . and she described it the same way that Leopold did now. Esau as the hairy big brother. The blood I still had left in me ran cold in my veins. "How do you know so much about me, Leopold?" Somewhere deep inside of me I already knew the answer, but I needed him to spell it out, speak the words in the brilliant light of a summer's day in the wild countryside of Austria.

"I will spell it out for you, Mama. If you need me to." He stretched to his full height, exactly my own height now.

The hairs on my forearms prickled and my long-suffering, battered heart began to pound anew. The blood on my lips tasted like rusty iron. "Don't call me Mama."

"But you are my mama. You made me. You named me."

I blinked hard, forced myself to keep my wits about me. I had heard fairy tales of demons forged of princesses' words and thoughts; heard of great rebbes who formed golems to save their humble Jewish folk from destruction.

But this was something different. "I didn't set out to create you, Leopold. I don't know any spells that could make you."

"But ah, your epic fury. Such bad temper is a luxury, in the path that you walk, Mama dear. Throwing sparks like you did into astral ether will surely seed the clouds with life. Who knows how many of my kind you spawned in the next world? Only I cleaved to you; you should be thanking your boy for that."

"No, Leopold. Oh, no . . ."

"Hah. I thought raising an army of demons was what you were aiming to do with your fancy book?"

My tormented heart skipped a beat. "An army?"

"Oh, yes."

"But even if I made you all, I couldn't lead you."

"If you ever get that book, you can. How do you think Solomon got that big golden temple all built? By himself?"

Wily Leopold, my deepest, darkest thoughts come alive and spoken out loud in the mundane world. Created from my evil impulses, he knew as well as I did what I desired but wasn't brave enough to admit aloud.

I took a deep breath and accepted the consequences of my evil, and hoped Raziel had taken himself away from me altogether so he couldn't see me choose. I understood my mother's curse now. My highest aspect of soul had sheared away, lost to me. I had come back, but not all of me. Some of my soul had sparked away to fuel the creation of Leopold and his countless escaped brothers.

"We go to raise an army, then, Leopold. But first I have to get mopped up somehow."

"You need help, Mama dear. But I am just a baby imp. I don't know how to find it."

"Well, where did you get this dress from? Let's start with that."

"From a girl."

He hesitated, and I leaned forward, my fear of him all but gone. "Are you lying to me, imp?"

He pulled a face. "So what if I am?"

"Don't do it, Leopold," I warned.

"Or you'll what, Magdalena? Get angry again?"

He knew as well as I that my anger would feed his power, give him dominion. I studied the swaying fir branches overhead until my vision cleared. The clean smell of the evergreen sap calmed me. "No, I won't let my temper get the best of me again. I'll send you away instead, Leopold. Take back your name."

"Y-you don't know how." His stutter gave away his fear.

"Oh I will, straightaway, I will. I may be untaught, but the talent flows in the blood the demonesses stole. So mind me well, and we'll get along. Just don't forget who's boss."

My lack of skills continued to worry me, ate away at my

peace of mind. I had to learn, and quickly, how to harness the power of my lineage, my book, my anger. If I didn't learn, my many enemies would break me.

I smoothed my new dress, admired the stitchery. No machine had finished the cuffs and collar . . . the energy of their maker hovered around the hems. I cautiously casted, to find the seamstress, and to my complete shock I found a vibration, faint but sure, far to the west—a gentle whisper of encouragement from kin.

"Not just a girl, Leopold. A witch. A Jewish witch, like me."

He shrugged, picked at his toes as he settled into a crouch again, and studied me without the merest pretense of circumspection. "Maybe she can help you, but I don't think she will. Stealing her dress was enough to do to her, no?"

6

Leopold and I did our best to clean me up. And then we traversed some of the loveliest countryside in Europe in our flight to the west. In the distance, the Bavarian Alps loomed over us, a brooding, white-faced glory hovering in the air, clouds made of stone.

The thin cotton of my new dress hardly protected me from the cool mountain air, even in summer, but I no longer cared. Before I was murdered, I felt the cold most particularly, and often felt chilled even when other people felt warm enough. But now, as we stumbled along, I no longer cared about the external temperature.

Leopold, who seemed to feel the cold more severely than I ever had, even as a girl, never complained, only shrank in size, burrowed into my hair, and snuggled up against the back of my skull. He and I spoke only a dozen words or so across our entire walking tour of Austria, but his presence proved a comfort, because he reminded me I still walked the earth, a mortal being. Alive. And as an additional benefit, he reminded me to drink water and eat what I could find in the fields: berries, bitter dandelion leaves. One glorious time, a field full of juicy peppers, ripe red and as voluptuous as a fever dream.

It is about 148 kilometers between Linz and Salzburg, and what would have taken me three hours by train instead took Leopold and me the better part of two weeks. During that time, I hid from the few mortal, nonmagical souls that crossed our path, and I slowly came to realize that I no longer had a place among the ordinary world of the living.

I did not dwell on the implications of that realization; all that mattered to me, and by extension to Leopold, was to get to Amsterdam so that I could find *The Book of Raziel*. And that was all I allowed myself to think about.

By the time we reached the outskirts of Salzburg, near the Bavarian border, my repeated casts had brought me into range of the helpful girl who had unknowingly supplied me with my dress. Trudy, pretty as edelweiss, only child of the chief witch of the local Daughters of Arachne coven, hidden away in dirndls and petticoats in the Bavarian foothills, on the German border.

Trudy was exactly my age, with white-blond hair and a cream-fed complexion. She looked like a Bavarian fräulein, a flawless daughter of the Aryan nation. But her eyes gave her away. They had the tired, haunted look of a deer harried by hounds. She masked the fear with a tight, perfect smile.

But I, who also lived by fear, could see its telltale traces. She and I both moved like ghosts over the land of the living, the world of those who refused to see the evil germinating all around them.

Bless them, the witches; they took me in without a word of protest. Trudy's mother, who refused to give me her name, had a face as soft and round as a cream bun, eyes deep-set, kind currants. She let me stay in the kitchen of their farmhouse, washed my hair and bloody feet in a bucket in the yard, gave me a new pair of ugly but sturdy walking shoes. But she refused to tell me of her coven and her clan, how they came to live unmolested among the folk in the foothills outside the Nazi town of Berchtesgaden.

The following morning, Trudy and I walked through the fallow fields, the sky a cold, brilliant blue bowl inverted over our heads, Leopold draped around my shoulders like a fox stole. I tried to get her to talk to me, tell me why despair hung over the coven's every word and deed, but she was more interested in giving me a tour of the surrounding environs.

The reason why became clear once we came to a scenic overpass, and stopped walking. Trudy pointed up into the clouds. "Hitler's stronghold is up that hill," the girl said.

✳ 12 ✳

We stared up into the haze surrounding the huge, silent mountains, and the cold alpine air stole my breath. "Hitler's stronghold. And you live in his shadow? How can you stand it?"

Trudy shrugged, as if she was trying her best to care but couldn't be bothered. "He is too busy to trouble about us, even to notice us. He knows we are here. He even befriended my little niece and invited her up to his mountain house, the Berghof, for her birthday. They had tea and cake together. I tell you the truth. Little Liesel is charming and sweet. Like her, all of us are too trifling for him to bother with."

I studied Trudy for overt signs of madness, but she seemed to believe every crazy word she said. She spoke slowly, rationally, as if she made perfect sense. We strolled along the forest path together, the pine trees waving in the brisk mountain breeze. Now that I had freshened up, finally gotten the tangles of blood out of my hair, we looked like two schoolgirls at liberty on a Sunday afternoon. The fatal calm of the alpine morning was like a goose-down coverlet smothering my face.

I needed Trudy's help, and I told her a fanciful version of my travels, the way I wish it had gone. With a flourish, I came to the point of my long story. I had laid it on thick; she had to help me. The trip westward had taken weeks longer than I had planned. And with every moment I spent taking the air near lovely Berchtesgaden, my enemies drew closer to claiming *The Book of Raziel*. Or they had captured the Book already.

"So. I must get to Amsterdam, and without any further delay."

"Of course we cannot do anything more to help you, Magdalena."

I stopped dead in the path we walked. Sunlight filtered to where we stood together in the gloom under the canopy of trees thick overhead.

She smoothed her already perfect hair, rubbed her arms as if she felt a chill too deep to banish. "I have my family, the same way you do. We live in our enemies' very shadow. If I step into your fight, even a baby step . . ."

I understood her point, though it was a bitter medicine to take. "You don't need any more enemies, that's for certain. But surely . . ."

I turned my head and studied the hills rolling serenely all around us. "Our enemies all work in league together, you will agree. They will come for you too, and not at the last either. For you are not only a witch, the same as me—you are also a Jew. The same as me. No matter how you look, what you believe, there's nothing you can do about it."

She winced and cleared her throat. "My family has lived here since time out of mind."

"That time is about to end, whether I can turn aside my sister's prophecy or not."

She shook her head against me, against the truth. "Surely they would have gotten rid of us, so close to Hitler's retreat. If they haven't yet, they won't."

"You don't want to see it, Daughter of Arachne, but by virtue of your simple existence you pose a threat to the supremacy of the Reich. No matter how ornamental and inoffensive you are, no matter how much you stand aside, nothing is going to save you. So fight."

The morning, crisp and clear and cold, seemed to grow darker under the weight of my words. But I fought for something bigger than myself, and that determination to resist my doom gave me a measure of comfort. Poor Trudy didn't even have that.

She paled as she considered my words, the roses fading from her cheeks. "But we trouble nobody, we are all but invisible."

"So you lie to yourself. But the man in the Eagle's Nest is ruled by fear, no less than you or I. Fear has no end—and to keep it at bay, he will destroy anything he deems a threat. Innocence is no protection."

I sighed, thought of my guardian angel, so far away and distant, a star I navigated by but untouchable except in my dreams. "Hitler really lives up there?"

"Oh, yes. It is no secret, Hitler's favorite getaway is up in those Bavarian mountains. His headquarters, the Berghof, used to be Otto Winter's place, Haus Wachenfeld. You should see it. It floats like a castle in the clouds. And far above it, the Eagle's Nest, like seeing the world from Heaven."

I had seen the world from heaven, and it was somehow far less picturesque than Trudy implied. But I tried not to vex the girl by pointing out how close to admiration her description sounded.

"Is it heavily guarded?"

Her bitter laughter drew my attention back to her lovely face. "What do you think, Lazarus? By the Liebstandarte SS bodyguards, by werewolves lurking in the forest. By demonic wards set over every single threshold. You have the sight, can you not tell?"

I cast my senses into the clean air, and a sudden rush of nausea almost sent me to my knees. The world began tilting sideways like a boat taking on water, and I reached to a pine trunk for support and missed.

Trudy had fed me well at breakfast time, with hot buttered rolls, boiled eggs, and warm milk with coffee and sugar. I was glad I had eaten before turning my attention to the Berghof and the Eagle's Nest perched high in the Bavarian hills.

Blinking hard, my eyes leaking with tears, I covered my face and withdrew my senses inward, away. The world returned to its pristine alpine clarity, and mercifully the urge to toss up my breakfast receded.

"Well protected, indeed," I managed to say.

When I opened my eyes, Trudy knelt beside me, her face a carefully composed picture of concern. "I want to help you, you know I do. But I have to keep my clan alive. We've already done too much."

By now, I understood that Trudy's exposed position posed a danger to me too. She and her coven had done all they could. "You're right. Send me away. If you know a friendly soul on the way to Amsterdam, send me to her. I will not endanger you further—by the Witch of Ein Dor! To live in the shadow of such a place every minute of the day."

Trudy shrugged, wet the tip of a forefinger and tested the wind. "It is only the devil we know. No worries, Lazarus. You fight your battles, and we will fight ours."

I was about to respond, to say that our battle was the same, when we both smelled the same rank rot in the same moment. The Staff.

"Go into shit," I muttered at him in Hungarian, and I rose to my feet. My new, ugly shoes were a little big but fine with some newspaper crumpled into the toes. I smoothed the dress Leopold had pinched for me, quickly skimming my fingers over the brushed cotton and the careful needlework.

"I'll draw him off; he's still far away. That's the sorcerer I told you about. He must be visiting Herr Hitler up in the clouds. That wizard's after me and my kind, not you."

"He'll know I helped you." Her voice was steady, but I saw the panic rising in her eyes.

"No, no . . . I'll go fast enough to protect you. He doesn't care, doesn't have time to take his revenge, and if he comes round later you'll smell him again before it's too late."

She straightened her pinafore, wiped the tears off her cheeks, but otherwise looked perfectly composed. "Do what you must."

"I'll take him off your hands, easy as you please. Kiss your mother for me, and thank her from my heart."

Upon consideration, I understood Trudy's strange half existence well. Sometimes, pretty lies are all we have.

I left her in the clearing and started hiking up the winding pathway to the Berghof, my limbs trembling with exertion with every step, my mind recalling the horrible visions my sister had poured like poison into my ears and that now I could not erase from my brain.

As I walked I stoked my heroic delusions. Why stop at the Staff? If I could survive an encounter with the wizard, and return from death's dominion too, why not confront Herr Hitler himself?

My ankle tingled with a sudden tug, but I ignored it and kept going. The tug turned into a bite, sharp but not excruciating.

Leopold had embedded his blunt imp's teeth into my ankle. "Ow! What the blazes are you doing?"

I shook my foot, but the creature, now no larger than a kitten, held fast, pulsed with the tempo of my agitation. "Mmph, mmph!" He refused to disengage long enough to make his meaning clear.

With a rumbling sigh, I reached down and pried his jaw open. His little chin felt cold and scaly to the touch, but though he waxed with my own evil, I could not fear him. To the contrary, his impulsive, wicked ways were all too familiar.

"Peace, Leopold! Let me do what I have to do."

"You forget yourself, Mama."

"I forget nothing."

I held him in my hands like a baby dragon crouched in my palms and I started upward along the path again. His screaming shriek sounded like a wailing woman at the edge of a grave.

The din was so dreadful, so disastrous, that I had to stop him before I went on. "What, Leopold?"

He smiled when he saw how he had gotten my attention, sat up and drank my impatience like my life's blood. "You seek your book. The Book!"

"Of course, so I can save my sister and fight. But my adversary waits for me here!"

He shook his head, clearly convinced I was too stupid to save. "You think Hitler is your worst problem."

For the first time since I had set off on the mountain path, my grim self-righteousness began to falter. "Well . . . *yes*. Hitler is the key to all. If he dies, Gisele's prophecies die with him. He is a madman like Napoleon—vanquish him, and the world will settle. He is so close."

"Think! How many thousands of Jews wish they could strike Hitler dead with their own hands. But you know all too well that is a fool's dream, no more."

It was my dream too, but I held my tongue. I had assumed Leopold's knowledge and abilities were limited to my own, that as my creature he was thus constrained in his potential and range.

His eyes glinted, and his lips parted in a delicate grimace of a smile. "I am indeed your child. And may the child not exceed the mother?"

The imp alluded to my mother and myself, and he appealed to my own pride as well as his intended path. "Ah, tempter. You can't stop me, not even with the truth."

"You know you mustn't. Without the Book, you will die long before you reach the front door. The Staff and the SS werewolves will surely see to that."

Leopold spoke my fears aloud, and my traitor body began to tremble from the top of my head to my feet in their ugly shoes. "Ah, but what about you, little protégé? I thought you plan on exceeding me."

"Of course my ambition matches yours. But if you die I die with you." His face, pleading, grew serious. "If you die here, you stay dead, and for very bad reasons. I am not ready for death, even if you are. Life in this world is sweet."

"I would die to stop the man in that palace in the mountains." I could see it now, half hidden by fir and linden trees overlooking a scenic valley.

"Don't die a stupid death, Magda. Smell the werewolves— they wait!"

As soon as he said it, the wind shifted and I could scent them all around us.

"Mama, go back down now and they won't risk crossing their wards to attack you," he wheedled, his fingers prickling against mine as he gripped them.

I hesitated. He was right, of course. But to know my nemesis was so close, just above my head . . . I didn't want to die, no more than Leopold did. But I had to stop the Staff and his master, Hitler. They were both so close.

Yet as I walked, Leopold's nibbles no more than a mere annoyance, my steps slowed. My body longed for coffee, pastry, a cigarette even, in Bathory's corner alcove of Café Istanbul. And though my world still existed, in daily life as well as in my memory, I sheared away from that blessed ordinariness. Life in Budapest still ran along its customary tracks, like the yellow tram I rode home from work in the light of dawn.

And in that moment I understood my mother as I never had before. Her unceasing craving for normalcy. Simple mortality. A life of husband, little girls, red balloons and bicycles on a spring morning at Heroes' Square.

My footfalls along the path slowed, then stopped. My

mother's way, the domestic paradise of husband and children, was not mine to choose. And Leopold, my little evil impulse, was true and right, the very embodiment of the voice I had fought to ignore every night I had escaped to the cafés, to my ardent Communist poets, to avoid my mother and her witch's knowledge.

To seek my death at Hitler's hands now, to openly fling myself into oblivion, was not my proper fate. It was false courage, the courage of blustering, innocent youth. I was only twenty in human years. Yet already I was no longer as innocent as that.

I stroked Leopold's head with the fingertips of my left hand. "Ah, my friend, my friend," I whispered, the salt of my tears delicious against my living lips. "I waste your precious time and mine. We must go on to Amsterdam."

I sensed the werewolf dogs glaring at us in the darkness of the alpine shadows, listening to every syllable we spoke aloud. They waited, longing to tear out my throat, and they knew I could not forestall them if I stepped into their demesnes. Another hundred meters, less, I could almost hear them whisper. Come, come.

I turned my back on them and retreated down the path, Leopold trilling with pleasure, a low growl of frustration rising all but inaudible behind us. They knew they could not touch me with impunity, not outside their wards, not with Leopold on my shoulder and the angel's blessing on my heart.

"Ah, Mama, Mama," Leopold sang, when we had gotten well clear of the path to Hitler's compound. "We live to see another day."

He took a springing leap out of my hands, clean muscled and wiry like a homeless cat. He landed in the path ahead, and sent up a puff of dust and fir needles.

He looked at me over his shoulder and he smiled. And in a

bright flash he grew into a man-sized form, contained within a burst of spiritual lightning. "I ascend, Mama, I ascend. I saved your life, a good deed, and now I ascend."

His words surprised me, left me bereft. "But why are you going now, Leopold? I need you, to help me get to Amsterdam."

Leopold smoothed his skull with his fingertips. "You never needed me, Mama. But I did a good to you, it raises me higher. I may go?"

I felt naked at the spot on my shoulder where Leopold had perched in our journey together westward. But the little imp deserved his freedom, his own chance to choose his path.

Our farewell was unexpected and sudden. I rubbed at my eyes and nodded, a little too quickly. "Go."

I watched him go forth with a mother's twinge at seeing him lift away from where I stood, planted like a tree on the hillside below him. All of us live on through our good deeds, but it shook me to see my wicked ones become sentient and alive. And thus, transformed.

"Be free, Leopold," I called, and the sight of him shooting into the sky like a firework, glowing marigold orange in the morning sunlight, made me gasp. "Bless you, Leopold, go in peace. Stay out of trouble!"

"But I am your child, Mama. Trouble, I love." He did a dancing little jig in the sky, exuberant as a Chagall painting, blazing as he rose and disappeared into the sky, a star falling upward. The spark of my soul that had sheared off to make Leopold pulled painfully away.

I was glad to see him escape the troubles of this world, even as I stayed behind to face them. "Good-bye," I whispered. And I waited for the Staff to hunt me down.

✳ *13* ✳

I waited, but the Staff never came. Did Leopold perform another good deed and draw the wizard away from me? Or did the Staff have other missions to accomplish, knowing he had failed to lure me past the wards protecting Hitler and into the werewolves' waiting jaws? To this day, the mystery remains unsolved, but as the day faded and the wizard stayed away, I realized that I was not destined to face him on the mountainside near Hitler's Eagle's Nest.

The Staff, gone, no longer represented an imminent threat to Trudy and her coven. I decided to come back down the mountain, thank her mother properly, and see if I could do anything to help them in their quiet desperation.

Instead, the country witches blessed me with their generosity and understated courage. Trudy and her family did what they could to send me swiftly on my way, in the hope that they could return to their peaceful, anonymous existence in the shadow of the Reich. Trudy's mother went so far as to convince her cousin, a wealthy bandleader, to lend me his second car.

I had but little experience behind the wheel of an auto— Bathory had a driver who would take me on errands, a gentle creature named Janos with moth-powder skin, who wore dark glasses day and night. But the roads, though treacherous through the mountains, were all but deserted.

After I got clear of the mountains, the motorcar ride to the border passed in a whir, my mind racing faster than the wheels could spin. The ease of my journey troubled me. I imagined the Staff observed every step I took back from the brink of the Berghof. He had let me go—why? The answer to that uncomfortable question evaded my conscious mind.

Once at the border, with a few well-placed bribes, I slipped into Switzerland, and from there procured a map and some gasoline. After a picturesque and rather uneventful tour of the Swiss countryside, I left the car with yet another witchy cousin in the gorgeous Lake Geneva town of Montreux. There I caught a train for Lausanne and from there to the great railway hub of Paris. Despite my murder, the demonesses had left my satchel and money intact, and when I converted my pengös into francs I was suddenly rich—and Bathory's credit was good everywhere.

Now that I was free of the Reich and had plenty of cash to spend, my fugitive taint was an all but invisible shadow. But in my dreams . . .

Whether I slept in a motorcar on the side of a Swiss mountain pass, a humble third-class berth on the train to Paris, or in the Hotel Bastille, with clean sheets and a tidy common bath in the hallway, my nightmares stayed the same. Every night, the werewolves waited for me, and their fangs ripped my body apart. The wizard stole my soul and tortured me for evermore. And over all my sufferings, looming high in the thunderheads, brooded the hate-filled face of Hitler himself.

I hid from sleep, avoided rest. And alone in the watches of the night, Raziel stayed with me, so close that I could almost touch him. I never called him down from heaven to travel by my side; the reality of Raziel in my world frightened me rather more than my fear-inflected nightmares of wolves, wizard, and tyrant. But the knowledge that Raziel existed, that angels watch over us as we stumble along our destined paths, was a talisman that I kept close to my heart all the way to Paris.

Daytime was another matter entirely. It did not do, my looking haggard. So on my second day in Paris, I resolved to look the part of vampire's emissary. Rather than invest in a cumbersome trousseau, I went to a certain fine boutique at 31 rue Cambon and spent my ready cash on a single Chanel suit with braided trim, and with buttons like coins, impeccable and perfect in every way. I all but bankrupted myself to match it with a pair of ravishing alligator pumps.

Thus armored in sartorial perfection, I went in search of the only man in Paris who could help me: Robert Capa, world-famous war photographer, the man who had made his fame capturing iconic images of the Spanish Civil War. He was also the boy who'd pulled my pigtails at the gymnasium, in another world, many lifetimes ago.

✳ 14 ✳

JULY, 1939
PARIS

I was lucky. I found Capa at a little round table outside the Café du Dôme; he sat alone, smoking cigarettes one after another, lost in the same melancholy reverie as the other denizens of the immortal city.

I found Paris's doldrums somewhat difficult to understand. Paris, unlike Budapest, was still a free city. Yet, Paris was wrapped in a gloomy pall, completely at odds with the glorious, not-too-hot summer weather. Geraniums bloomed with wild abandon, feral cats haunted the charming bistros, and the echoes of that lovely, melancholy melody, "J'attendrai," trailed after me, whispered out of radios propped in open windows.

Capa had apparently succumbed to the same sullen tantrum as the rest of the city. I smacked him on the shoulder, the way I'd once done as a bratty girl at our Sunday family séances. His little brother, Cornell, had liked me better, but Capa was the only Hungarian I knew who now lived in Paris, and I needed all the help I could get, no matter the source.

"Hey. Greatest photographer in the world. Give a girl a cigarette, will you?"

His eyes smoldered and he wheeled on me, glowering, his thin lips curled into an unspoken retort. Behind his displeasure I detected desolation, and I remembered: his father had just died a few weeks before, and his breathtaking fiancée, the "Little Blonde" Gerda Taro, had died in the Spanish Civil War not all that long before that. In this, Capa prefigured us.

My heart gave a little twinge, a pinch of remorse. "Sorry, Endre," I said softly, calling him by his original, Hungarian name. "Budapest sarcasm doesn't sound like wit here in Paris, yes?"

Capa started, ran his blunt fingers through his thick black hair. He shook his head, as if to get the dreams out. "My God, it's Magdalena Lazarus, isn't it."

He squinted hard, took my chin in his fingertips and tilted my face up to the shifting twilight for proper inspection. "Fantastic. Something about the planes of your face . . . completely different."

I said nothing, realizing that a professional photographer with such an expert eye would surely see the troubles written clearly on my face. I let him examine me, and enjoyed the pressure of his fingers on my chin, the rustle of his body in his thin silk shirt.

"Your skin is etched in marble, Magda. Uncanny."

I shrugged, not sure whether to take his observation as a compliment or not. "Well, you look different too, my friend. It's been a long time since you went away from Budapest."

He sighed and let go of me. "Long years. Bad years."

I kissed him on both his cheeks, reached for his hands and squeezed them hard. Like the rest of us, he'd lost a lot of family since 1933, but for some reason his heartbreak moved my stone-cold heart with pity. "But you are still ever the lady-killer, Capa."

He half smiled, an unlit cigarette still tucked between his lips, and I saw that my flattery pleased him. "But not of you, little Magduska, Lady Lazarus. You were always immune to my lady-killing."

I plucked the cigarette from between his lips and snatched the lighter off the table. "Immune, surely no. Resistant, perhaps."

The Zippo felt heavy and cold in my fingers, and I luxuriated in the ritual of flicking, lighting, deeply inhaling the smoke. "I need your advice, dear Capa. Do you have a moment for me?"

His half smile broadened into a low, throaty laugh. "For my beautiful friend from Budapest, always. But only if you tell me all of your secrets: why you have come to Paris. How long you plan to stay."

I took a long, slow drag on the cigarette to calm my jangled nerves. "Oh, I'm just passing through, on my way to Amsterdam. Family business."

Capa really was the world's best photographer, and a master of the human face. His photos of the Spanish Civil War and the ghoul attacks in Guernica were published the previous winter in *Life* magazine, and rightly had made his fame. I had tried to keep my voice casual, but Capa's eyes were too sharp.

He leaned back, closed his eyes, and smiled, his thoughts far away. When he opened them again, our gazes met, and he conveyed his hidden pain to me, a knowing and unspoken kinship with the hunted ones of this world.

I knew he saw the shadow of death over my mask of unstudied elegance. I had been at pains to look the part of a sophisticated Continental traveler, but Capa, like me, could see through the surface disguises we all employ to hide ourselves. And he didn't need magic to do it.

"It's really bad in Budapest, isn't it." He merely stated the fact, didn't bother to dress the sentiment up as a question.

I affected nonchalance, but Capa, with his melancholy eyes, could see through it. "It's bad everywhere." And I shrugged and smiled; no point in bewailing our collective rotten fate.

"If you need money, Magda, I must warn you that fame and fortune are two separate creatures."

A fat, buttery croissant tempted me on Capa's table. My stomach rumbled, hopefully too quietly for him to hear. "Oh, no, don't worry about it. I have my way to Amsterdam mapped out. I only wanted to know if you could introduce me to anybody you know in Amsterdam, any Hungarians. I have my formal introductions all lined up . . ."

I hesitated, saw Capa still followed me. "But I wouldn't mind having a secondary plan in case the first falls through. I know you passed through there in your travels, after . . ." After Gerda died, I almost said.

"Yes, after." His smile, so sweet and sad, could have melted the heart of any other woman in Paris, I am sure.

I gave him the privacy of his grief and took a peek at the cluster of chairs and tables assembled on the pavement outside the Dôme. It was as perfect a Montparnasse café as anyone could imagine, with both human and magical customers, real coffee, and sausage and pastry in wild abundance. No matter where I ended up, at least I could say that, before my life ended, I had spent some time in the City of Light, in Paris, in the year of the Christian God 1939.

I sighed with bittersweet contentment. "Not bad, this Dôme place. Reminds me a little of Budapest."

I made him laugh, and I saw he enjoyed my ability to coax mirth from him. "Almost. Paris has no Café Istanbul."

I smiled, thought of my precious vampires. "Yes."

Capa waved at the waiter, a Frenchman adorned with an elaborate mustache, and he ordered me a coffee and seltzer without my asking. As we watched the waiter shamble away, I wondered, not for the first time, if I would ever see Budapest again.

Capa's soft voice broke into my thoughts. "Listen. My friend Lucretia will help you out—as long as you don't bother her with too many questions. You'll have to keep your wits about you, understand? She isn't Hungarian, either. Belgian, I think."

"You think? Some friend."

Capa refused to banter with me, or to take up my teasing tone. "No, it's complicated." Ah, everything was complicated with Capa.

How comforting that some things hadn't changed. I beamed at him, patted his arm. "It's good to see you again, Endre. Like having Budapest here with us."

Capa lit a new cigarette. "Budapest is not such a good friend to me. Or to you."

My coffee arrived with a flourish from the waiter, and I made a great show of dressing it up with sugar, stirring it, taking slow, preparatory sips. I never felt cold anymore, but I could not get warm, either.

"You're in deep trouble, Lady Lazarus." Again, a statement, not a question. "I'm no good at rescuing fair maidens in distress, I must warn you."

"Fear not, good knight. I am used to taking care of myself." But my voice caught on the last word.

I decided to take a chance on getting at the truth. Capa thought of me as a little brat anyway. He could always laugh me off, and I would laugh along with him. I leaned forward and lowered my voice. "Tell me, Capa. What's your secret? How do you walk right into danger and out the other side?"

He took my hand in his, stroked it like a dove nestled in a nest. "No secret. If I only knew . . ."

Ah, he meant Gerda, his doomed fiancée, dead in the Spanish war. I bit my lip; I didn't mean to poke him. But he didn't seem angry. He sighed and shrugged, his eyes still downcast. "I guess what you do is, you just read the wind. When it's time to move, don't hesitate. Just go. You might not survive, but at least you move in the right direction."

He reached for my hand and played with my grandmother's red-gold ring, twirled it around my little finger. "This ring is cute, shaped like a ribbon tied in a bow. I want you to use it to remind you of what I am going to tell you now."

I looked into his eyes, and he looked up into mine. "Forget about being good," Capa continued. "We don't know each other so well, but I recall you are trying always to be all things to all people. Believe me, you can't."

I swallowed hard, my mouth suddenly cotton-dry. "But what about the people who depend on you?"

"No. Even worse. You can't save anybody in this world, Magda. Not a single, solitary soul. Forget it. Live your life, *your* life. Give up your imitation of a hothouse flower."

His last words puzzled me. "Hothouse? Who mentioned a hothouse?"

"Oh, nobody. But I remember your father from when I was only about ten and you were a little sprite. He was already fading, you know, but he wanted nothing more than to hide you and your sister away. He was wrong. You're more like Queen Anne's lace, meant to grow wild."

"Oh, a weed. Thank you so much."

His grip tightened over my hand. "No. A wildflower, not an orchid. Stop trying to please your mother by being a perfect ornament—she's dead. You're not. And as for your little sister, she will have to make her own way just like the rest of us."

He released my hand at last. I rubbed my knuckles and reached for my coffee, and cursed myself in a most unladylike way when I spilled half of it into the saucer.

Capa, mercifully, laughed at me so that I could breathe again. "Just go to Amsterdam. Do what you must. I will tell you all about Lucretia—but you better forget about being good if you plan to get along with her."

✳ 15 ✳

I don't believe in coincidence. The Lucretia that Capa knew turned out to be the same Lucretia, leader of the Daughters of Arachne coven, who Trudy knew as her distant cousin in Amsterdam. She and I were meant to meet, indeed.

My mission to Amsterdam intersected with Bathory's machinations, but they did not entirely coincide. Lucretia would help me, for Trudy's sake if not for Capa's. But my train for Amsterdam did not leave until the morning.

I decided not to take a room. I could sleep on the train when the time came, and in those days Paris didn't sleep either. The Seine, sister to the Danube, snaked through the heart of the city of Paris. It smelled of algae, of chlorine, of unfinished dreams. It was dangerous to wander down to the river on the Left Bank, but danger was no stranger to me, and Capa was right—none of my virtuous ways, my attempts to become either an upright daughter of Hungarian society, or her mirror image, a wicked and purely doctrinaire Communist, had done me a single drop of good.

The darkened houseboats stretched along the river's edge, slumbering silent in the dead of night, witches' time, my time. I haunted the night of Paris, and she haunted me. I willfully refused to send my sight along the path where rats scrabbled and people with no home wandered. *Let my enemies come. Let them.*

I saw the face of Notre Dame reflected in the shimmering, dark water. A breeze rose and skittered along the quay below me, rattling the closed-up wooden kiosks where vendors sold used books and trinkets by day. Not a single human soul revealed itself in the night.

Ah, Capa was right. About everything.

On impulse, I reached heavenward, took a deep breath, whispered

RAZIEL

And obediently the air before me shimmered, opalescent. His wings manifested first, unfurled over me like a canopy of light. His heavenly form filled in next, encased in a tight, double-breasted suit with a chalk stripe—dove gray and perfectly tailored. Gisele herself could have done no better.

His fedora appeared next, cocked rakishly on his still-iridescent head. Finally, his face shone into existence, etched into my memory as well as the air, his visage as perfect as an El Greco saint's.

Raziel's face, still and serene, remained remote and closed to me. For once, I didn't care.

"Beware, Magda. This way is death," Raziel whispered, directly into my mind. He settled into manifestation with a barely audible sigh.

"No, to the contrary, my dearest angel. I'd rather be alive than saintly but dead."

He blinked hard and smiled, a crooked little smile that looked out of place on his angelic face. He straightened the hat on his head, stretched his wings to their full, breathtaking span, and then carefully folded them like a paper fan against his broad back. "What does it mean—'be alive'? To one such as you, or me?"

Raziel strolled closer to me, like any acquaintance in the street, and the breath caught in my chest, like all of the oxygen in Paris had shot up to heaven in his place.

He shook his head, shot his cuffs, and licked his lips. "Tell me, Lazarus. What led you to break your solemn oath so easily?"

Wickedness was much more attractive and easy in theory than in actual, dangerous practice. My heart fluttered like a butterfly trapped inside my chest. And all at once, my emotions broke free, that butterfly escaped into pure delight. Instead of convention or the orthodox Party line, I stood alone, with my true, honest desire.

"I just wanted to see you, angel. And I wanted to thank you before it's too late."

The corners of Raziel's eyes crinkled when he smiled, as if merriment set him free from sainthood too. He had a dimple high on his left cheek.

Raziel drew nearer still, and I smelled musk and cinnamon, heard a low murmuring of bells like a musical gust rushing toward me as he came. "What else is an angel for but to serve as a messenger of good tidings? We rejoice to receive these messages as well as to deliver them."

His reply threw me into a grave confusion, a dizzy springtime fever of emotion. Far below us, I heard the soft slap of the Seine against the houseboats moored along the river's banks.

I took a deep breath and tried to regain my bearings. "But I thought calling you, compelling you, was a dreadful sin. A twisting of cosmic law, no?"

He laughed out loud, a lovely, terrifying sound. And his mirth pierced me, shot me through the heart with a strange, inexplicable longing.

Raziel leaned against the railing and looked over the side to where the Seine flowed far below us. We stood close enough that I could study his long, soft eyelashes. "Mortal souls have called upon the Almighty and his Heavenly Host since time out of mind. Calling an angel to your side is no sin; to answer your call is why I am created."

"But—Vienna. You were so angry when you appeared on that platform!"

"Of course, I came to Earth filled with a mighty and righteous wrath. But not against *you*, Magda."

I blinked hard, the sudden rush of tears surprising me as much as his revelations. "I always thought anger was a grave sin, too."

"So many sins! From what you say, everything you do is a grave sin. Your very existence is a sin."

I blinked my traitorous tears back with difficulty. I had thought the price of returning from the dead included a blast of heavenly wrath as well as a good percentage of my eternal soul. For the first time since I had returned to life and earth, the night air caressed my living skin, my senses opened to the world again. "Life is so good, it's worth sinning to live."

"But you have committed no cosmic crime, my girl. You have the right to live, to fight to live. And the Almighty Himself granted you this gift of return."

Why *had* I returned? I thought of Capa's face when he spoke of Gerda, my mother's when she spoke of my father—love can be cruel.

Carefully, I kept Raziel at a distance so that I could calm my racing, galloping pulse. "Honestly, Raziel. I broke all my frightful oaths simply to bring you here to thank you, with all of my heart, before I go to Amsterdam and start sinning for certain. And I also wanted to invite you for a cognac. No more."

He hesitated. "Cognac?"

"Yes. Or if you are not allowed to drink spirits, at least a white wine with seltzer or a strong cup of coffee. I want to toast the fact that you exist, Raziel."

He looked away, quickly, as if my words stung him, across the river to the black, shadowy face of Notre Dame by night. Out of the corner of my eye, I saw a couple, little more than shadows in the night, stroll along the path and down the stairway to the river's edge.

"Love can make people do funny things," I said, half in a reverie. "But love is all that matters in the end, isn't it?"

He smiled then, though his smile was melancholy. "But you were speaking of cognac, not love. Why not? Let's have a drink in Paris—I'll toast you, and you toast me."

✳ *16* ✳

Heaven is a crowded café, decorated with smoke and light and condensation caught against plate-glass windows filled with darkness. With white linen tablecloths, and smiling waiters who don't sneer at you because you are a woman, a Jew, or both. With coffee flowing in an endless, sweet river. And filled with languorous, beautiful, benevolent souls.

In the midst of my Heaven sits an angel, Raziel. Refusing a cigarette but more than content with a crock of French onion soup and a small espresso in a gilded cup; an angel with a diabolical smile, diabolical because of the emotions this Raziel summons forth from me.

We had wandered into the Café Alibi, and French hauteur, applied democratically to all patrons not known to the establishment, cloaked us in an anonymity that worked better than any spell. Raziel kept his wings tightly furled and out of sight, his godlight at a low wattage. Still, every female in the place hardly failed to notice him.

"Where do they go?" I asked him, after the waiter had settled us in an obscure corner.

"Go? They?"

I leaned forward, and whispered conspiratorially, "Your wings."

His smile broadened, and his whiskey brown eyes dazzled me with his warm, barely suppressible radiance. "Ah, those. They are made of light, you know. Everything is made of light, but my wings—they are at a higher frequency than this place, than the rest of me. The everlasting love of the Almighty, clouds of unknowing . . . Anyway, I turn them down like a wick in a gas lamp."

His analogy made me smile too. "And they fold away just like ladybug wings. Charming, and practical too."

He laughed aloud, and so did I. Some ladybug he was, Raziel. I leaned over the tiny round table and studied his features, memorized them for a talisman against despair. "Ladybugs are good luck, you know." I dared to touched his forearm with the tips of my fingers, and a warm glow ran through me like an incandescent light.

His smile faded away. "You sound like you are saying goodbye."

I took a long, camouflaging sip of my café au lait. "Aren't I?"

"Magda. Always call upon me—I hear you best from the midst of the fire."

"Is that so." I replaced my coffee cup in its matching saucer, admired the steadiness in my hands. "But what about those poor devils trapped in that hell. That . . . Mauthausen. Are their guardian angels listening to them? Or are they too far away to hear their cries for mercy, their prayers?"

I watched the sea of living mortals churn: smoking, kissing, fighting, drinking, drowsing, hating, despairing. Life surged all around us, and Raziel was my island in the midst of it. "Why do you come to me? What about the children slaughtered last year during the Kristallnacht? Didn't those sweet babies deserve to be saved?"

Raziel squeezed my fingers, and unwillingly I shifted my gaze to look at him.

His eyes, huge and dark, looked deeply into mine. His voice was so hoarse I could scarcely understand his words. "Don't you think I ask the same questions? Do you think that the Almighty Himself deigns to whisper all the answers into my ear?"

I had never heard Raziel even whisper a word of doubt before now. My heart began to pound, and the noise of the café retreated to a low hum as we leaned closer together. "Oh, Raziel. I had hoped you would have a more enlightened view on our wretched human affairs. Some crutch for me to lean on."

When Raziel spoke, his smooth baritone voice was still husky. "No. Unless that crutch is me."

"But, Raziel . . ." I bit my lip, tried again. "I can't lean on you, not that way. That couldn't be what God had in mind—could it? I thought compelling an angel violated the witches' creed, and Divine law, too."

His eyes flashed with a danger I could not identify, and I braced myself for a divine stroke of lightning, for a smiting.

No divine retribution struck me where I sat, but Raziel frightened me enough. His fingers inched out and re-captured mine. "I cannot tell you God's plan. But I come to you because you call to me, have the power to compel me."

"But why do you not rebuke me for summoning you?"

"Because. I *want* you to summon me. Even compel me to stay."

My cheeks burned with the shock and I spilled my coffee. As I mopped up the mess and ruined a lovely linen napkin, I considered the implications of what he'd just said. Raziel was tempted to fall, to walk alongside me on Earth. That truth put our earlier adventures into another light entirely.

His fingers slid up the length of my arms to the tops of my shoulders, and he pulled me away from the damp disaster of our table. I could feel his breath, hot and sweet, on my face. "No one, Magda, has ever called me by name to Earth. Not the Witch of Ein Dor, not another angel, not the wizard Rabdos Staff. I have come to deliver specific messages, and left thereafter. I came long ago to give a gift once, a balm to a suffering soul.

"But I never drank coffee and debated philosophy with mortals in a Parisian café before. Never joked about my wings before."

I thought he was going to lean in and kiss me, and Heaven help me, I was going to let him. But he closed his eyes against me, released my shoulders, and pushed his chair away. Little drips of coffee ran in rivulets off the far end of the table.

That cinnamon-scented kiss, withheld, burned my lips as much as if it had happened. Capa was right, but I didn't care: Goodness would have to trump passion, at least for now. I couldn't let him do it. "I've put you in danger, angel mine. Gisele is charge enough."

"Do not presume," Raziel interrupted me, in a low, choking

growl. "I am angel born, but I am a primal spirit of the air. Protected. But—"

"Exactly. You have to stay protected."

"Let Raziel take care of Raziel. And you as well."

"But," I protested, "you have taken care of me from the second Heaven. That is where you properly belong."

Raziel's gaze pinned me like a butterfly to my chair. "No. No more second Heaven for me, no longer. You and your clan are my destiny and my charge. And unlike those slaughtered innocents who ascended straight to the throne of the Most High, you, little star, will not ascend so easily should the wizard have his way."

My program of flouting convention had gotten me nowhere but on the verge of the kind of trouble proper mamas warn their girls about. I covered my confusion by withdrawing a compact and lipstick from my new beaded bag, and even though it was rude I painted my lips right at the table, in the full view of my bewitching guardian.

I pressed my lips together to smooth the coral lipstick to the lip line, checked the rest of my makeup in the mirror—

And read the wind.

"We have to leave," I muttered, my fingers suddenly as cold as death.

"You cannot run from me," Raziel began to say, but I lunged for him and we toppled to the ground just as the gunfire erupted from the front door. I did not know if angels' bodies were immune to gunshot, but I did not want to find out.

The concussive sound of breaking glass and the rising shriek of ladies' screams drowned out anything I could have said, any rational chain of thought. I draped my body over his, chest to chest, and I buried my face in the wide expanse of his arms, closed my eyes against the screaming pandemonium.

Almost immediately, the gunfire ceased, and we were in more danger from broken glass and the stampede of panicked Parisians fleeing from the café. After a moment, the smell of gunpowder faded and the smoke began to clear.

I wanted to stay wrapped in Raziel's arms. But I snuffed that tender impulse like a cigarette, and dared to take a quick look around the café.

A man's body sprawled facedown in the broken glass, blood pooling out in a circle like a spell of death all around him. The headwaiter's face popped up over the surface of the bar like a ragged Punch-and-Judy puppet, his chubby cheeks streaked with sweat and dirt. He shrieked in broken French, "The Fascist dogs have got Hilare." And then he dove under the bar again.

A flash blinded me, and I flinched until I realized it was a photographer's bulb and not another round of bullets. A silhouette of a lithe, athletic male figure crossed into the room, and again he shot his camera like a gun.

I blinked hard against the flashes of negative light filling my eyes, strained to make out the man's shadowed features. And then I laughed, a maniacal giggle dancing at the edge of madness. Of course.

The man taking photos was Capa.

6

"This is why I can't stand Paris right now," Capa said later, another unlit cigarette dangling from his lower lip. "The Third

Republic still stands, yes. But these fascist thugs run around the city, shooting it out with the Communists. It's not as bad as Budapest, not yet. But it doesn't take a mystic—sorry, Magda— to see which way the winds are blowing."

Capa, bless him, had rescued us from the floor of the Alibi and installed us at his customary table at the Dôme. He bought us both something alcoholic and fortifying, some kind of brandy or port or something. Raziel, who had refused a cigarette earlier, now puffed away at a thin Cuban cigar.

I watched Capa study Raziel with his photographer's eyes, but if he perceived Raziel's celestial origins, he did not remark upon them. He twirled the black enameled ashtray in a little circle, around and around like a children's carousel.

He kept looking up at Raziel, but Capa spoke to me. "The city's balanced on a razor's edge. It's time I went to the far shore, to America. I'm on all the wrong lists, my girl."

I took a long, shaky sip of my brandy drink. "It's a roll of honor, Capa, and you're at the top of it."

He acknowledged my shameless flattery with a little half smile, indicated Raziel with a nod and a waggling eyebrow. "Is this who you were really worrying about, before?"

It was my turn to smile, though secretly I still felt like throwing up after the scene in the café. "Even a wicked girl hides her secrets."

Capa threw back his head and roared, tapped Raziel, backhanded, on the shoulder. "Watch yourself, mister. She's worrying over you for good reason. This is a free spirit, this Magdalena Lazarus. Easy to sell your soul to be with one like her. Believe me, I know."

Raziel stubbed out the still-smoldering end of his cigar in the ashtray, narrowly missing the back of Capa's hand. The sweet smoke rose up like a king cobra.

Capa leaned in, and he whispered, "Sir, you are in dangerous territory now, the land of the fugitive. A land of mortals, souls that can die."

Raziel only stared, a whisper of a smile playing along the sensual curve of his lips. And in the silence, something dangerous passed between Capa and the angel—some strange mixture of jealousy and brotherhood.

"We live in the shadow of death these days," I said finally, to break their silent interplay. "That gives us all a certain kind of freedom."

"You learn fast, girl," Capa said under his breath. "I'm afraid for your friend, though."

Raziel looked at me and back at Capa again. "I am no innocent on holiday, Mr. Capa."

Capa raised his hands, as though Raziel were aiming a gun at his heart. "I have no claim on Magdalena. I wouldn't dare. Catch her if you can. All I am saying is, innocent or not, be careful what you wish for."

Raziel's laughter rang like church bells in the rain. "I have no claim on her, it is she who has a claim on me."

I couldn't help grinning at both of them. Here we sat at the edge of disaster, and these elegant creatures still resorted to wit and repartee. There was a certain desperate gallantry to both of them that I deeply appreciated. "Now you both speak of me as if I weren't sitting here. I can't stand it."

My pleasure faded when I saw the expression on Raziel's

face and I considered the truth: to Raziel, my café Heaven was in fact a descent into an unprecedented level of Hell. And he had fallen this far on my account.

"How can we sit here joking in the midst of disaster. That poor devil, Hilare," I said, to change the subject.

"Hilare was the lucky one," Capa muttered around the unlit cigarette clamped in his teeth. He flicked open his battered Zippo lighter and the end of his unfiltered Gauloise bloomed with a tiny flame.

As I watched the smoke rise from Capa's nostrils, it became ever clearer to me that Raziel had to return to his proper sphere, turn away from the dark road I now had to travel. The realization was sudden, perfect, complete in itself, sharp as a shard of broken glass lying on the floor at the Café Alibi.

"You saved us, Capa," I said.

"No one can save anybody, Magda. I thought I made that clear, earlier." He squinted down at his Breitling watch. "Or should I say yesterday. The sun is up, by now."

I flashed a smile at Raziel. "Ah, yet another sleepless night. Someday, I'll sink into a big, fluffy, down-filled featherbed and sleep the divine sleep of the gods. That's all the Heaven I'll ever need."

Raziel winked at me, slowly. "Perhaps Heaven is overrated." His face stilled, and the noise of the café suddenly seemed an eternity away.

I couldn't tear my gaze away from Raziel's face, even though Capa watched us with his knowing eyes. My words were for my countryman, but my sentiment was for Raziel. "Thanks for all your many kindnesses, Endre. I mean, Capa—the world's most famous photographer. I kiss your hands."

"Sounds like you're saying good-bye."

I swallowed hard and looked from mortal to angel and back again, and I made up my mind. "In fact, I am. In Amsterdam awaits my doom. It's only fair I go down to it alone. Better not to take anybody else with me. Not even you, dear Raziel. Farewell."

I turned to Capa, held out my hand, and bemused, he shook it. "I'm no seer, Endre—my baby sister's the one for that—but you're right about one thing. You should get out of Europe as fast as you can. Or you'll end up as dead as Hilare."

He paled, and I reveled darkly in the pleasure of shocking the unshockable Robert Capa. I rose slowly, and left him and the angel sitting together at the table.

✳ 17 ✳

It was such a grand farewell. Eva would have been so proud.
Except Raziel wouldn't stay put, in his assigned place in the
tableau. I had walked no more than twenty feet from the Café du
Dôme, when he somehow stood in front of me, blocking my way
as sleepy-headed working people stumbled over the cobblestones,
rubbing the dreams out of their eyes as they scuttled off to work.

"Magda."

I drew myself up, with as much authority as I could muster.
I am tall; as a young woman I spent most of my days hunched
down, trying to make myself smaller to match the men in my
life. But Raziel physically loomed over me.

"You cannot run away."

"Can't I? The night is done, Raziel. Thank you for saving me, though honestly only the Almighty knows why. I'm off to Amsterdam now. I don't need your help anymore. Good-bye."

"I'm coming with you."

I blinked once, twice, trying to clear my head of the night's magic, regain the clarity of daylight, and make sense of Raziel's words. "Why? I mean, what can you do, really? You deliver messages, as you say, sweet, wonderful Raziel—a celestial postman from the Almighty. But you are forbidden to open the letters yourself, to read them in advance of delivery. And you are not allowed to write a reply."

He stood, immobile, taking my words like blows.

I swallowed hard, wished with all my heart he wouldn't listen to me. "I have already released you, angel of mine. You belong in Heaven, creature of light. Go, ascend, trouble me no more."

Raziel crossed his arms over his chest. His expression clouded over. "How do I trouble you?"

I didn't want to answer him. A pigeon fluttered between us with a great clatter of dirty wings. "Because. For one thing, you can't help me with my job. All you can do is remind me, so kindly, that I'm going straight to Hell when I'm done. And for another . . ."

I hesitated, then decided on the truth. "I—well. My feelings for you are not exactly, shall we say, angelic. I seem to remember my ancestors, and your brothers, got into a lot of trouble over that sort of thing."

His face flushed, as if I had slapped him. "Is that the only reason you want me to leave?"

"Last night was a miracle. But I don't want you falling out of heaven over me. Please, go in peace, be my star in the night sky."

Raziel uncrossed his arms, held them open . . . as if to show me he carried no weapons. "No."

"No?" I had to laugh at that, a low laugh that hurt the base of my throat. "You sound like me, with your big 'no.' I'm a bad influence on you, angel. Now, please, go. My train leaves in less than an hour and I'm certain there are officials to be bribed, conductors I need to flirt with."

"I am staying. I cannot hold back anymore. For all the reasons you say."

The thought of Raziel sharing my fate, Gisele's, out of some noble martyrdom made me dizzy. "Are you kidding? I'm on a fool's errand—you are the one who's made that fact perfectly clear. The only way I'll ever make it is to pretend I am invincible. Untouchable." I took a deep, shuddering breath. "And you remind me I am not."

Full day had come, and Paris looked like a perfect rosebud in the pink morning light. If my angel had been a city, he would have been Paris: breaktakingly beautiful, golden. Not for me to keep.

"I'm not leaving you," Raziel insisted. He closed the distance between us, and I averted my eyes from his unbearable virtue. "I will go with you into the lions' den, and I will close their mouths."

I could feel his breath on my cheek. When I opened my eyes he hovered so close that I tingled with anticipation of his kiss.

I couldn't let him kiss me, or we were both doomed. "The Almighty didn't tell you to stay, did He? And if you defy Him to stay, what kind of celestial message is that?"

He drew away, and rubbed a square hand over the sharp edge of his jaw. "I'm coming with you, and I am protecting you. Stop asking so many questions."

My traitorous heart leaped at the news, even as I worried for him. "But why? You told me before that you are not allowed to make your own decisions."

"I don't care if I'm allowed or not. I'm coming with you anyway."

6

The implications of Raziel's decision haunted me all the way to Amsterdam. I had wanted our night in Paris to be a sweet farewell, a memento mori of a mortal girl to a celestial creature who belonged in Heaven. But not everything was up to me and my frantic machinations.

In any event, I hardly needed protecting on this leg of the trip. The borders between France and the Netherlands seemed porous compared to those of my native land; in Paris, before finding Capa, I had procured an official-looking forgery, a letter from the Hungarian consulate assuring the reader that my passport had been oh so innocuously lost in Paris, the follies of youth, etc., la la la. A few official-looking, sufficiently blurry stamps, and the border guards hardly gave me and my defunct, lying papers a second glance.

As for Raziel, his papers were flawless, and his gleaming, prosperous self gave me a reflected aura of respectability that helped to ease the way.

This new train trundled along the tracks from the Gare du Nord in Paris to Amsterdam Centraal, bathed in summer sunlight. But the way seemed dark to me. What battles awaited me in Amsterdam, what transgressions would I have to commit to prevail against an enemy such as the Staff? And how could I live with myself if Raziel damned himself to destruction because of me?

We pulled into Amsterdam Centraal, we alighted from the train and together we rushed through the station, the huge curved ceiling stretching like the heavens over our heads. After washing up in the ladies' powder room at the station, I looked remarkably put together for a woman on the verge of madness.

Before leaving the station, I changed some money, then we took a taxi to Het Spui. The skinny houses congregated tightly along the narrow streets, right up to the edges of the byzantine tangle of canals, like sober burghers marching backward into time. I would have chewed off every last fingernail had I not worn my prettiest yellow gloves this morning.

The slap of rubber tires against cobblestones almost drowned out Raziel's low murmur. "What next, Magda? Do you plan to take rooms?" Bless him. Raziel meant to protect me, not tell me what to do.

The thought of what next made my stomach churn. I took a deep breath. "No rooms, no need of them. At least not yet. We go straight to the bookseller, right now. If I fail to get the Book . . . well . . . I mustn't fail. If I am delayed, I will look to Capa's friend Lucretia for help."

I wouldn't let him interrupt the flow of my words, for if he did I would have to think about the implications of what I said. I continued, in a low, fast murmur. "Once we get the Book, we need to get out of Amsterdam as fast as we possibly can—I expect we will be pursued. With any luck, we'll be back in Paris tomorrow morning."

He took my hand in both of his, squeezed tightly, and said nothing. My heart pounded so hard it hurt. The fundamental questions—What would I do with the Book once I had it? And what would become of Raziel and me?—hung in the air between us, unspoken.

✳ 18 ✳

The angel and I stood together on the pavement as the hump-backed taxi scuttled away along Spuistraat. We stood alongside the Singel, and inky canal water slapped up against the quay near where we walked. Together, we slipped around the corner and hesitated before the door of the bookstore, the already-hot pavement strangely deserted.

Raziel stepped forward and touched the closed door, drew his hand away. "Here is the place of danger," Raziel said.

I looked at him; he looked at me. I tried to smile. "Danger? With you here? I am in no danger, thanks to you."

His smile was sad. He took the hat off his head, examined the brim a little too intently. "My power stems from the Almighty," Raziel began, his voice quiet. "As you know, I serve only as a messenger."

He looked up and the breath caught in my throat. He was about to fall; I couldn't bear it. But I needed his help, needed it desperately. "Raziel, you don't have to . . ." I did not voice my hopes and fears aloud. I had hoped he had come with me to Amsterdam to join me on my quest to recover the Book, and feared that to do so would forfeit Raziel's place in Heaven.

He stepped close to me, kissing close. "You do not understand, Magda. Here, the Book is trapped in evil. I cannot reach it, not as a servant of the Almighty."

Raziel hesitated, and I studied his tense, drawn face. He meant to leave Heaven for good; I was too desperate to stop him. "Let me try, Raziel. I've been surrounded by evil for half my life."

He interrupted me with a wave of his hand. "You are trying to protect me again, Magdalena Lazarus. But I do not need your protection." The sleepy-looking bookstore loomed over his shoulder; in the far distance I heard a faint cacophony of bicycle bells like birdsong.

Determination sharpened his features. "I told you I would no longer stand apart. But that does not mean I will throw myself into the fire to be consumed."

He looked back down at me. "Magda. The Book cannot save you from your fate. It will draw you ever deeper into a dance with evil, that evil that desires power and seeks the destruction of all that is good. I must try one last time to dissuade you. Your best bet is still to run."

"You're right. But I've come too far, dear angel. I've failed you; I should never have called on you in Paris. But I can't stand apart, either. I just can't."

Raziel replaced the hat on his head and sighed. "If I go in there now, Magda, the wizard will be able to capture me."

"Capture you?" I took a step backward, thunderstruck. The thought of Raziel trapped in the Staff's clutches sickened me. "But the Staff is a mere mortal, a wizard living beyond his natural years through sorcery. How could he . . ."

"Capture me? Use me? Through his very sorcery, a perversion of the pathways of power. If I go into that bookstore and fight the wizard for the Book, I no longer go on the Almighty's errand, and must fend for myself. And I will lose."

I wondered whether Heaven would judge me more or less harshly than the Staff, when my days were done. Either way, there was no way Raziel could go through that door. I could not bear the thought of Raziel bound. "You have no sorcery, no magic of your own."

"No, I don't."

"For goodness' sake, you can't come with me, then." I sighed, near tears, thoroughly disgusted with myself. "I never learned the Witches' Creed, not before it was too late, and now I understand it too well. I did wrong calling on you in Vienna. I did worse, calling you down to Paris and tempting you to stay."

"No, Paris wasn't wrong. Vienna wasn't either." Raziel smiled again, with more assurance this time, and began restlessly pacing the cobblestone pavement. "But I'm in. We need to figure out a plan."

He stopped pacing, and the intensity of his gaze almost melted me into a puddle. I nodded wordlessly for him to go on, a lump caught in my throat.

His smile widened. "How about this? You go in that door, unleash your magic at full force and retrieve the Book, whatever remnant of it that you can find. I'll . . ." His smile faltered, and he seemed to choke on the words. "I'll stay back. I won't descend and renounce my role as messenger, not yet. I will bide my time, and will wait until you have the Book to fight at your side. But, Magda . . ."

I felt like I was going to faint. "Yes?"

"If you call on me, I will come for you. And I will fight until my dying breath."

"Your—*what*?" My heart constricted painfully over the thought of Raziel choosing death to save me.

. "I will fight for what is right, Magda." He swept close to me, took me into his arms. "And I am willing to pay any price. I never understood, until now, why angels fall. Always thought my brothers descended purely as slaves to evil impulse."

His arms wrapped me in warm safety, though no wings unfurled to protect us from the world. At the moment, Raziel did not seem like an angel, not at all. "Don't come to harm because of me, Raziel."

"You mustn't come to harm either. Too much depends on you, once you go through that door. Love is never wasted . . . do not forget that, no matter what happens now."

Love. Raziel hugged me close, and the cinnamon scent of his skin surged my body into life.

"Farewell, Lazarus," he said, his voice rough. He lifted my hands to his lips and kissed my fingertips. "Work your wonders. When you have the Book, only whisper my name and I will come."

It was a plan. Ours. I waved and smiled a watery little smile; I didn't trust my voice to even say the single word good-bye. He drew away from me, smiled encouragingly—

And faded away.

Raziel still watched over me from above; he called upon the

power of the Almighty Himself to strengthen me in my path. But nevertheless, my body shook as I crossed, alone, over the threshold of Ulysses Knox's bookshop. A little bell attached to the door sounded, I clutched my satchel, which contained Bathory's letter of introduction, and I silently rehearsed my little speech in my head.

The place was as quiet as a chapel, the books like meditating congregants. As I walked past them, I could feel the words in the books calling to me; some of the volumes trembled as I trailed my fingers along their spines.

Was it my death that had strengthened my affinity for the written word? Or was it the intensity with which I pursued my mission? It did not matter—I saw now that the demonesses had spoken literally when they said my blood would speak to *The Book of Raziel*.

I wandered among the towering stacks of books planted between the shelves, heard the murmur of voices echoing far away. I found a splintery, narrow door closed tight at the back of the store. Slowly I reached for the doorknob, and my battered heart began to pound anew. My fortune, for good or ill, hid behind this door with Knox in the back room, "for employees only" as the sign on the door announced in both French and Dutch. The door was not locked.

I could tell Knox was not alone—the murmur of voices behind the door put the lie to that vain hope. I gathered my courage and swung the door open without knocking. But nothing could have prepared me for the sight of his company.

They sat all together, as if for a workers' party meeting. Three demonesses crouched upon battered wooden chairs, disguised as prim ladies in long dresses, surrounding a solitary gentleman like vipers hidden in teacakes.

With my ordinary sight, the three ladies looked like genteel tea drinkers who swooned over a first edition of Tennyson's poems in translation. But when I blinked and Saw them, their true aspect became revealed to me, and I recognized them immediately: we had last met in a blood-stained copse of fir trees next to the train tracks outside Linz.

The gentleman with them stroked his mustache and seemed at ease with his visitors, but my nerves crackled with the danger that engulfed the mortals in the room.

But the demonesses were not the worst shock. Across from them all, her merry blue eyes twinkling, sat, seemingly unafraid, none other than my beloved Eva Farkas.

I saw stars and hiccupped in my surprise, and Eva and I exchanged a single wild glance. The sparkle in her eyes sputtered out, doused with recognition of me, and the inability to disguise her fear.

My darling friend was afraid, afraid for me. Why?

The man, whom I assumed to be Knox, shifted in his chair, saw me swaying. Built solid, with a walrus mustache and an enormous American expanse, he looked nothing like the slender, clever man I had built up in my mind on my long journey westward.

My fancy memorized words of introduction fizzled away into nothingness. But I held steady, my resolve lending me courage. "Good afternoon, kind sir," I said in French, to match Bathory's letter.

Knox stroked his impressive mustache with his fingertips, inclined his head in a slow, wordless greeting. Eva blinked hard and cleared her throat; never, in all my years of knowing her, had I ever before caught her blushing. "Monsieur," she said, in her flawless, sparkling French, "this is the friend I had mentioned to you. Count Bathory's assistant."

Knox looked up at me sharply, and his open American face flushed as red as ground paprika.

What had Eva told him about me? How did she get here in one piece? And did Eva know she sat, defenseless, amongst a cluster of Nazi demonesses that had murdered me once and intended to destroy all of us?

I composed my features into a soft, hopefully charming and inoffensive smile, and I retrieved Bathory's letter of introduction from my unfashionably battered satchel. I ventured into the soft light shed by the Tiffany lamp standing on the corner of Knox's heavy wooden desk. Knox accepted the letter from my fingers, and if he noticed the bloodstains and the damp, curling edges, he gave no sign of it. As he read, I cast a furtive glance in the direction of my triple nightmare, the demonesses.

So lovely were they in their human casings, so vile and hateful underneath. They smiled at me, flashing their demon fangs through their disguises while Knox's attention remained on Bathory's missive.

Undoubtedly they were here to get my book from Knox first, by any possible means. I shifted my gaze to Eva, whose attention remained fixed on Knox and the letter. After a moment she glanced at me, and a tentative smile fluttered over her lips and away.

She ignored the frantic question my stare contained: What in goodness' name was she doing here in Amsterdam? And who was looking after Gisele?

Knox folded the letter reverentially between his fat fingers, interrupting my runaway train of worries. "Ah, Bathory, old friend," he rumbled, in a French deeply inflected with an American accent. "It would be my pleasure to assist you for his sake, Miss Lazarus. For his sake and for your own."

The moment for which I had returned from death had finally come. I took a deep breath and swallowed hard. "I am glad, for I need your help, Monsieur Knox. I am here to save my sister's life, for a start."

I faced Knox head on, and though Raziel restrained no lions for my sake, the knowledge that he watched me from above and trusted me to do right gave me more strength than I would have previously believed. "But I cannot address these matters with you, not in our current company." And I shot a significant glance at the troika of nastiness sitting across from him.

Bathory trusted this man, so I expected he understood far more than it seemed. But his next words shocked me out of what remained of my composure. "Miss Lazarus. These three ladies are here by my express personal invitation."

By invitation! If Knox, knowing what I knew, could sit and confer with demonesses in the employ of Hitler himself, then my mission would not find success here. He was either in league with them or so hopelessly ignorant and naïve that I could not rely on his judgment.

I backed against the door, ready to run for the street if it came down to a physical fight here, in the depths of the book hunter's stronghold. Bathory was near-immortal, my beloved benefactor, and a vampire of the world. But he could be betrayed, in the end, as easily as anybody else.

My fury leaped up like a gasoline-fed fire. "My book has

gone missing since 1701, kind sir; I do not think it will resurface so easily. Not without my help. You see, that book belongs to me and my family. It is mine by right, and I have come here to claim it."

The eldest demoness leaned forward, and her deep-set eyes glittered in her imperfect human disguise. "By right, little one? An amusing arrogance you have. It belongs to whoever can find it, and to the one who can muster the power to keep it and command it. That is the only right that matters now." She smiled wide, licked her lips as if she found me tasty, a little snack, an amuse-bouche butterfly for her lizard jaws to snap in two.

I refused to be drawn. Instead, I shifted my attention, tilted my head to hear the whisper of intuition that spoke to me. "When last we met, you did not properly introduce yourself. But, Obizuth, I know you now. You are a daughter of Lilith, and it is time for you to hold your peace. I too have been granted power."

Obizuth's face creased in a hideous grimace; because she and her sisters had bested me so easily in our first encounter, perhaps she had assumed I did not have the strength to summon their true names. It was important that she understood me now.

I turned to Knox, my jaw clenched so tight I had trouble speaking. "I beg of you, sir. A few moments alone, so I may speak freely."

How could I convince him to listen to me? Remembering Bathory's letter, I crossed my arms, spoke slowly and deliberately. "Bathory has sent me on a number of errands, sir. They have nothing to do with me and are too volatile to repeat in the presence of anyone else but you." I paused. "And they mean a great deal of money."

Knox's impressive eyebrows gathered together in surprise. I had piqued his curiosity at last.

"That's different. I didn't know Bathory had non-book business for me." Technically, Knox was wrong, but I was certainly not going to correct him.

He rose from his seat, surprisingly graceful for so portly a man, and kissed the demonesses' limp, white hands one by one in farewell. My stomach turned as with my witch's sight I saw the truth of what he kissed—long scaly fingers; dirty, bloody claws. But we all maintained the pretense of civility. How perfectly all of us in Europe practiced the art of false courtesy.

The three inclined their heads. Their leader, named Enepsigos, turned to smile at me. I remembered her well; she was the one who had delivered the death blow in the wilderness outside Vienna. "We shall meet again, Miss Lazarus. Very soon. And it will be for the last time, *ma chère.*"

I barely acknowledged her or her sisters as they left, only allowed myself a long, blissful sigh of relief when I saw the back of them disappearing through the doorway, and through the bookcases out to the street.

Knox offered me Enepsigos's now-empty cane-backed chair, abandoned next to the place where Eva still sat.

I preferred to stand with the door at my back.

Eva rose to stand by me. I kissed both her cheeks and her rosy lips. "A sight for sore eyes," I said in Hungarian.

"Sweetie, you know I am with you until the end." The fact she spoke her benediction in Hungarian, our native, homely language, gave me almost as much comfort as her trust and her crazy courage.

Knox scooped up another packet of letters with his thick,

hairy fingers: clean paper, unblemished by mud or blood. He slid the packet along the length of the heavy, ink-stained blotter to where I could reach it.

"I don't understand Hungarian and what you two are saying," he said, his voice shaking. "But this is the stuff that Bathory sent along with Miss Farkas. She didn't read it, but maybe you should."

I took the packet from him and opened it up. The same spidery handwriting, the same wet-looking strokes of fountain-pen ink:

Via Hand Delivery
Mr. Ulysses Knox
My Dear Sir:

No word from my first young courier. Alas, I now believe she never made it through the fire to reach you with my original missive. Since I have not yet been assailed by fascists or demonic ghouls, I trust that my first letter has also been destroyed with her, and I send this second one to you in the care of courier number two: a very nice, ordinary Hungarian girl named Eva Farkas who does not care about magic and who needs absolutely nothing from you.

There is a book. An ancient and malign book—and since books are your especial expertise, I come to you in search of assistance. This book was first reproduced in print, in Amsterdam, in 1701 Anno Domini or thereabouts. But I need the original, the handwritten version used to make the bound facsimiles.

The book's name is THE BOOK OF RAZIEL.
Penned by an angel, treated as mere legend, but real,
quite real, I assure you. The book is talisman against
fire, against violence, against death in childbed. To as-
sist you I have gathered the relevant local and univer-
sal legends; please see the attached.

But. Most important, Knox, The Book of Raziel, in
the possession of a person of power, may be used to
command an army of demons to serve its wielder. So,
the book is a magical instrument of doom, exquisitely
dangerous, priceless once it has been recovered and de-
canted, like a fine wine, for our imminent feast of war
and destruction.

I work with a group of revolutionaries in a Soviet
location—no need to specify—whose resident seer has
predicted the book's reappearance and recovery. In the
words of my Byzantine friend: It is a visitation. The
beginning of the End, perhaps. And according to him,
an American is currently in possession.

May I persuade you to procure and sell me this
literary superweapon, for a premium, choice price? I
assure you, I will outbid any other potential customer,
and I seek the book's recovery for a noble cause, though
I well realize such scruples will not move you in the
slightest.

As that is all to my advantage, I rejoice in your
avarice, kiss your hands, and implore you to send word
via Miss Farkas only.

Salut,
Bathory

I riffled through the thick packet of supplementary papers, and then stopped reading. I glanced up at Knox. "This is just silly. Why doesn't Bathory simply call you on the telephone?"

He snorted with a whoop of barely suppressed laughter. "He does, oh believe me, he does." Knox sighed and played with a cracked and reglued stone gargoyle paperweight no larger than my fist on his desk. "But Bathory believes he cannot speak honestly, that his conversations are being eavesdropped upon."

His gaze met mine, and goose pimples rose all along my forearms. Bathory had his own enemies, after all. Of course he would be watched, by the Horthy regime or someone . . . or even perhaps some*thing* else. "I see. From what he says in his letter, couriers must be pretty faulty, too. At least my friend Eva reached you in one piece."

"No, in your boss's mind, paranoia is nothing more than just good sense. Bathory predates Herr Freud by a good two or three centuries. He trusts his couriers, you two girls, more than he trusts the phone lines. Smart fellow."

Knox's eyes bored into me, and his unspoken message—we are under surveillance, watch out!—rang in my ears. He indicated the packet half opened on his desk with a toss of his meaty chin.

A fine sheen of sweat slicked his ample cheeks, and I realized with a jolt that my formidable-looking American friend was in fact terrified. "Take the whole pile, m'dear. Read it at your leisure, then destroy it. Amsterdam is a free city, at least for now, but the borders here are porous. Watch who is reading over your shoulder."

I wouldn't allow his fear to deter me from the purpose of my mission. He knew as well as I why I had come. "Bathory must at least have hinted in that pile of paperwork at my own reasons in coming here for that book."

Knox patted at his beefy face with a big linen handkerchief. "Ah, the *Sefer HaRaziel*. Written in the *brillenbuchstaben* script, am I right? You want the original copy. If Bathory's right, finding it could mean death for all of us."

I sighed and plunged in, invisible listeners or no. If I went too far, I expected Knox would stop me. "Yes, and I would be happy to take it off your hands and leave you out of danger. It's mine, for one. And Bathory needs it to assist his clients."

"Of course. The revolutionaries Bathory's talked about."

"Yes. You must know what Stalin is capable of, yes?"

"Of course."

I swallowed hard. "Good. Now for my sister's sake, I need *The Book of Raziel*, Monsieur."

The polite smile faded from his lips. "You read what Bathory had to say, and I made my own discreet inquiries. It would be a disaster for that book to get into the wrong hands."

"The Book is still mine. Of course, any weapon can be wielded against its rightful owner. But I will not relinquish it so easily once I have it."

He cleared his throat, rose from his seat to his full, impressive height. "I'm sorry, my dear. But I don't think I'm the fellow you or Bathory take me to be. Those—ladies—could carve me up like a Sunday roast without their hardly turning a hair. And never mind their master."

So he did understand. Even as my estimation of him rose, my spirits sank. "You must help me," I whispered. I knew I sounded as pathetic as the Azeri man who had begged Bathory at the Istanbul, but pride was a luxury I could no longer afford.

"Whatever you and Bathory have to offer me, it's just not enough. Don't you know what you are up against?"

I swept the packet of letters into a neat pile, bound them up, and clutched the bundle to my chest. "So you are going to side with those Nazi demonesses instead? Give me the chance to prove to you that I am capable, though of course we all know time is running out for me, for everyone. But don't throw your strength behind the Nazis. For the love of God!"

His face twisted with pain. "I'm not America personified, you know. I'm a private citizen, with no obligations to pass these letters on, help a partisan witch, finance a vampire anti-Soviet revolutionary group, none of it."

"But you love freedom, you must. How could you side with the Nazis, with those demonesses?"

His cheeks grew red, as if I had spit in his face. "I want to help you, by God I do." His voice was a half-strangled whisper. "But I don't think I could survive double-crossing your enemies."

He rose to the doorway and held the door open: our audience with Knox was at its end. "I will tell you those demonesses are not Nazi. But, I'm sorry, I can't do anything more for you. Not now."

✳ 19 ✳

When Eva and I reached the pavement outside the bookstore, I saw that the demonesses had vanished like characters in a strange, disjointed dream. I took a deep breath of the cool, late afternoon air, scented with the tang of canal water and fresh paint, and resolved to make my way to Lucretia's address, there to untangle the mystery of my failure with Knox.

Eva's smile effervesced into a laugh, like champagne bubbles. "You have a knack for showing up in dangerous places. It's not just me."

I adjusted my gloves to hide the trembling of my lips. "Eva, you have no idea. Just no idea how close you came to being incinerated."

I looked away, across the arch of the bridge stretching over the canal. "How did you manage to get to Amsterdam so quickly? And what about Gisele? You've left her all alone!"

Eva avoided my gaze and shrugged, and we started wandering on the pavement, alongside the canal. "You left Gisele behind first, you know," she said with a sigh. "Don't worry. I came with her blessing. As for how I came, I took the train, you silly girl. The Orient Express, straight from Budapest."

"But your papers. They had to be as flimsy as mine."

"Even worse, I'm sure. But it's amazing what a smile and a little luck will do."

"Well, what are you planning to do now that you delivered your message?"

She stopped short, looked away again. A peculiar expression passed over her face. "I was thinking, maybe . . . Zanzibar."

I tried to sound reassuring. "Zanzibar sounds like just the place for us by now. But I have a friend of a friend here in Amsterdam, and I hope she can somehow help me with the Book."

Eva shot me a sidelong glance, and for the first time since we had found each other in Amsterdam I saw her mask of breezy insouciance slip. "Please, take me with you."

I squeezed her fingers a little too hard. Maybe she was right and Zanzibar was a more reasonable destination. But Gisele waited for us both in Budapest. I had finally made it to Amsterdam, and the only person left who could help us now was Lucretia de Merode. Running away could wait. "You come with me, and I'll watch out for you. Zanzibar isn't going anywhere."

☙

When I arrived at the address that Capa had supplied, the decrepit-looking brick building drowsed in the fading light of day's end. I rang the buzzer, and the porter, an ancient half-blind lady encased in black lace, shuffled ahead of me until we reached a tiny, dusty anteroom.

The shabby opulence of Lucretia's brothel took my breath away. My work for Bathory had taken me places I could not bring myself to tell the girls about, but this . . . this woman's house of wickedness was a new world.

Eva's expression was bemused. "So, are you planning on becoming a working girl, Magduska? Can I join you, if so? Though I would make a terrible lady of the night."

Eva. I wanted to hug and throttle her all at the same time. Our Hungarian was as good as a code language in this place, so I didn't see the need to hold back. "What are you doing, ordering me around like a gendarme, no less." My stomach rumbled with hunger, but my desolation at my failure with Knox trumped my body's demands.

Eva's incandescent smile could not hide the sadness lurking in her eyes. "Come on, Magda, show me your sunshine." I rolled my eyes at her Pollyanna imitation, and she snorted in derision. "I am not joking!"

A regular girl caught up by extraordinary events: Eva had moxie, certainly, but what was my nonmagical friend from Tokaj doing in the midst of a supernatural lightning storm?

Eva read my expression, and her face grew serious, all traces of levity gone. "I heard what Gisele had to say, the same as you. What am I supposed to do, pretend I didn't hear it? Sit at home and wait like a good girl until they come to chop off my head?"

She made an impatient little sound and slumped against my

shoulder. She smelled like tea roses. "I've been busy too, Magduska. This is bigger than the three of us. You can't just keep a secret as big as that."

I groaned. I should have known the situation was far out of my control, had been from the beginning. "Oh, Eva. I wanted to keep you clear of this whole mess."

"The last time I checked, darling, you didn't rule the world. I'm not clear of this mess, and I never was."

I grabbed her arm, shook her gently. "Don't be dense. You're blond and cute, can pass for an Aryan princess, in Hungary, Amsterdam, anywhere! Of all of us, I could have kept you clear. But it's too late for that, now."

Eva clutched me close, whispered in my ear. "No, not too late at all, silly goose. Don't you see? We could still slip away; we got this far, got through the hardest part. My friends are better than Bathory at forgery, bribery, whatever you like. We could go on the lam, get out of Europe altogether, so easily now."

Her tone remained calm, ordinary. "But we won't. There's Gisele, of course, too sweet and otherworldly. And more than her. We can't just run."

"We should," I said, and we both laughed. "If we had any sense, we would. But we're both fools."

I drew back, searched her face. Something bothered me about her little speech, and after a moment, it dawned on me. "And another thing, Eva. What in Heaven's name are you doing, acting as Bathory's courier to Knox?"

Eva suddenly looked so tired. "I could ask you the same question, you know. Bathory sent me, but I also come as an emissary of the Zionists. They want me to tell the world about Gisele's vision, try to get people outside to listen."

I could not keep the horror out of my voice. "Tell everyone."

"Yes, and I *have*. Don't you think the Jews of Amsterdam, of Poland, of the Soviets and in America, that all of them should also know?"

Eva astounded me. "I thought . . ." I trailed off lamely, struggled to compose my mind. "I had trouble believing Gisele's words, myself. I thought nobody would credit them secondhand. And I thought spreading around her visions would—"

Eva's laugh was bitter. "Would what? Make them come true? Magda, you know her voice had the ring of truth. She's too innocent to queer the message to suit some agenda or even her wish. I believe her, and the Zionists did, too. And Knox believed her, too. All you need to do is listen to Hitler and believe *him*. It's not that big a leap, really."

"But don't you see? That's why Knox won't give me the Book. He must think the Book itself will hasten the war. But that won't matter: the war is coming. You heard what the Witch of Ein Dor said. You know that book is our only chance."

"She also said we were all a bunch of dead ducks."

Her turn of phrase made me smile and roll my eyes to Heaven. "I refuse to accept that. And you don't accept it either, Eva, otherwise why did you bother coming all this way?"

She shrugged. "We all fight with the weapons we have."

"So, how do we fight now? What do we do?"

"Well, first we talk to your lady friend Lucretia. And we do not give up, Magduska!"

I hadn't planned on surrendering just yet, but I held my tongue and shifted my attention to the fantastically faded bordello in which we hid.

"I don't sense much magic here," I said.

A rustle behind a beaded curtain made both of us start. More than the sound, I detected the magic of the madam before she appeared. Magic speaks to magic. Most of the girls living here had no more magic in them than Eva did, but the madam made up for all of them by herself.

As a born witch's child, I had my own odd notions of what it meant to be a worker of magic. Trudy and her family, simple country pagans, only reinforced those assumptions. So meeting her city cousins, the Sisters of Arachne, only shocked me the more.

At first glance, she looked no more than twenty-five. But as she drew close, her rounded cheeks and creamy complexion revealed a tracery of fine wrinkles like netting over her skin, and wise, tiny eyes, set deep. She looked like a benevolent mama elephant ready to stomp on two frightened mice.

Her French bore a strong, mysterious accent. "Ah, the Lazarus. Welcome, welcome, my dear." She bowed from the waist.

A slight movement about her person sent a bolt of tension into my shoulders. It was her earrings. At first glance I took them for large gray pearls, luminous and soft like the full moon behind clouds. But when I took a second look, her earrings were in actuality living spiders, with gumdrop-sized abdomens, perched over each earlobe. They wiggled their long, silvery legs, and then they seemed to realize together they were being observed. Their long legs curled around her ears like filigree, they fidgeted a moment longer, and then became earrings again.

The lady caught my gaze and smiled. "A trick of the light." And her smile widened to reveal tiny, pearly teeth.

"Of course, a trick of the light and shadows," I agreed. No need to antagonize this powerful witch unnecessarily.

I said, "Eva, we are privileged to meet Lucretia de Merode."

"Not the dancer?"

"No. Perhaps, Madame, you are a relative of hers?"

The mysterious lady's smile widened still more. "You speak of Cleo de Merode? Why yes, I am her great-great-aunt."

And my sense of wonder grew. For that meant Capa's friend and Trudy's cousin must be well over one hundred years old.

I nodded slowly at her, truly impressed and a bit awed. "Forgive me for intruding upon your private enclave. It is only by necessity."

"Of course. We must stop the Nazi dogs together, together." She swept the air with an expansive arm. "Please." And she motioned for us to enter her parlor and seat ourselves.

We pushed through the shimmering beaded curtain. No gentlemen callers were present at this unfashionable hour, though prostitutes clothed in flimsy lace and translucent silk peignoirs dotted the old-fashioned embroidered cushions and drifted along the thick Persian carpets, looking half asleep. Some of the ladies sipped steaming cups of tea and nibbled languidly at thickly buttered rolls.

"Pay these pretty mortal flowers no mind," Lucretia said. "They speak no French, or hardly any. We may speak freely among them in any case."

Despite my admiration, there was no way I would reveal the details of my journey to Madame de Merode, no matter how beautiful her manners or mesmerizing her living jewels. I sat at the edge of an overstuffed scarlet divan with puckered armrests, and I tried my best to relax, to savor the homey smells of tea and butter and the loveliness of the blowsy ladies resting like sleepy butterflies all around.

I leaned over to Eva to warn her against eating any of the refreshments, and saw her curled eyelashes fluttering as she slouched in a man's winged armchair and sighed long and luxuriantly. As I watched, she half sang something unintelligible and laughed under her breath.

I turned my attention to Lucretia de Merode. "We have entered your parlor indeed, Madame," I said, with a ghost of a smile tickling at the corners of my lips.

"It is safe enough for *you*," she replied, an edge of something dangerous playing in her voice for the first time.

I sat straighter on the slippery cushions, leaned forward to drive my meaning home to Madame de Merode. "It must be safe for my sister Eva as well. She stays with me."

Her luscious, overripe lips pursed in exasperation. "Tut, tut, Lazarus. She is a ravishing flower, no wonder you clutch her to your breast like a boutonniere. You know it is within my rights to claim her."

It was a shame: Lucretia de Merode was too dangerous to trust, despite her connections. Thank you anyway, Capa, I mentally muttered over the miles to my daring friend in Paris. "I know no such thing, Madame de Merode. I thank you for your kind hospitality . . ." and I rose to grab Eva's hand and go.

"Peace, Lazarus!" When I glanced at the witch again, her beautiful glamour had all but dissipated and I saw her true. Beneath the diaphanous exterior boiled a core of molten iron.

Slowly, I sat back down, considered my next step. Raziel could not violate the witch's wards without touching off a magical battle. Eva was drugged into a happy stupor.

But I was out of other ideas. This witch madam had the power and the determination to help me fight my enemies and regain my inheritance. And her relation to Trudy and her Bavarian coven inclined me to trust her. Her dangerousness was an opportunity; I decided to rely on Capa's judgment after all.

I stated the obvious. "We share a common enemy."

Her laugh tinkled like broken glass. "Of a certainty. We are sisters, you and I. Of blood and vocation. And we seek the same treasure. We are after more impressive quarry together, after all."

When I said nothing, she leaned forward, and I could see how deep were the pits of her eyes. "The Book." She could not keep an edge of excitement from creeping into her voice, and she licked her lips slowly, as if she could taste the Book's power, throbbing somewhere as yet undiscovered.

This time I could not restrain a groan. "Who is this Ulysses Knox? And why does everyone in Europe know my family secret, better than I?"

Lucretia's long fingers stroked the spider babies at her ears. "Ulysses? You have met him. He is a hunter of rare books."

"You know that is not what I mean."

Lucretia studied her elegantly manicured fingertips while her spiders fidgeted and played with the jet-black tendrils of hair tucked behind her ears.

She spoke to her open palms, not to me. "He is a Mason. An American of great antiquity, one of the first ones, with connections to the Illuminati. He is a magical cousin of that general, Henry Knox, in the American Revolution." Slowly, she looked up at me, her chin tucked low as she smiled. "Ah, but that was before your time."

I swallowed hard, held absolutely still. Madame de Merode was a marvel; her spellwork was profound enough to hold at bay death's advance. I could only return from the place where death still held dominion; this petite, extraordinary person had never gone there, and there was no sign that Lucretia de Merode would ever visit the country of death at all.

Her answer only led to a labyrinth of more questions. "Is he a spy?"

Lucretia extracted a nail file from an invisible pocket hidden somewhere within her voluminous skirts, and she set to repairing her already-perfect manicure. "Perhaps, but I would more accurately describe the man as a patriot. His business is to traffic in spellcasting books and grimoires, and he is the primary dealer of magical books in Amersterdam. Knox publicly claims to be in Europe for himself only, but he is no more here for selfish reasons than you are—no matter how loudly the two of you protest the fact."

"Will you help me find the Book?"

Her eyes flared into life at the prospect, and she met my gaze with a greed she did not bother to disguise. "Most certainly, with pleasure."

"Why?"

Her smile grew hard, and the wrinkles over her face grew more pronounced, as if the skin underneath was straining against a fine netting pulled tight. "Those Nazi bastards. I want them to die, every last one of them."

"Ah, another patriot." I was immune to the hallucinogenic effects of the spiders' parlor, but the surrealism of the scene only increased, melting all around me like a Dalí painting. Despite the running colors and the increasingly discordant tones of my hostess's voice, I clung to the truth with the passion of a true believer.

I did not care how those who killed my family met their ends, or who claimed credit for the deed. By now, I knew in my marrow that war could not be set aside. My ancestral grand-mama from Ein Dor had spoken true. But that harsh decree only meant I would fight until death claimed me for good.

Lucretia de Merode's laughter echoed weirdly in the over-heated room, and Eva startled awake with a little snort. "If I could wield that book myself, Lazarus, I would have uncovered it and used it long before now, yes? It must be you, young and green in your witchery."

I could not keep from shuddering. "September the first, the window closes. So my ancestor has spoken to me. If the Book remains hidden after that date, it will remain hidden forever, and our fate is sealed."

"Ah, but it is too late for *that*, my dear. Did that rascal Ulysses not tell you?"

My heart began thudding in my chest, a throb echoing it at the base of my throat. "Too late?"

"Those demonesses. They have already located it, here in Amsterdam. They now need only to claim it."

Suddenly, I understood Knox's eagerness to keep my three murderesses close. I buried my face in my hands. "And I chased them away myself. I *am* a vengeful fool."

Lucretia whispered something in a language I could not un-derstand, and I looked up in time to see the twin spiders leap from her ears, trot neatly down each of her long, soft arms, and down the hem of her diaphanous skirts. They skittered through the deep pile of the Persian silk carpet under our feet, and dis-appeared into the lurid shadows of the seraglio.

"All is not yet lost, my lovely creature. You must hunt your hunters, and I will teach you how to do it."

✳ 20 ✳

And so Lucretia did teach me, as I had never allowed my mother to do, and the days passed in a slow dream. That first afternoon, after we had tucked Eva up to bed in an unused bedroom high up under the eaves, she and I settled in her private sitting room for my lessons.

She stood before me, shimmering in the starlight filtering in through the thick, ancient leaded glass in the window. She looked so infernally lovely that her question surprised me more than it should have: "Do you know what is a midrash?"

"Do I know . . ." My voice trailed off, and I sat down uncertainly at the edge of her impressive, high and fluffy bed. "I must confess I don't."

"It is nothing more than a story, little mother. I want you to relax and open your ears, so I can relate to you the midrash of the lovely Lucretia de Merode, that is, me."

I leaned back on the cushions and forgot my shyness, for her contralto voice soothed me even as it instructed.

"In the beginning, there was lust; in the beginning, there was envy and desire. The ways of women, the methods of managing the body's hunger; the ways of witches, the way to channel and manifest man's will.

"When the Lord created the world, His holy sparks emanated throughout the universe. Witches bring these sparks to life, and it is our free will to decide whether we bring them back to the Almighty, or rend the earth and snuff the sparks into darkness.

"We Sisters of Arachne call upon the living breath in metal. We call upon the holy sparks that imbue the bones of the Earth with the breath of the Maker. We weave the holy words into a web of power. We catch the holy sparks in a net of magical speech.

"Dear little heart, the spine of our magic is in the word. The Lazarus line, so ancient, derives its power from the Hebrew tongue. All languages retain their native magic, but Hebrew is the Word that the Lord spoke when He separated the sky from the sea, and moved along the surface of the water.

"How can you not know your Mother Tongue! Ah, the debased age in which we live! Little star, I cannot teach you your inheritance, but I can give you a tale of when your auntie Lucretia was young, another unlearned witchling.

"Your power resides within your soul, your breath, little star. I, a courtesan, first discovered that power in the act of love with men. I capture the sparks that men throw off, and I whisper the words of power to weave them into webs of spell.

"I grew up in my mother's house of sin; in Venice did I come of age. A great price the first man paid to lie with me, an untouched maid of thirteen.

"My mother taught me the power of no, and of yes. She gave me the power to weigh the bargain, set the price, and choose the winning bid. I did not need the entire language of my courtesan creed to wield that basic power. Those men, who thought they could force me to say yes, they did not understand the depth of a woman's power.

"The strength to prevail, my love, does not rest in no or yes. The greatest magic is an ability to bring a no or yes to the lips of the men who surround you. Thus, your vulnerability contains your greatest power.

"Such complexities of lore I have no time to teach you: the magic of numbers, of herbs, of runes, of time. Your magic grows from a different root than mine, it originates from the word no. A Havdalah word, a word that separates, defines, clarifies. I cannot teach you all of your magical language in the remnant of time we have together. So hold on to your no, dear witchling.

"I will teach you the spells by rote: animate them with your no. We will learn the spell of erasure, the spell of binding, and the spell of the word of Solomon. First I will teach you the bare words, stripped of meaning, pure of sound. Then we learn the meaning of the words. Finally, we teach the meaning of the silence: the moment before a word is spoken, the moment after.

"But, my sweet, first you must understand that I cannot teach you how to wield your magic at its apex. I will give you the basic elements of magic: your breath, your no, will give the magic life. I wish I had the time to teach you proper, Magdalena

Lazarus. But time slips through our fingers, whether we make full use of it or not. So, we begin."

6

By then, that first afternoon, I had fallen asleep in the gentle cadence of her words. But I had found a safe haven in which to rest; I served my craft of witchery in repose as well as in action. The spiders returned that night, and they verified my story and vouched for my trustworthiness, by ways I still do not understand.

Magical Amsterdam lay hidden within a maze of canals, arched bridges, and cobblestone streets, treacherous and labyrinthine. But blood calls to blood; one morning, too soon after I had come to my refuge in the brothel, my living blood tingled and burned like fire in my veins.

The demonesses were using the life force they had stolen from me in the Austrian countryside. And my book returned their demonic call, responding to my blood, stolen or no. Too soon, it was time for me to seek my fate.

Before I arose, I wrapped myself in scented sheets in my tangled bed and, my skin burning with the call of my blood, I thought of Raziel. The country of the heart is not measured in meters; spheres of heaven separated us, but he and I walked the same darkened, shadowed path.

I made my hurried farewells. There was no question of Eva coming with me; it was a comfort to know she stayed safe with Lucretia. When she tried to speak, I hushed her, kissed her cheeks, and held her close. I thought of Capa, knew I needed no more reminders, and I twisted the red-gold ring off my pinkie finger and gave it to my dearest friend from Tokaj.

6

My blood had spoken, but I did not have an exact address. I took a cab and directed the cabbie from street to street, frightening him as I navigated by my inner senses, not a map. We finally arrived in front of a huge, abandoned-looking warehouse at the crumbling edge of the Nieuwe Zijde district. My fear drew me forward, the true north of my magical compass.

The very air smelled of blood. Something horrible rose up from inside the big brick building rearing up in front of me, something coppery and diabolical and hungry for my soul.

I threw open the heavy double doors. My blood all but boiled; a tremendous urgency to expend the wordless magic I possessed rose up in me like sap.

The main floor of the warehouse, dark and cobwebby, seemed deserted. A rush of human ghosts brushed past me like a cloud of bats, desperate to escape the building via the thin sliver of light I had admitted by throwing the doors ajar. I left the front doors wide open so they could cross the wards of the place and seek the light, and I ran through the main level to a wrought-iron staircase at the back of the echoing silence.

I heard a clatter and stopped dead in my tracks, a shuddering gasp trapped in my throat. I turned, but all I could see was my own huge shadow stretching behind me. When nobody attacked, I ran, echoes radiating all around me, and found myself in a towering two-story-high warehouse, stuffed to the rafters with books.

And guns.

I ascended the huge iron staircase as quietly as I could, whispering Arachne endearments to the metal to silence the echoes and keep my progress a secret. The sound of my footfalls died away and I reached a stifling, dusty second level, lit only by the dappled sunlight filtering through filthy, gigantic leaded windows.

The demonesses three clustered around a bound volume that glowed hot white in the darkness surrounding us. I drew up short as they turned, and bit my lower lip so hard I tasted blood.

This wasn't the Book that called me.

Their leader, Enepsigos, pointed at me and screamed something incomprehensible, a shriek of primal triumph. They clustered around me, blocking my exit back down the stairs. "Ah, little sister," Enepsigos hissed. "Too late. Always too late, for you."

I said nothing, only licked at my bleeding lip and fought to catch my breath. A wind rose to a mighty shriek all around us, but it left me untouched. The bound volume, still glowing white-hot, tore itself from Onoskelis's golden fingertips and soared like a messenger pigeon into my open hands. The burgundy leather felt hot to the touch; I could not read Latin, so the leather cover's stamped subtitles didn't speak to me. But I flipped the book open and a surge of energy pumped through my body.

The Book of Raziel. Written in smudged pencil in German, underneath the printed Latin on the title page.

The demonesses keened and moaned in the still-punishing wind that whipped against me. I read and reread the title page in triumph, in wonder . . .

With a sense of growing dismay . . .

The words were *printed*. With a printing press. I expected a scroll dating from King Solomon's time—in other words, not a bound printed book at all. A roll, lambskin or papyrus, something different. Not a printed, bound volume.

The three demonesses hurled themselves at me, and I threw them back, using nothing more than the whispered word "no."

My blood and their violence both proved that my book was here, somewhere, in this warehouse. But the book in my hands, coveted by the demonesses or not, was not the Book we sought. It had power inherent as a copy of the original; all words contain power. But it was not the Book we were killing each other to find.

"A disappointment, isn't it."

That mild, slightly reproving German mutter almost brought me to my knees. The Staff. Hitler's wizard. I should have known he would come, on an errand so important.

I tore my gaze away from the book, and saw him standing on a chair halfway across the cavernous room. All of the fury of my magic hadn't ruffled a single gray hair combed over the bald, oily head.

"Ah, of course, Herr Staff, our paths have crossed again." My careless courtesy was not all pretense. I had died and returned, and the shock of it, like a first dive into a cold lake in August, had somewhat fortified me against the prospect of dying again.

It would have been an arrogant mistake to underestimate him; I still could only imagine how much agony the ancient sorcerer could inflict. But my family's gift for returning to life had indeed passed to me, and through my own magical efforts I had earned the right to return. It was a small comfort, but it was real.

"You will now release the Book to me, lovely one."

I clutched the book I held to my chest. "And what if I say no?"

"I have ways of making you say yes. Scream yes." The Staff floated off the chair and halfway across the warehouse before touching lightly to the ground, the remnants of his hair greasy and stuck to his skull like the hairstyle of a rotting corpse.

The book grew hotter in my hands, and I clutched it tighter to me, a glowing ember. Even printed, even an ersatz copy of the original, *The Book of Raziel* retained innate power.

My family was no paragon of religious observance. We celebrated Easter the same as Passover, we ate bacon and put cream in our chicken goulash. But my mother had taught me a single prayer during her time of life, as a talisman against mortal danger. *"Sh'ma Yisrael . . ."*

The printed Book trembled in my hand like a living creature, and I dimly registered the fact that the demonesses swatted wildly at the air, as if the sounds of the Hebrew words were stinging insects scourging them. Through my half-slitted eyes I watched them cover their ears in agony and flee down the stairs. How they roared!

But the Staff did nothing. After the metal door slammed shut behind the last demoness fleeing the building downstairs, his smile widened and he applauded me, slowly.

"Ah, brava!" he said, the sneer in his voice low and sickly sweet. "You drove the ladies away this time! Vanquished them! All the better."

"The—better?"

"Why, yes! You have changed, little mousie. You have returned from dead. Or have you?" He smiled, revealed his awful, mossy teeth.

I swallowed hard, refused to reply to his taunts, however much they fueled my own unspoken fears.

"You know that little trick with the prayer would never have worked the first time, in the fields," the Staff remarked. He removed a toothpick from his breast pocket, poked between his molars with it, and then flicked it out as it grew from a splinter to a sapling to a small tree trunk of a wizard's staff. "The Psalms were a failure."

"Ah, but we both know the Sh'ma comes from the Torah itself," I retorted, playing for time as I backed away toward the staircase behind me. "And the Psalms were composed by mortals. The word of God trumps the word of man, no matter how sublime."

"It is not the holy speech that makes the difference. It is you. You have bartered your soul for power, *ruach* gone to the Angel of Death. I myself have done nothing but the same." The taunt in his voice grew stronger, the mask of his suave amusement slipped. "Your baby lessons, learned well, so quickly, but they are not enough to master me."

He snapped his fingers and the Book leaped in my hands; I held on and with difficulty kept the Book nestled against my heart. "I am playing with you, little one," he said, stepping ever nearer.

It sickened me to hear him say it; dreadful as he was, we were the same kind of creature. "Why waste your time playing with me, Herr Staff?" My voice shook like leaves in a storm, but I held steady.

"Why indeed? I told you the first time. I enjoy watching you suffer. Your terror is sweet nectar."

We stared at each other, at something of an impasse. I wondered: if I gave him the printed, mistranslated copy of the Book, would that partial surrender get me out alive?

The demonesses only sought my blood as a catalyst, while the wizard seemed fascinated with my ability to die and return. If the wizard killed me, I would have a much harder time returning—if indeed, I could return at all. If I could not wield it, the Book would not stop him, and the Staff would easily kill me and devour my soul. I swallowed hard, inched toward the stairs.

He waited, fiddled with his now-massive staff, did nothing.

"What do you want of me?" I finally asked. "The Book you sought is here, and as you say, it is child's play to take it away from me."

"What do I want? Everything." His voice sounded affable again, as if we were discussing lunch instead of the fate of my soul. "I want your book. I want the *real* Book—of course we both know the book in your hand is only a copy."

The hairs at the base of my neck prickled with an animal revulsion as he went on. "I want to use your blood, body, and soul to activate the Book, the real Book. Make it mine to serve me. You will be a fitting sacrifice."

He stopped talking, mercifully, and we stared each other down, time suspended.

"You cannot use me," I said. "I will escape into death before I let you use me that way."

"So you think." He shrugged, shuffled closer still. "You raised a demon, and probably a score more, in your last adventure in the next world. You are more like me than you want to admit. You could learn still more, avoid all these unpleasantries."

In an instant he had somehow closed the gap between us and I smelled the foul puff of the wizard's breath as it caressed my cheek.

"I'll grant your sister safe passage, a safe journey to America. Knox will make sure of it!"

I swallowed hard, tasted bitter satisfaction in recognizing the obviousness of this last lie, and forced myself to look into his face.

The Staff grinned and nodded, evidently thinking he had gained ground. "I'll swear the most terrible oaths, bind myself with irrevocable spells. In fact, you can bind me yourself."

I remembered Madame Lucretia's lessons. In my vulnerability lay my power. "We both know I don't have the strength to bind you, Herr Staff."

By now I had retreated to the landing at the top of the stairs, even as the Staff had followed me close, step for step, and made any escape impossible.

He stroked my hand where I clutched the banister. His fingers closed over my wrist. "Give yourself to me willingly, undamaged, and I will make sure Gisele is protected. You will suffer. Your suffering is part of the bargain no matter what you decide. But I can swear to you that Gisele will be safe."

A hornet's nest of lies swarmed around the Staff's pretty words. My sweaty left hand slipped along the leather spine of the book I still clutched, and I saw the name of my only true protector shining in gold leaf against the embossed red leather: *Raziel.* My lips moved silently, shaping his name, but I refused to utter a sound.

Call him! Call upon the angel! A sudden urging assailed me with an irresistible intensity.

I tore my gaze away from the cover of the book, saw the rapt expression on the Staff's face, and it occurred to me that he wanted me to call upon Raziel once more: my last, desperate thought had echoed too loudly inside my skull, sounded a bit too German-inflected.

The wizard wanted Raziel to show himself now. Maybe he believed he could vanquish the angel himself, but with a sickening, sinking sensation I realized he wanted the angel for something more sinister than mere destruction. Raziel had spoken true: the wizard meant to enslave him in service to the cause of the Reich.

There was nothing for it, I would have to die once more: the wizard's cruel lie about protecting Gisele was nothing more than a false dream.

My wrist was still trapped inside the Staff's knotty fingers, and I twisted my hand in vain to free it, fought a wave of panic that surged over me as I struggled and the book tumbled to the dirty floor.

I shook my head in admonition, forced myself to smile, and had the satisfaction of seeing the grin fade from the Staff's lips. "No. I don't know why you want me to summon the angel, but I won't."

His eyes narrowed, and any pretense of his civility was gone for good. His fingers darted upward and clawed into my shoulders, and the Staff shook me like a terrier worries a mouse. "He's your only hope, damn you!" Hot spittle sprayed from his lips onto my face, where it burned.

"No," I whispered, and I reached with my summoning to the true *Book of Raziel* with everything I had.

The walls blazed up in a moment, as though some thoughtful hausfrau in Hell had just switched on the ovens. The paint blistered on the hand railings and I yanked my hand away from the hot metal just in time. Sweat poured down my face and I closed my eyes and called to my book without words, with simple unbridled longing, the sigh of a half-asleep lover for her soul mate, gone missing from her bed.

I opened my eyes. The walls glowed with pinpricks of light, orange stars. I abandoned my only physical escape and, with a dreadful effort, wrenched away from the wizard's claws. As I raced to the middle of the room, I stretched my palms toward the far wall, even as my nearly broken left wrist throbbed with pain.

Some misguided mortal soul, long ago, had used the pages of my book to insulate the warehouse as wallpaper. A Jewish star burned through the heavy coating layers of paint, the incantation double-ringed with Hebrew words I could not read. I ripped into the wall with bare fingers, pulled the outer layers of nineteenth-century newsprint away from the ancient pieces of parchment, and I cupped the drawing in my palm and held it outward against my foe.

It was an amulet; how I understood that at the time, I do not know. But it was mine: I held an amulet to bind and compel evil spirits—I held it in my hand, held it at the ready.

The Staff swooped upon me. I called upon my ancestors, but they could not help me, not from beyond the grave. My family ghosts gathered at the edge of the second Heaven, clustered all around, maiden aunts and bent old great-uncles I

didn't recognize, and they wrung their hands and cried griev-
ous tears until I released them once again.

Next, I sent my power deep into the spongy ground underneath the warehouse, into the old, mossy bones of Amsterdam,
and I called to the spirits of the land to hurl out this horrible
sorcerer's vile toxin. Alas, wherever I sent my witch's summoning, I could only find water, the flow of water rushing away as
fast as it could from the pestilence that was the Staff. And the
air spirits that still remained inside the warehouse only huddled in horror against the ceiling.

I held the amulet out from my body, a spiritual firearm, but
I could not activate it, not without knowing the Hebrew incantation, not without even knowing how to read the letters. I
whispered the Sh'ma over and over, but it was not enough.

My eyes met the Staff's, and time ground to a halt. We stood
only a couple of feet apart, and he held his hands open wide, as
if he were defenseless. "Go ahead, Lazarus. You have the remnant. Go, animate the Book. That is why you came all this way,
nein?"

"Aleph, bet, gimel, daleth . . ." I whispered, and the corre-
sponding Hebrew letters began to glow in my palm. But then, I
had to stop, for those were the only Hebrew letters I had ever
learned.

The letters flickered and died in my fingers. The Staff licked
his lips and smirked at me, and I backed away, knowing he
would close the gap between us in another instant. In that final
moment, when the wizard lifted his staff, I held the amulet up
between us. Lucretia's magic was not enough to defeat him,
and it was a mistake to believe that I could even fight him for
long with her magic instead of mine. Only my own, still-

hidden magic would do, and I had to find it myself. But it was too late for that now.

He threw his staff aside, and the wizard grabbed my already-broken left wrist, bent it back. I smothered a cry as he plucked the Book's amulet out of my other hand with a smooth, fluid movement and tucked the slip of paper into his breast pocket.

And then the Staff was upon me, a furious, punishing juggernaut. In desperation, I screamed for the Witch of Ein Dor, and she came. But she could only hover outside the rippling, cracked leaded-glass windows and shout inaudible curses and shake the ancient, rattling panes.

I tried to protect my head with my hands but he slapped them away, beat at my face with physical blows and with malign, poisonous magic. Again and again he pounded on my ears, in my eyes, and he screamed: "*Call the angel! Make him appear, you little bitch! Make him fall, you Jew whore!*"

The world faded around me and I sank to my knees, the spectral forms of the ghosts and the witch glowing brighter and brighter in the gathering darkness. Raziel's name twitched on my lips, but I held my breath, would not call him.

"*Make him come! Make him die too!*"

Sometimes the only victory is in defeat, the only honor is to run away. This time, I ran away to death, not Zanzibar, and I left the wizard beating my pulverized face with his staff and his big, hard, bloody fists.

✳ 21 ✳

Dead, again.

My flight into death this time was a grim victory. The Staff had certainly done his best to ride that fine line between torture and murder, and I had only managed to slip away because I knew the way to the next world far better than I did the geography or the native spirits of the city of Amsterdam.

Gray ether wrapped me in sepulchral silence, the profound nothingness a blessed relief after the vicious pounding I had taken. I bobbed like a cork in the swirling mists, and I basked in sweet oblivion.

And now I understood the temptation to let all of it drop, forget the miseries and passions of earth and simply fade away into eternity. Already, my mortal travails seemed far away and irretrievable, more a historical oddity than a screaming injustice I had to rectify.

I took a look around. The same endless plain stretched out to infinity, the same soup swam with primordial spirits. I whispered my own name, and it dwindled away into nothingness.

A thread of impatience spooled into a barely contained panic. I had to figure out how to get out of this place, escape from this moribund peace and launch myself back into the struggle of mortal life.

A voice called to me, rising through the soft fuzz wrapping me up like a flannel sheet: "Magdalena . . ."

Raziel. Golden light bled into the cottony gray that surrounded us. A pair of golden wings unfurled in their full glory, and the rest of Raziel filled in after them.

When I saw the look on Raziel's face, my shadow heart twisted. "My magic wasn't enough," I whispered. "Not even close."

"Your magic is plenty enough, if you can learn how to release it," Raziel said, his voice soft but rumbling, like thunder building far away.

His eyes blazed, his hands clenched and unclenched. Slowly it dawned upon me that he had watched every turn of the battle from this safe but ineffectual vantage point. I could not imagine the agony of his watching my demise, without being able to take a step forward to intervene as I suffered and died. And I knew that, no matter what, Raziel would never tell me. Never.

"Raziel . . . ," I began.

His brows knitted together and his nostrils flared. "You do not understand the frustrations of angels."

I kept my voice gentle. "I have to go back again, as much as I wish I could stay."

I thought of Paris, and regretted calling him all over again. "If you think I should stay with you . . ."

He shrugged. "I will descend, whether you return to Earth or not."

His answer left me thunderstruck. "But what about—"

"My sacred duties? The Almighty knows my heart. Surely He will forgive me for what I must do."

I tilted my head, considered my beautiful, terrifying messenger of doom. Ah, the Almighty. "Is He up above somewhere? Truly? I have met in my travels angels, demons, vampires, witches. Goblins and werewolves. But never once—*once*—have I seen a drop of evidence that the Lord even exists."

"How do you think all of us got here?"

I practiced drifting as an astral spirit: being a disembodied ghost has its pleasantries. I rose up over Raziel's head, floated upside down like a confused balloon. "Perhaps He has better things to do than worry about us and our little tragedies. Perhaps He has moved on from this world to create another, hmm?"

The angel shook his head and laughed. The sound echoed through the astral mists and tinged the gray with sparkling golden light.

"You might be surprised," he finally managed to say once his rolling laughter had faded away. "Take it from me, Lazarus, take it on faith if you must. The Lord Almighty does exist, though not in a form you could meet and amuse the way you do me. He withdrew from the Earth and its environs so that the children of men could truly be partners with Him if they so choose."

"But why? What a crazy way to create a world!" I reached down, and our fingers interlaced. My astral feet trailed up behind me, as Raziel tugged gently at my fingers like a kite string.

He shrugged and laughed again, though less uproariously than before. "What does it matter why? You are in terrible trouble. What do you have to lose? Believe in Him, call upon Him for help. I cannot show you the way back to life, and your spell will not work this time. Not given the way you died."

Raziel looked deeply into my eyes, and on the astral plane our souls grew close and twined together like flowers in a garland. "The Staff has more power than any demon, Magduska. He exercises his free will just as you do. I do not know if you can master your magic in time to defeat him, but you are the only one who has a chance."

My astral cheeks grew hot. "You called me Magduska," I said. "Only the people who love me the most call me that."

"I know."

We floated together in the silence, without even the pounding of my living heart to break it.

I could not tear my gaze away. "I'm going back, then," I said. "I best get started."

I smoothed his cheeks with my fingertips, and put the palms of my hands over my eyes to block the incendiary sight of his beauty. I declaimed the spell my mother had unwillingly once spoken on my behalf—I was proud to remember every syllable, every last inflection. But though the ether trembled all around us, I still remained.

My hands slowly dropped from my eyes, and I turned to see Raziel shaking his head. "You see? That spell of your mother's isn't going to work."

I squirmed in the astral soup, resisting the truth of what he said; resisting the truth of my feelings for him, too. Here I was, dead, and the angel's very words called me back to the challenge of life. "If I pray to the Lord for help as you suggest, I might not like the answer I get."

A trace of mirth flickered in his eyes, though his expression remained solemn. "What other choices remain?" Raziel drew closer. "Just try."

So I did. With a sigh, I looked up and said, "I know I sin through willfulness. But You made me this way! If You do exist, Lord, the One who made my beloved little sister, please send me a sign!"

I waited. Nothing.

I turned to the angel, my tone exultant, the reality not so much. "Are you satisfied?"

He snorted. "Did you ever think perhaps that I am the sign He sent?"

When I shrugged, he shook his head as he beheld me, a crackle of static in his peaceful void. "I can no longer remain in my celestial domain, safe. And watch . . . what I have to watch. The only choice I can live with now is to descend."

Oh, Raziel. "It's not all bad, life." I had to force out the words, husky as they sounded. "Chocolate is so good it tickles the nose, angel. The spring breeze off the Danube is rare and fine. Even better than coffee at midnight in Paris . . ."

His smile pierced my heart. "I plan to find out for myself, if I can."

I hastened to focus on practical details rather than the coffee of Paris. "Your plan was good in Amsterdam, so let us keep to it if we can. I'll find my way back somehow, and I'll fight the Staff again. You mustn't descend to Earth until I defeat him."

I could see he didn't like that idea. "Magduska. Time is running out. There is no more time for me to wait." He unfurled his wings and I gasped. "I will not allow the wizard to have his way with you again. I forbid it."

The light all but blinded me, even in my spectral state. "Raziel," I finally managed, "this is what the wizard wants."

That stopped him cold. The magnificent wingspan trembled, and Raziel folded his wings back away, like a barfighter who returns his knife into his boot. "He thinks he's won, Magda."

We now talked of trouble just as I, Eva, and Gisele had schemed for our survival on the dangerous streets of Budapest. "Yes—and the Staff's overreaching is an advantage to us. It makes him careless. But if you go charging down after him, he'll grab you for sure, just as you said. Bide your time. We'll think of something."

He chewed on the inside of his cheek, mulling over my words. "It's too dangerous," he said. "Let me return your specter to your sister Lucretia de Merode in Amsterdam. She may have some ideas. Perhaps she will invite you to inhabit her mortal body and you could wield your magic together."

It sounded like an excellent plan, all the more impressive given the fact that Raziel was unused to exercising his own will to live by his wits alone. But before I could assent, a sudden chill bit into me with iron fangs.

As if my words had conjured him, the Staff wavered in the ether in astral form, a clot of darkness at the edge of my line of vision. He had pursued my soul into the next world.

Fighting a groundswell of panic, I blasted the wizard with

my mother's spell, really put my magical muscle into it. He shielded his face from the force of my prayer—for prayer my dark spell was, however impious.

I squeezed myself into a needle of light once more, to escape back into life—but this time, I strangled within the eye, unreleased. Instead of shooting into my body, back into the Earth shadowed with darkness, I was trapped inside the light.

Even now, I could see the Staff's horrible teeth, twisted like a car wreck into a smile. "Going back so quickly? I don't think so, my dear little Magdalena, fallen one. I promised you I'd drink your soul like blood. And so I will."

I writhed in his grip, but could not free myself. "No." No: what I had, all I'd ever had. "I curse you; my soul will stick in your throat and choke you for all eternity. Every spell you ever work will turn in your hand and smite you. I curse you now, Staff, for now and evermore."

The Staff sneered at me, though his expression did look somewhat uncomfortable. "What matters your little curse, Magda? Your ancient grandmama of Ein Dor cursed me too. The Temple fell anyway. Curse and curse again."

His face grew serene, almost contemplative. "Every evil thought drags you into a lower emanation, brings you into my dominion. I drink your hatred too, little girl, and it strengthens me in my purpose."

"No. I refuse to serve you."

Locked in struggle with him, I sensed his power; ancient, complex, seasoned. Stronger than mine, by far. He pulled tighter and I gave a little cry. "Of course I have the power to make you serve me. You yourself will animate the true *Book of Raziel*, enliven it for me with your hatred, your negation. You refuse to let go, you insist on subverting God's will. Don't give up now, there's a good little scout."

He banked my rage and pain and suffering like a fire, a locomotive's coal-fueled engine. Righteous or no, my fury was trapped inside his magical snare.

He reached out, and his hard, bony fingertips pinched me between them like a flea. "You come with me."

The Angel Raziel leaped up before us, his sword outstretched. "Release her, wizard."

I twisted to see his face one last time. "Raziel, you promised! Stay back—it's you he wants."

The Staff shook me like a terrier with a rat, but I had reached Raziel in time, the angel understood. Raziel lowered his sword, bent his head.

"Magduska," Raziel said, his face a study in agony. And then, slowly, he faded away.

The Staff had me in his clutches again. But this time, I was the one who claimed victory.

✳ 22 ✳

The Staff returned with me back to Earth, painfully compressed as I was, to Knox's warehouse in Amsterdam. He took the amulet of the fragment of the original Book that I had found—written in Raziel's hand? Adam's? I did not know. I craned to see my broken, dead body, but I could not find it.

And he trapped me inside the amulet, the way any demon is trapped, the way Solomon enchained Asmodel, Enepsigos, and the other demons and demonesses he enslaved into building the First Temple of Jerusalem.

How I fought him, how I strained against my prison of Hebrew and ink! But to no avail.

I was trapped inside my own book of spells.

He rolled me up and, whistling, tucked me into the silk breast pocket of his well-tailored suit jacket. The curve of the parchment crushed my soul against the tailored hem. "Very good," he said in German, his voice sounding pleased.

I strained to make out the dimensions of the prison in the shifting shadows. In my current, compressed form, the inside of the amulet looked like a half-lit, arch-domed mausoleum. A huge improvement over death in the warehouse, even an improvement over the gray and formless void of the second Heaven.

But my amulet was still my prison.

Silence echoed all around me, the living Hebrew setting off sparks of heavenly emanations all around my still-living soul. I looked way up: the words arched like a cathedral far over my astral head, and whispered echoes of the holy words vibrated all around me.

I was imprisoned inside my inheritance, yet this magical prison was still mine. The wizard had bent it against me, but it was still mine by right. How to claim it for my own, to use it against my enemies and bind them in their turn?

Even as I considered my circumstances, doubt nipped at my astral body. Who was I to wield this power? It had done in no less a personage than King Solomon. Who was I to defy the Angel of Death?

But then I thought of Gisele and Eva; of Trudy, and her family; even of Leopold. I thought of Raziel. And I thought: who was I, *not* to wield this power?

Who was I to sit on my spectral hands and refuse to fight against certain evil? God had abandoned me to my fate, His reply to my prayer was clear enough. But I would happily go to Gehenna in the end, rather than forfeit my God-given chance to stop Gisele's prophecy from manifesting in the world.

To hell with all of it. No one, not God in Heaven nor Trudy in Salzburg, had the right to tell me that the noble thing to do was to shut up and simply die. I could not accept I had to spare the world the embarrassment of my existence, and forget what God or Something Else had created me to do:

Wield my inborn power, grow in it, glory in it.

I gathered my strength and tested the Aleph hovering immediately before me:

א

The sharp edges of the letter burned, like a knife left on the surface of a woodstove. I drew back my astral hand, and focused myself into a more coherent physical form. Easier to be careful with my astral form if I kept clear in my mind where my limits existed.

Rabdos had confined, but not bound me. I risked much by my "tinkering," as Eva would have put it, but I had no real choice—I had to break out or end up a tool of the evil that threatened all that I loved. The matter was as simple as that.

Even as I counted alephs, I fought the melancholy that pulled me down. In my heart of hearts I had believed that I could prevail through youth, luck, and sheer stubbornness alone.

But I had no time to indulge in despair. The Staff surely was on his way to some place of power, in Berlin or elsewhere, a place where he could put me to maximum use. I was no student of military strategy, and had no certain sense where Hitler planned to strike. Under no circumstances could I call upon Raziel again.

What to do? In a burst of dark inspiration, I hissed, "Leopold!" and the letters all around me crackled with static. I stayed well back from their sharp edges, but I didn't give up either. "Leopold . . ." I summoned my creature with everything I had.

I heard a prickling, thonking sound, like a stick pulled by a running child against a wrought-iron fence. And then I saw his little face, peeking through my letter-shaped prison bars. "Mama. Mama! The wizard caught you after all. The bastard."

I sighed. "Leo, I need to ask you a favor."

He tilted his eyes, squinted up his face so he could see me. I drew close to the light to meet him. "I need—well, I need to get out of here."

Leopold laughed and buzzed around like a fly, too little for the Staff to swat at or even notice at all. "Why, Mama? They say to keep the angels close and the devils closer."

I crossed my arms, tapped my foot impatiently at Leopold's baby talk. I was fully prepared to argue with him unto oblivion, but then his words sank into me like a restorative, a magic elixir.

The Staff planned to use me, not destroy me, not yet. I would abide, call my forces when the time came. If I could call Leopold, I could call his brothers too.

"Leopold, you are a genius!" I whispered.

He groomed his fine mustache with his long fingers. "But of course, I am my mama's son." He winked at me, beamed with pride.

"I will stay in the amulet, stay and learn. Safer here, at least for the moment, than anywhere else. When I need you, Leo, I will call." I thought of the Witch of Ein Dor and her fabled

army of demons, and for the first time since I had been captured, I smiled.

"The favor is this, then, Leopold: can you find the many
brothers you said once that I sparked? And can you gather
them together?"

He gave me a look so skeptical and droll that I wanted to
laugh and cry together in my consternation. I recognized that
expression, had tried it out in the mirror many a time in my Budapest girlhood, in an effort to look sophisticated and debonair.

"I will be your demon general, Mama," he said. "I await your
call to arms."

Past the horizon of my sight, the vibrations of the wizard's
footsteps rumbled, and with a surge of hope I realized my very
bondage could prove a belated answer to my prayers.

✳ 23 ✳

Why in the name of the Witch of Ein Dor had I defied my mother while she had lived? Why had I resisted the long, slow, boring process of acquiring the ancient, superstition-riddled knowledge of my people?

The answer hid within the question itself. I had believed in the promises of rationality and science over the dingy, backward reaches of my mother's magic. But now . . .

I guess the times in which we live are dingy and backward indeed. The Hebrew words arrayed against me mocked me with their very incomprehensibility; my power lay hidden inside their unknown meaning. The alephs glowed, familiar and attuned to me . . . *at my service.* I focused my concentration, welcomed all the alephs to join me—

And they slipped out of their formation, the change sending

huge tremors through my prison. The amulet still held—I had not altered the words surrounding me enough to change their meaning. Aleph is a silent letter, and allies though my alephs were, they could not speak the spell into a different intonation, a different effect.

But they did infuse the enclosure with the world's light. They left holes in the amulet, open windows through which I could project my sight and hearing. I surged up against an aleph-shaped pinprick of light—it was tiny, a sliver of brightness, but in my current disembodied form, I thought I could perhaps squeeze through and escape that way, find a safe astral corridor back to my dead body and return again, pick up the burden of mortality to fight another day.

The words around me creaked like ancient timbers, strained by the defection of all the alephs. I peeked through the pinhole, tried to pass through, then drew back with a huge gasp of shock, one I hoped the Staff could not detect.

We had indeed traveled far. My captor was in the midst of a personal, heated conference with Adolf Hitler, the Führer himself. And as I watched their private conversation, it dawned upon me that the portholes revealing this tableau must also expose me to any magical being that would happen to notice.

(Stop him)

The words echoed through my mind, an imperative echoing through my dark, light-pricked prison: Summon Hitler's soul into this amulet and seal it up tight, somehow. The thought of spending eternity trapped inside a paper amulet with Adolf Hitler struck me as a peculiar damnation, but I would willingly accept it, if I could only stop him from the course the whole world assumed by now he meant to take—

War. Total, irrevocable war.

I inched up to my aleph-shaped peephole and risked another look, as I tried to stay as invisible as I could be.

The Staff and Hitler stood alone, in a brilliant aleph-shaped tableau. It was an alpine summer's afternoon, on a stone patio overlooking a cascading hillside and a meadow below it, dotted with edelweiss and linden trees. I trembled, focused on cohering. We were at the Berghof, Hitler's famed retreat overlooking Salzburg, which I had trudged past on my way to Paris only a few short weeks ago.

The exquisite view would have taken my breath away if I had any left. I strained to see the outlines of the great stone house rising behind the terrace where Hitler and his wizard stood contemplating the world, supplicant at their feet.

Of course they spoke together in German. "My mission is accomplished, my Führer."

Hitler paced without speaking. His face was stern, like in the newsreels, with a shock of oily hair that fell into his eyes, his puffy-lidded eyes squinting into the far distance. I watched him stamp the flagstones under his well-shined boots, and I considered with wonder that this dough-cheeked, cloudy-eyed man held a knife to the throat of the world.

A low bark echoed along the evergreens, and a German shepherd bounded along the patio, its long thin tail waving like a flag.

Hitler knelt, and the dog licked his neck slavishly, while the dictator returned the beast's caresses. I gulped and forced myself completely still. This bounding, blindly loving creature was Blondi, famed throughout Europe, and she was Hitler's paramour, the werebitch Eva Braun.

Her story had filled the nonmagical world with fear when it came out in the magazines; I had read a profile in the *Pesti Hirlap* myself. Ordinary folk at least pretended to live their lives free from magical associations. Braun's open transformation into a creature of the Reich warned the free people of Europe what Hitler might do should he obtain dominion over them: compel their obedience in order to consolidate his power.

Hitler had offered Braun, a regular woman, up to the great Eastern Werewolf Pack in order to bond with them and establish himself as their pack leader supreme. As his mate, she was the highest offering Hitler could make short of becoming a werewolf himself. Though he called himself "Wolf," and admired the werewolves' fierce loyalty, Hitler would not allow himself to be turned and thus potentially come under the dominion of any other wolf.

His Nazi wizards had helped her to survive the Change. Unlike most of the European weres, her primary form was animal, and she only took human form under the full moon.

The dog stilled, and I watched her leathery nose wrinkle. A low growl arose in her throat, and for a terrifying moment I believed she had sniffed me out and knew she was being watched by an enemy. But no, her teeth-baring hostility was reserved for my own nemesis, the Staff. One of the magical ones responsible for turning her.

"Hush," Hitler said, his face half buried in the ruff of hackles raised along Blondi's trembling shoulders. I saw he loved her, and it annoyed me—I wanted Hitler to be all monster, one hundred percent a nightmare, without even a glimmer of humanity to redeem him.

It was easier to kill a monster than a human man, no matter

how bloodthirsty. But I did not need Gisele's gift of foresight to comprehend his utter ruthlessness. A single glance revealed the evil in the man who knelt in the soft breeze.

With difficulty Hitler calmed his canine familiar. He looked up at Rabdos's face, and his puffy eyes narrowed. "You disturb her." He hurled the words at the Staff's head, sharp as a surgeon's scalpel.

The Staff's heart, wizened as it was, still beat so hard that it shook my paper prison, rocked both him and me. "Forgive my presence."

The wizard bowed slightly from the waist, and his dreadful fingernails scraped against the outside of the amulet. My astral stomach turned at the dry scratching of his nails and the oily unctuousness of his voice. "Forgive me my enthusiasm. But I clutch in my hand an amulet, an ancient tool of binding and of destruction."

Hitler's lips thinned. He bent to Blondi's twitching ear, muttered some all but inaudible endearment. And with a final low growl the dog trotted across the flagstones and down the stone stairway, out of sight.

When I returned my attention to Hitler, he had drawn closer, unbearably close to where I huddled in my jail, all but helpless. "Destruction." His voice was filled with an unholy note of triumph. "Speak, tell me of it."

"This little scrap of paper is what remains of an ancient volume compiled in the time of Solomon's Temple, a book called *The Book of Raziel*. It contains many spells, my Führer, formulations, incantations, amulets such as this."

My prison trembled like a leaf, trapped in the wizard's curling fingers. "Even without knowing how to work the magic, this paper will protect the bearer, from fire, in surgery, in childbed.

"But in the proper hands, it may do much more. A wizard may capture spirits, trap them inside the amulet, bend them to his will."

He hesitated, and Hitler hunched his shoulders and scowled. "And you have done such, to the demons and the like?"

"It is so. The Book has been reproduced endlessly, and with every repetition, it loses some of its integral power. Of Sapphire was the Book first inscribed, just as the words of power were encased in the Ark of the Covenant. This little scrap was inscribed by a worker of great power, long, long ago. It has touched the Sapphire Heaven, it contains the true magic of Raziel.

"From this scrap, I may call up the entire Book; the magic of all is contained in this bit, like an oak tree hidden within a tiny acorn. I may grow it back entire, through my magic, and when it has grown to its full, the Book can be used to command legions of demons, not just one."

A low cackle of pure delight escaped from between the Staff's cracked lips, somewhere above his clenched fist, out of my sight. I was glad to miss the expression on his hideous face. "In days of old, I was pushed aside, deemed too impure to even touch the Book, let alone inscribe the magic into words. But I have outlasted those who underestimated my power, and I will destroy those who doubt my magic now."

Hitler flicked back the limp lock of hair that had fallen over his left eye, and his smile was small, hard. "Tell me, wizard. Tell me what destruction I now can wield."

"You may compel the Jews to their own doom. They can not lift a finger against your race or the Reich now."

Hitler nodded. Lost in reverie, his eyes began to glow orange as the nod faded into a rhythmic rocking, and his nostrils flared wider than any human nostrils could open. "Can you steal their power with this regrown Book?"

The voice was lower, more guttural than Hitler's public voice, and the words were slurred as he spoke them. I was used to Hitler's hysterical rantings, the screams of his adoring mobs only fueling his insane rages. But this voice sounded hungry. And souls were its meat.

The Staff prattled on, his words spilling out a little too quickly. "I can compel the angel himself with this amulet, well watered with the witch's blood." His hand trembled as he unfolded the parchment to show Hitler the double circle, the six-pointed star trapped within.

Hitler's laughter echoed over the countryside like the footfalls of a giant. "Hah! Raziel. He and I, we have an old rivalry to resolve, wizard. The time has come at last. Bring the remnant to Berlin and grow the Book. Do it!"

The wizard's pulse raced so loudly I could barely make out his reply. "Yes, my lord. Of course, of course." The Staff paused. "Come out of your host, my lord. Let me speak with you directly."

Hitler's scratchy laugh was deep, hearty, and genuine. "Oh no, let me speak through channels, as usual, wizard."

The Staff cleared his throat with a phlegm-filled hack and trembled at Hitler's bizarre outburst. "Even so. My pleasure to speak with you, in any guise."

The wizard's suave innuendoes baffled me. And apparently, the Führer too. Hitler tilted up his chin, squinted back at him through his puffy, sunken eyes. "You speak rubbish, wizard.

Tell me of what you hold, quick. Tomorrow I go to Berlin to meet with Ribbentrop about the Soviet delegation."

The paper crackled all around me as the wizard shifted his body. "The Book contains an ancient, implacable magic. It will secure your power, over the Jews and over other demons."

The Staff's fear infected me with its virulence. Something was horribly wrong here, even more terrible than I could have imagined. I struggled to grasp the import of the Staff's repetitions and Hitler's words—and then realized to my horror that they were not Hitler's words at all. I had heard spoken the conspiracy not of two beings but of three.

I looked again at Hitler's face, and with a rush of understanding stumbled away from my tiny window on the living world. With my second sight I saw the ancient demonic face superimposed quite decisively over Hitler's human features, overshadowing and occupying them. Though, may God help me, I believe the malevolent human face of Hitler frightened me more than the demon that possessed him.

"You will restore the Book and compel Raziel at the earliest auspicious time," the demon said, his words slurring over and through Hitler's lips, darting from outside into Hitler's mouth like a snake or a probing tongue.

It was Asmodel who spoke, the demon Raziel had once spoken of, the one the Staff had invoked on the platform in the Vienna station. He was a most ancient and malign demon, one who hungered to punish humankind for Solomon's presumption. And now Asmodel inhabited the soul of Europe's wickedest and most powerful man.

Miserably, I huddled inside the circle of words, glad of the faint protection the holy incantations offered me. Then, as quietly as I could, I whispered the alephs back into their former places.

They hovered, slightly out of alignment, and the darkness grew to all but total. I could still hear the harsh clatter of German-speaking voices, but mercifully I could no longer watch the demon working Hitler's features like an infernal ventriloquist.

"Long have I awaited my revenge on Raziel," the demon growled in Hitler's staccato German. "Do not delay, wizard. The summer is nearing its end. My hunger drives me to the East."

The echo of Rabdos's frantic heartbeats almost deafened me as he backed away from Hitler and his resident demon, still gazing over the verdant alpine hills surrounding the Berghof.

The newsreels could not capture the malevolent charisma of Adolf Hitler in the flesh. He was not a huge, physically impos-ing man. It was the force of his will, what Nazi wizards call the *vril*, that radiated from him in soul-crushing intensity. After only a few moments in his presence I was exhausted, my soul light almost completely extinguished by the force of his smoth-ering power.

The world seemed huge and cold outside my dark prison. I held to myself and what I believed in, but both of these things now seemed small and insignificant.

Inaction, the destroyer. The enforced lethargy of the amulet was robbing me of my own *vril*, my own will to action. The fact that the Jewish tradition called that drive the *yetzer hara*, the will to commit evil, didn't matter. I had to escape, keep moving, stop Hitler, and I would use any means to accomplish my ends.

The Staff's racing heartbeat made thinking all but impossible. I held close to the letters like wooden beams in the hull of a tossing ship in a stormy sea, and I waited for my chance. Waited in the darkness of my own despair.

Desperation creates strange phantoms, creatures of despair and hope. And, surrounded by these specters, it is all too easy to make fatal, irreversible errors, commit grave sin, succumb to self-delusion.

None of us, saints or sinners, can know the will of God while we walk the earth. The best we can do is reach with all our souls for what we love and what we are willing to die for in order to save. For all we know, our failures serve God's wish more than our supposed successes ever will.

✳ 24 ✳

I sat in my darkness for I know not how long, without the faithful markers of hunger, thirst, sleep, or wakefulness to trace time's passage. After a time, the wizard's heartbeat faded away, either returned to normal or too far away from my curled-up parchment prison for me to detect.

I spent that unknown time counting the letters surrounding me. I did not know all of them, but I counted them, nevertheless. The more I could discover about the structure of the spell that bound me, the more I could gain a purchase on it and bend it to my advantage when the opportunity arose.

I tried not to think about where the Staff was taking me, or of the passing seconds, the hours I had already spent separated from my body. Lazarus lore held that I had only three days to return to life. My soul hovered in eternal time, not Budapest time, and I had no way to tell whether three days or three weeks had passed since my encounter with the Staff in Amsterdam. So I restlessly counted the alephs, the bets and the daleths, and I tried not to reflect upon the fact that only living human beings can work magic and effect spells.

As I caressed the lovely curve of a Kaph, I heard murmuring voices. They drew me out of my lonely exertions. It was German, spoken sinuously, sibilantly.

The demonesses.

I whispered the alephs out of order again, peeked through the negative space into the world. And the jolt of what I saw almost blasted me into ghostly smithereens: we sat not in Berlin but in Café Mephisto, in Budapest, not a kilometer from my beloved Café Istanbul, from my home on Dohány Street!

This was my chance: somehow, fate had placed me in my native place of power, with the opportunity to study my enemies, to understand them and their particular evils. I tried to view the scene with the Staff's ancient eyes.

For once, I withdrew my witch's sight and saw the demonesses as they wished human mortals to behold them. And now I saw how, in the fertile magnificence of the German Reich, his demonesses had bloomed like desert flowers. I, again, could not easily see the Staff—evidently he had placed the amulet, all curled up, on the table in front of him—so I considered his three venomous flowers as they clustered around the tiny marble table, sharing a single Sacher torte for breakfast and drinking weak coffee from delicate porcelain cups.

The Café Mephisto catered to a demonic clientele the way my Istanbul welcomed the vampires and Café New York was home to the artists. The Staff stood before them, behind me; the

voices of the other demonic patrons made a low music humming in the air.

Above, a frantic sparrow flew among the ceiling arches and
the crystal chandeliers, lost in the opulence of the ceiling fans.
The demonesses paused in their breakfast libations, coffee cups
poised in their delicate fingers, and the Staff settled into his chair
with a grunt.

The Staff shifted in his seat, and the ornate carved wood
groaned for mercy. "My lovely ones, I trust you find Budapest
to your liking."

I watched the three women-forms murmuring to each
other. My task now: to study each of their particular brands of
evil, to learn the heart of each of my enemies. I needed to become a connoisseur of evil in its many manifestations. But could
I master their machinations in time to escape?

The clink of silverware and porcelain, the low growls and
hushed voices echoing in the high-ceilinged room, bathed me
in a symphony of civility and gilded charm. The creature sitting
next to him was as lovely as a peacock: Enepsigos, the demoness
who had inflicted the first death blow outside Linz.

The Staff reached across the polished surface of the table,
pulled her long, limp hand into his lap. "Now that I have captured the Lazarus and recovered her ancient magic, your long
nightmare will end at last."

"It will be interesting," Enepsigos said, her smile at odds
with the menace in her voice. "To wield the knife of that magic.
To taste that power. Interesting, indeed."

"The werewolves will not stand for this," Onoskelis said. Her
outward appearance, now that I gave myself the opportunity
to admire it, was extraordinary: creamy skin and butter-yellow

blond hair proclaimed her a sweet maiden of the Fatherland. Her beauty obscured but could not erase her hideous true aspect: another cruel illusion in this world.

He took the coffee cup out of her hand, drank the horrible coffee dregs left at the bottom. I had swilled the coffee of the Café Mephisto myself, and I remembered demonic coffee as nearly undrinkable. "No, the werewolves are sworn to Hitler as pack leader supreme. They will follow his orders, and those of their superiors, unto death. That is their creed."

Obizuth, the third, considered his words. She was the oldest of the demonesses arrayed around the table; the weakest, yet the one who had seen the most, endured the most. Obizuth frightened me by far the most. "That is not our creed. We do not follow mere orders, but live for freedom and for revenge."

The Staff's laugh was more awful than my memory of the coffee. "Freedom? Let me remind you who holds the power at this table. Was I not the one who bound Asmodel myself at first, at Hitler's own command?"

Enepsigos's hand stilled in his. "Yes, of course, Rabdos," she said, her face demure under the netting of her hat. She knew as well as I what agonies he could inflict with a word or a single incantation. And of course she knew his potential once the full power of the Book was within his grasp. After all, she had been present with him at the Temple of Solomon. So Raziel had taught me, on our long journey west of Vienna . . .

The Staff would not be thwarted now. "Now is the time to bring the power of the ancient book to hand. With this remnant, I will call the rest of the Book back to life. Rewrite the Book as I restore it, with magic, to suit my own will. A magnificent feat of magic, rare and sublime. You will soon see."

Obizuth pursed her lips, played with the edging on her gloves. "And you need us, still, to work this sublime feat of human wonder."

"Of course. And you three will be instrumental in giving life energy to what will be new. Or . . . you will taste my anger as you have before." He pulled Enepsigos's hand up, squeezed a little too tightly, and the diamonds in her rings caught the light and glittered cold and merciless in his fingers.

The silence deepened, and it became something menacing when I realized all three demonesses were squinting down at me, studying the amulet. If they saw the alephs gone all askew, they gave no sign of it.

Obizuth, the eldest one, dared to poke at my prison with a pinkie finger, even as she looked up to fearfully study her master's face. "So. The little Lazarus is trapped inside—now, there's divine justice for you!"

The three demonesses laughed together, in a horrible, discordant harmony. "Can't she get back into her body as soon as you let her out?" Onoskelis said.

The Staff snickered through his nose, his face out of sight somewhere behind me. "No chance of that. Before I left the warehouse, I set it aflame, with her body in it. She is nothing but ash now, she and the books together."

His words and their import echoed through my mind:

My body was gone.

I pulled away, my mind reeling. I could not return to life: there was nothing for me to return to. I was doomed to die now for good, or to exist as a ghost, or serve as a trapped tool of Hitler. The best I could do was escape and seek my punishment in Gehenna. Perhaps reincarnation did exist as the Chassidim claimed, and I could return as a mouse and infect Hitler with the plague. That could work, but too slowly . . .

I sank to the bottom of my paper sepulchre and listened to them squabbling; I had to focus on their words. The demonesses whispered behind their napkins, a sound like wind rushing through an empty valley filled with bones. "Ach, Rabdos," the creamy blond one, Onoskelis, said. "Such rare books, magical ones, destroyed."

"Yes, destroyed." He sounded nettled, and I could hear his body rustling in his bamboo-caned chair. "Out of that American's hands, too. So much the better."

"The end is near," the Staff continued. I heard the soft clink of his espresso cup, the way he sucked the hot liquid through a sugar cube. At the edge of the table, I saw a napoleon pastry half toppled on its plate. It occurred to me that I could never nibble a rumball or a napoleon again . . .

For me, the end had already come. It gave me a strange freedom, the knowledge that my body was gone. I would have to find another avenue, some backward, impossible way to escape.

I ventured my way to the very edge of my prison, knew I was exposing myself to my captors, but I was too intent, too heedless by this point, to care.

The Staff's voice dipped low, went scratchy. "Hitler will strike by September first if not before. Poland."

I understood as well as the demonesses what the wizard meant. He meant to invade Poland, annex it as he had Austria, Czechoslovakia, the Rhineland.

"But why are we here, then?" Onoskelis, the youngest demoness, looked confused as she slowly licked her demitasse spoon. "This is no Poland. Horthy is a good little Hitler!"

The Staff chortled, took a more confident-sounding sip of his coffee. "My dear, Horthy can only aspire to be a pale facsimile of our Leader. We are here to hide the amulet from prying eyes, away from the field of action. The last place anyone dangerous would look for it is here."

Enepsigos, the cruelest of the three, narrowed her eyes and glared at her human master. "This fragment of the old Book is not much use, *here*. Surely Hitler means to, put it and us to better use than that!"

The Staff's gnarled fingers scratched at the edges of the amulet, and I shuddered. He chortled as he spun me around, and the Café Mephisto whirled in my sight, caught in a crazy whirlwind.

Mercifully, he stopped to smooth the amulet out, and for the first time I saw his wrinkled, yellowed face looming huge above me. "Magic is an art, my precious pet. It waxes powerful in the proper hands. I am old, my love, you know it well. As a young man, I watched Solomon himself wield the Book to suit his purposes."

Obizuth's face was closed and still, but I caught a flash of reptilian yellow in her deceptively mild human eyes. "We all watched him, wizard, watched you, too. Watched Solomon bind Asmodel just as you. And we watched Solomon fall, in the end."

I watched fear coat her face like a creeping slime, and knew the Staff had pinned her with one of his hard, cruel gazes, one that hinted of the pain he could easily inflict as punishment for any infraction or none.

His voice was low, but it crept along the edge of the table, a malign creature born of his lips, ready to strike. "I watched

King Solomon bind and torture demons to work his will as he built the Great Temple of Jerusalem. I have bound you and your sisters, lo, a thousand years and more! Is not the land of mortal earth sweet and lovely, my pretty girls!"

His voice stretched taut, a near whisper now. "You know what I mean to do with her. Do not forget your master."

A heavy silence crushed us in its jaws.

When the wizard spoke again, he sounded almost normal. "I have rooms for us at the Hotel Gellert, across the river in the old city, in Buda. We will rest until the full moon, and then we use this girl to draw our quarry."

Enepsigos dared to sneer. "Our quarry? You mean to capture her little sister?"

The Staff chose to ignore her sourpuss, instead rolled the amulet up. All of them disappeared from sight, though I could hear them through the displaced alephs. "What use is the saint, the little one? No. I mean to capture the Angel Raziel himself."

The demonesses and I gasped in unison. They, creatures of air, winced in pain at the angel's very name; I cringed at the thought that the time had come all too soon, the moment I had long dreaded. The Staff was ready to capture Raziel, to bind him and bend his angelic spirit to the sorceror's service.

The Staff polished off the last of the toppled napoleon with lip-smacking gusto. "Once we bind the angel, we compel him to serve *my* will. *Mine.* Not only Europe, but Hitler himself, his resident demon too, all will serve me. Asmodel believes he has gained the upper hand. But no."

His shadow fell across the Hebrew-shaped bars of my prison. The parchment rustled, and I saw his enormous eye looking down at me, a mere handsbreadth away. His foul breath stirred the edges of the amulet. He smiled—smiled at *me*—and I, who thought I was past fear, clutched at the letters to keep from fading all away in sudden terror. The wizard knew I had heard every word; he did not care.

Unless I somehow found the key to this prison of incantation, it would become much more crowded. All of us, angel, Hitler-possessing demon, and mortal, stuffed into the Staff's satin breast pocket like an unholy passport.

✳ 25 ✳

Time had another meaning in the land of the dead. Our gravest misdeeds lived through all eternity, hatching the day the Almighty moved over the surface of the darkness, and will be resonating through the universe after the final trumpet sounds. So why struggle and twist in the trap of our fate? My efforts to avert the witch's dread decree had only hastened it.

The beautiful façade of the Hotel Gellert mocked me in my tribulation. Its magnificence had not faded since Hungary's defeat in the Great War, or in the worldwide Great Depression that had followed. If anything, the rococo facades and wedding-cake spires looked bigger and grander now than they had the last time I had seen them as a girl, in better, simpler days.

The green-striped awnings and sweeping marble columns contrasted dreadfully with my circumstances. I met my end surrounded by pink marble, the delicate fronds of potted palm trees, ornate gilded fountains, and filigreed window boxes. As the Staff and his demonic entourage swept through the grand lobby, my vantage point obscured and incomplete, I sat paralyzed, and more alone than ever before or since.

The concierge's voice, wheedling and cracked, speaking German so fast I could barely understand, bade the Staff and his lovely ladies welcome. He swept us up the grand staircase to the mezzanine, and after his offer of coffee was coldly rejected, he ushered us into the elevator, escorted us personally to the hotel's grandest suite, hoped it was suitable, on and on he went until I hung on the edge of a scream.

Mercifully, the genuflecting concierge faded away, and with a rustle of silk and paper, my rolled-up prison came to rest on a flat surface somewhere in the room. If I looked out as far as I could see from the single curling aleph I could displace, the elaborate crown molding and the crystal and brass chandelier shimmered above me like a faraway horizon.

I waited in the sudden profound silence for I don't know how long, an eternity of gray emptiness more foreboding than the second Heaven. Time ended, stretched away into infinity.

I held on to my memory of Raziel, hoarded the blessing of his absence like a treasure. I ached for him, I wanted him to come and rescue me, I wanted to lay my head down and bawl like a baby.

But nobody could save me, not even Raziel. So instead I remembered him as he was in Paris, and my panic drifted away, along with my life, all nothing more than dancing cigarette smoke in a Parisian café with no windows or customers. I was no longer Magdalena Lazarus, wayward daughter, beloved sister, malign witch.

But what was I?

A crinkle of paper, and then a whisper rattled the Hebrew letters like a chain-link fence in a punishing rush of wind. They peeled away one by one, and with a curious sense of detachment I watched them go.

As each letter went, more of my earthly surroundings revealed themselves. A grand suite at the Gellert, a glory of green satin, sweeping balcony outside French windows, sheer curtains glowing in the inky moonlight. All of it gorgeous, all as transient and inconsequential as a soap bubble.

"The moon is cruel, but I love her," a voice said in German.

By now I hated speaking German, replied in Hungarian. Screw the voice if it didn't understand me. "I don't love anything, anymore."

"*Nein?* Why are you still here, then?" the voice replied in surprise, still in German, still hateful. But mercifully, the voice did not belong to Staff.

My curiosity worked on me, got the better of me. I leaned out to look for the source of the voice.

Obizuth. The eldest demoness, naked and bathed in moonlight, cruel and pale as the moon. Her long white hair tumbled over her bony shoulders and down her reptilian back, and overspread her ankles and the marble floor. She drank champagne from a fluted glass, her mailed, webbed fingers etching little scratches along the gilded rim.

When our gazes met, she smiled. Obizuth had no interest in

hiding herself from me. I drew halfway out of my amulet prison. "Where are the others?"

"Gone to take the waters. The hotel management kindly closed the baths to the public so Rabdos and the girls could swim alone, together."

I flinched at the languid wave of the hands, her apparent friendliness. "Why didn't you take the waters, too?"

Obizuth tossed back the last of her champagne, twirling the leaded flute between her scaly fingertips. With exaggerated gentleness she perched the empty glass on the top of the black grand piano that hulked in the corner. "Somebody had to guard you. But really I stayed back so that we could have a little chat, Lazarus."

The breeze off the Danube picked up, and the long, sheer drapes blew diaphanous into the room, wrapping her naked body in wisps of white chiffon.

Her diabolical beauty left me cold. How tired I was of marble and chiffon, of the gilded accoutrements of power and corruption. "Enough with the glamour by moonlight, just spit it out already."

Obizuth's laugh, a low scratchy growl, rattled my paper cage. "Your confinement has made you savage, my little pet. So come out. Now."

No one had ever summoned me against my will, and the sensation was curious, a sick compulsion I could not resist. Bit by bit, her summons dragged me along the edge of the amulet and around the circle of the Hebrew script until a gap between two words afforded me enough room so that I could squeeze through.

It hurt. I saw stars despite my resolution not to cry out in pain or shock. And then the hurt faded, and I stood in the moonlight, my full size again. I looked down at my hands, saw silver and starlight. I was a creature of the air.

"Not so nice, the summoning, eh?"

I said nothing. When I finally looked up, Obizuth was only an arm's length away. Her vulpine features no longer frightened or repelled me; to the contrary, she haunted me with a strangely familiar beauty.

"Knox told you about us, yes?"

I tried to ignore her aquiline nose, the slope of her tiny, firm breasts. "Some. He just hinted about you, really. About your true—sympathies."

She trailed the long fingers of one hand up the length of my arm, and I gasped. I flicked my hair behind my ears and tried to move away as discreetly as I could: how she laughed at me! "My little mousie, the Staff has the three of us in his thrall. We are trapped, as surely as are you."

"Well, you certainly murdered me with gusto—nobody forced you to enjoy killing me." I refused to speak German, and she wouldn't speak Hungarian, so our conversation limped along in two languages, a deformed linguistic mismatch.

"Nonsense, you should be thanking us. You needed to die to claim your full power—or did your old grandmama from Ein Dor forget to mention that?"

Obizuth's outburst shook me like a leaf in the wind. For once, I wished the demon spoke truth: nothing now could save me except my own power made manifest.

I turned away, and she sidled closer. "Besides, we are desperate. We must have the power of your book!"

I turned to her. "Who? And why?"

"We three. And with the power of the Book we will be free. Surely now you understand."

Her voice wheedled and pled. Altogether, I preferred Obizuth murderous and cruel; the implications of her sudden genuflections disturbed me. "You don't need my book to get away, and you know it. Go ahead and repent. Ascend to your Maker, answer for your sins. That will set you free, book or no book."

She shuddered, her reptilian features creasing with fear in the quicksilver moonlight. Her long, thin tongue darted at her lips. "No, no. No facing the Maker."

I had to laugh, though I honestly didn't wish her harm, not even now. "I guess you just don't want to go free badly enough."

Her yellow eyes narrowed. "Why don't you take your own advice? Not so sure your Maker would approve of you either, yes?"

Her hand shot out and captured my forearm in a viselike grip. The empty champagne glass on the piano wobbled and fell to the floor with a tinkling crash.

I yanked my arm back, but she held me fast, and I realized with a sudden jolt that Obizuth could reach from flesh to spirit, manhandle and capture a ghost.

I stopped struggling. Her fierce grip on my ghostly arm raised a number of disturbing questions. I put my free hand over her claw, and my ghostly grip met her demonic one. We touched. That wasn't supposed to happen.

I shrugged and tried to look unimpressed. "You're right, I admit it, you and I have something in common. So tell me what you want from me."

"Freedom. Freedom! Surely you now understand how desperately we three wish to escape."

"I bet you do. So that you could start smothering babies in their sleep again, no doubt."

"No, no, we forget revenge. All we want now is the moonlight, the pleasure of the open sky."

Slowly Obizuth let go of my arm. How had she touched me? I rubbed at the shimmering skin of my forearm, and muttered, "Why, for Solomon's sake, do you think for a second I could do the slightest bit to help you?"

"You do not see?" Her eyes widened, and I saw the elongated pupils narrow into vertical slits. Her yellow eyes glowed like streetlamps. "Knox never explained!"

"No, he didn't. I'm hard-pressed to help myself, obviously. I can't avert the witch's prophecies. My witchcraft is no match for the wizard's sorcery, and I'm dead. Dead!"

"But you don't understand. You have power enough to beat the wizard. And we sisters have granted it to you!"

What Obizuth said was absurd, a fantastical lie. But she spoke so earnestly, it was impossible to dismiss her words out of hand.

She nodded, her lips pressed together hard. "Knox stayed out of it because he feared you, wanted to protect us from you, the Lazarus. Kind American mortal he is."

Protecting the demonesses—from me! I could not keep the skepticism out of my voice. "Go on, tell me your tale, quickly. Before your friends get back here."

Obizuth watched me warily with her yellow lizard's eyes as I swept along the room's shadowy corners, stretching my ghostly legs.

I paused at the open French doors. I could have passed right through the glass as a spirit and entered into the night; I too wanted to rise up into the moonlight and fly away, alone and free under the stars, freed from my lineage and my determination to master the Book, even now.

I looked back at her, and her inscrutable eyes showed me no mercy. But I sensed with foreboding the pain hidden behind those strange amber irises, the suffering the Staff would inflict if he should return to find me, his golden goose, flown. Obizuth would pay the price for my flight.

She caught my hesitation, and her lips curved into a slow, knowing smile. "You are weak, your heart is your downfall, you mortal girl."

My unspoken reply echoed in the silence: She knew as well as I that I was no longer mortal.

Her smile widened. "Are you ready to hear the story I have to tell?"

"I don't know. What does it portend, for my people or me?"

She shrugged, her bare shoulder glowing like a bone. "I don't care about you, your stiff-necked people, or your doom. I want that miserable worm the Staff ground into dust. And you're the girl to do it for me." Her eyes flashed, deadly as knives.

I nodded for her to begin.

"When the world was young, the daughters of men loved the sons of God. Asmodel, beloved of the Almighty, worshiped beauty, pleasure, and the passage of time. And a girl, a silly thin-armed girl by the name of Obizuth, tempted him into loving her.

"Long we lived, outside the Lord's sanction. Our children, Fallen Ones, drowned in the Flood, fell victim to God's armies, died one by one before their limitless time, each death a murder of my human heart. By the time the last one died, felled by a shepherd boy with a stone shot between his eyes, I had sold away the last of my soul and could no longer walk the earth, or love at all.

"My Asmodel could stay no longer. He descended into the lowest levels of being, what you mortals call Hell in your ignorance, and I became something I did not recognize: a scaly thing, a creature born of air and night. And I, who no longer had sons, took my revenge on the daughters of men, that they may know the torment I now refuse to suffer.

"I have forgotten more than I can tell you, creature trapped like a cricket in a cage. But if you unlock my prison, I will unlock yours.

"You say you cannot defeat the Staff. That your magic, too weak, can only strike through the hands of a living, mortal soul.

"To that, I reply:

"*One*, the love that has broken you will set you free;
"*Two*, you are the rightful heir of the Book, no matter what its form; and
"*Three*, you are a daughter of women, not of men. I speak in riddles, but consider now what I have to say."

I indeed considered what Obizuth had said low and quickly, like an incantation or a curse. She had called me a daughter of women, not of men: did she mean I was now a demoness myself?

Her obtuseness wearied me. "I still don't understand. I thought only living mortals may work magic, throw spells, commit necromancy. That's why you can't beat the Staff, why you can't kill me in human form except with your bare talons."

"Yes, good girl." She drew close to me, her skin smelling of soap and sulfur. "We are sisters, you and I. You are both mortal and creature of air, now. No one can stop you. Not unless you let them."

"I'm only a ghost, Obizuth."

"Still you do not understand." Her voice held a note of pure amazement. "How do you think the Lazarii obtained the power?"

I stared at her, still uncomprehending. And then, with a gasp, my mind flooded with understanding.

Raziel had spoken of the Fallen Ones, the Nephilim, not with loathing but with tenderness and regret. Obizuth had called me a daughter of women. The descended angels had taught mortal women how to compose spells and collect their power in writing.

I finally knew. A fallen angel lurked somewhere in my family tree.

Obizuth laughed at the conflicting emotions battling for supremacy within me. "Now at last you see, witchling. Now you know why you still remain, more than a ghost, a creature of air."

She smoothed her fingertips along her bony temples, combing back her long hair. "At the moment the Staff takes you for the sacrifice, rise up and call upon me, the same way that you summon your winged one. Together, we will crush him into nothingness and fly into freedom, each our own way."

I stared into her eyes, and she leaned forward and kissed me lightly on the lips. And though I kept my eyes open, I saw endless desert plains, a blackened sky, a cracked white earth. I suddenly understood why the Staff kept such dangerous creatures within his physical reach. Her touch contained worlds of torturous delights.

Obizuth drew back, and her hot breath caressed my ghostly cheek. Perhaps she did not lie: if I could whisper alephs aside in my current state, maybe I could do more than die and die again, a sacrifice under the waxing moon.

"Knox spoke up for you," I whispered. "And Bathory spoke for Knox. That will have to be enough for me. So. We are sisters for this battle, Obizuth."

✳ 26 ✳

Before the Staff returned from the baths, Obizuth had outlined for me his master plan. He intended to summon and bind Raziel, using my torment and agony as bait. Now that the moon had waxed to the full, his sorceror's power was at its apex. Under Buda Castle, built directly on the main ley line running through the old city, ancient caves gathered the subterranean energy of the earth spirits clustered underneath the surface, where the mortals rushed above, through their brief, modern lives.

Raziel. If the Staff captured him and used his celestial life force to reanimate the Book, it would be rewritten to suit the Staff's propensities and his power. Forged to his specifications, bent to his purposes, the Book would become a devastating locus of power: the Staff could summon and bind an army of demons, snuff mortal souls, and compel magical creatures to die, the way that Raziel had defeated the werewolves in Vienna on the station platform.

I had to keep Raziel out of the wizard's clutches. Throwing my lot in with the demonesses who had murdered me seemed a small and bearable price to pay.

Since time out of mind, shamans had descended into the caves to unearth secrets and bend the power of the lines to human will. As we ourselves descended, the power of the caves hummed through my prison like an electric current; I didn't need to wiggle letters out of sync to know why my thoughts wavered and crackled with a curious, half-painful static, like an electric shock that originated inside my astral body.

My tomb grew hot, so hot the letters began to glow orange. With the change, my curiosity grew fearful, and I ventured forward to watch the ancient cave paintings stir into life, the stags wheeling and stampeding all around us.

Rabdos stood hideously naked inside a magic circle carved into the living rock. Candles set at the four compass points guttered in their places, half buried in the crumbling dirt. I saw with first and second sight as one, now; demonic energy crackled in a circle of fire above the stone.

And with a horrible keening wail the Staff summoned me from out of the amulet, the only scrap of protection I had left. Because of Obizuth I was ready, and I was so far resolved to die that I was no longer afraid. Instead, I gloried in a vengeful rage, and I shot out of my lair with my own volition.

If Obizuth was right, I was descended from Fallen Ones, angels that had turned away from the Almighty to walk with women on the Earth. Now that I was a creature of the air, a strange mix of demon and unquiet ghost, I intended to goad my wizard nemesis to his own destruction.

I braced for battle, for the moment of soul sacrifice, and hoped that Obizuth had spoken true. The Staff marched counterclockwise within the stone circle, his feet backlit by the smoky candlelight.

I had learned one important lesson in all my travels: if you stand up for what you believe, you will be swarmed by enemies. My adversaries had become my badges of honor, and I would not cede them, not to Obizuth, not even to Raziel.

I drew myself up to my full height, stood in the middle of the magic circle, and I screamed:

"MENE MENE TEKEL UPARSIN!"

With every word I grew, until I reached my full size. The writing on Nebuchadnezzar's wall formed the basis of the curse that Lucretia had taught me. I screamed it, really projected it outward, and the cave itself trembled.

Even through the thicket of Hebrew words, the Staff's gaze met mine, and he did not look in the least surprised. "Ah, your fortitude is most fascinating."

He hesitated; both of us paused in the midst of our battle. He and I were kindred spirits, driven by the same delight in wielding magical power in service to a greater end. Much as I hated him, I understood his joy in claiming that power for his own.

The Staff began to laugh, and he shook his head: perhaps his thoughts had run in the same direction. "Come my pets—

devour her!" he commanded, his eyes bloodshot and weeping big, flat tears. "Enepsigos, Onoskelis—Obizuth! My beauties! Rip her apart. Scatter her soul to the four winds . . . with the angel here, we need her no longer."

He turned to them, his expression expectant, his too-round eyes still wide. The three demonesses stood still against the ragged stone wall of the sorcerers' cave, their inhuman faces flickering in the red candlelight as if they were characters in the cave paintings come to life behind them.

The Staff's face curdled with rage. Obizuth laughed then, her bony features lovely and possessed by red vengeance, and her sisters joined her in her terrifying merriment. My body filled with painful static, even as the battle turned in my favor.

Did Raziel feel this way as he went on his great and terrible errands? Even as I played my part, I wondered at the role I was meant to fill.

I had no physical body, so my ferocity was pure. I had no future, so I inhabited the present with my entire being. I no longer had any illusions or apologies, so I saw my enemies true.

I wheeled upon the wizard, enchained him with the full fury of my spirit. I no longer feared to stare him down, and saw even the demonesses draw back as I cornered Rabdos the Staff and crushed him with a towering rage.

He screamed and backed away from me, his skin smoking with steam, his face beginning to lose its shape. Desperately he clutched the paper amulet, to use against me as I had once tried to do in Amsterdam. But the paper ignited in his palms, and the primordial magic contained in my prison shriveled away to ash.

Aghast, I watched the Book's final remnant burn. But nothing would deter me from my vengeance. "Your own wickedness imprisons you," I spat, and my anger threw hissing sparks into the air between us. "Rabdos Staff, return to your Maker: Rabdos, Abdos, Bdos, Dos, Os, S. Be. Gone."

Our eyes met for the last time, and a smile marred his ruined lips like a stain. "My death means nothing, Lazarus. The Book has a life of its own, lives on after me. You are too late. And you cannot avert the Lord's hammer."

I leaned in so that he could see I was not afraid. "It doesn't matter, Rabdos. And as for the Lord, banishing you from life is a good deed all by itself."

The demonesses three descended upon him then, slashing, screaming, tearing, and I was treated to a reenactment of my own death at their hands.

I did not flinch. I did not waver. After terrible punishment, the Staff's soul untangled itself from its mangled, murdered body, and it drifted upward, blighted as it was. And then it lost altitude, sunk lower as the Staff's encumbered spirit screamed again.

A huge wind arose in the sealed chamber, and the candles guttered out. The three demonesses wheeled into the air and punched through the ancient stone, and they screamed too, screams of unholy joy. The crone paused, hovered near the cave's ceiling.

"I thank you, little sister," Obizuth hissed, opalescent in my witch's sight. "Now, release us."

My fury had abandoned me, and I flickered like a candle about to go out. "Yes, yes—you kept your word. Go, leave. Trouble me no more."

She descended to where I stood near the shredded remains of the Staff's body. "We go, daughter of women. But beware to meet us in a dark wood, beware Berlin. Sisters, but enemies still, you and we."

I tried to come up with a suitably frightening retort, but they vanished before I had time to say another word.

I hovered in the center of the broken circle, surrounded by melted wax, the stink of the Staff's broken remains, and complete darkness.

The Staff was dead. But so, still, was I.

✳ 27 ✳

I searched the darkness for the Staff's spirit, but he did not linger in the labyrinth beneath Buda Castle. Once I was sure everyone else was gone, I sank down, into the stone itself, and my astral being all but disintegrated with profound weariness.

Silence filled the air like the peal of an unearthly bell. Then Raziel began to glow, brighter and brighter, until his light filled the entire cave in which he still hovered.

And I, who had thought myself past all caring and human desire, felt my ghostly eyes prickle with tears. I had not called Raziel. He, as promised, came to me, of his own volition.

"Fear not, Magduska. But rest not, either. Your work has only just begun."

I considered the angel's words. With the intercession of the demonesses, I had defeated and dispatched the ancient wizard

Rabdos Staff, a feat that had eluded the Witch of Ein Dor herself. And yet, the Staff's parting curse was nothing more than the truth. Hitler and Asmodel, the Führer's demonic tool, still planned to wreck the world, within days, Book or no Book.

"What more can I do, dear angel? I can haunt Hitler, I suppose, but his demon will swat me into the next world like a swamp gnat."

I warmed myself in Raziel's light, and the fact of his presence filled my field of vision, the entire sweep of my mind. He was back, my beloved angel. He had come back to stay.

"You are still here," I whispered, soul to celestial soul. "Surely your job is done, I am dead, you can go back to Heaven and watch over Gisele, yes?"

His features, all but hidden by the brilliance of the light he emanated, grew sharp. "I can, but I have not yet begun to do my job on Earth." He spread his wings, beat at the stale air in the cave with great violence.

"How can you, a celestial servant of God, harbor such a violent fury?" I wasn't trying to be smart with him. I honestly could not reconcile his anger with his angelic status, a creature of the higher realms.

"My rage is righteous." His arms opened wide in silent invitation.

I flew into his gentle embrace, and his arms wrapped around my astral shoulders. His anger protected me. I grew calm inside the loving storm of his fury.

"I am at peace," I said, a small voice inside the whirlwind that was Raziel. "You don't need to fall. Not for me."

He sighed and held me closer, and his rage burned hot as banked coals, a physical manifestation of his forbidden will. "I am a messenger of the King on High. He promised not to abandon his human children to evil. And yet—"

"It is not for you or me to judge," I finished his thought for him.

"No, I do not judge. But the smallest act can tip the balance one way or the other."

"This time, Rabdos was the messenger," I said, my voice a little too gentle. Raziel drew back so that he could look into my eyes.

I took a deep breath and kept talking. "The Staff spoke true: the decree remains, the prophecy cannot be averted. So why fall now when it can do no good?"

His lips thinned, and his hands rubbed against the length of my arms. "Because I can fight to save who I can, Magduska. Perhaps that is message enough."

I could not keep the sarcasm out of my voice. "So you descend to save the entire world."

We both knew the real reason Raziel would fall. "You presume, Raziel," I said, my voice gently mocking. "And so a whole bunch of demons fell, as you once warned me."

The tension corded in the muscles of his arms. My astral fingertips feathered along the cables of his back, under the immense, sheltering circle of his wings.

"Raziel," I said. "You cannot save my life. My body is destroyed, I am no more. But you can still save Gisele. If you watch over her, I will be grateful and accept my fate. And if I could somehow be allowed to serve as your assistant in the second Heaven, I would do a good job. I have some experience in that regard."

He stroked my hair, and I surrendered to his ministrations, rested my cheek against his chest. We swayed together in the shadows, a slow dance in the middle of the wreckage.

His lips touched the top of my head, and everything in the world stopped. We stood completely still, and our souls all but merged in the darkness surrounding us.

"To rest in peace is not your fate," he finally said, his voice sounding reluctant to impart this news.

It was my turn to sigh and rustle. So my dream of repose with an angel in the next world was only a sweet temptation, and he had rightly roused me from the possibility. He understood me better than that. We both knew I would not rest now, not when Hitler was poised to strike.

I shrugged and smiled up at him. He needed me to have courage, so I pretended to have it. "I see, as a ghost, it is my fate to battle on. So be it. But what about you?"

"I am not the key. It is you. And you must battle on as a human woman, alive. You can still return to life."

My astral limbs went numb, jolted with his words. I pulled back and studied Raziel's huge, deep brown eyes. "No, you're joking. My body's burnt up, it's been three days, all over."

His face went so still it looked like it was carved from stone. "No. You may yet return, Magda. For a price, one perhaps too terrible to pay."

I didn't want to ask, but he pulled at my hands. "Come," he said. His expression became remote. "To do it, you will need Gisele's help. Come, I will show you."

❦

I returned to the Jewish Quarter of Budapest in a slow dream, led by an angel. The same narrow pavement, the same winding back streets, wreathed in morning mist. The local stray cat, a golden beauty with green eyes and the injured air of a deposed monarch, saw me move through the morning haze and, with a screaming yowl, shot into the alleyway behind the apartment building on Dohány Street. Otherwise, the neighborhood reposed in the silence of dawn.

The pillars of the Great Temple glowed pink in the morning light, and I looked far above my head, at the Hebrew inscription over the great carved double doors.

"Take words with you and return to the Lord," Raziel intoned, translating the words for me. I half turned, reached for his hand, and held on tight.

"From the book of the prophet Hosea," he continued, his face tipped upward to read the inscription, the curve of his cheek caressed by sunlight.

"Maybe the Great Temple is trying to tell me something."

Raziel's only reply was a squeeze on my ghostly fingers. I roused myself to drift along the half block to the door of my apartment building. I half floated up the long, narrow stairway to the splintery front door. My house key had burned up in the warehouse fire in Amsterdam, along with the rest of me.

Lucky for me, I had no need of house keys anymore. I faded through the battered wood, the sensation strange, like passing through a soap bubble, and Raziel came through with me. I drifted through the entryway, my mind a furious buzzing emptiness. Came to a stop over the threadbare needlepoint rug in the parlor.

Gisele, I guess, couldn't sleep.

I watched her knitting needles dancing in her fingers, as she swung in her rocking chair, her kitty circled asleep on her lap. In her nightgown, wrapped in a moth-eaten blanket in the little apartment on Dohány Street, the only thing unchanged after all of my travels: same creaky floorboard under her chair, same hideous green and yellow embroidered curtains, same faint smell of chestnuts, sausage, and jam.

Her nimble fingers twisted the yarn back and forth as she hummed a toneless little tune under her breath. My girl's soft tumble of black hair curled along the tops of her round shoulders, and her brown eyes, mild as ever, focused on something invisible to me in the middle distance.

There is a Hungarian saying: It is sometimes better to look in the window at a room than to go inside. I didn't want to disturb this precious sight, this fleeting scene of Home. I had taken this place, the syncopated rhythm of rocking chair against bare wood, too much for granted in my life. I had not expected to see my sister again, and more than anything I wanted to leave her in peace, alone but undiscovered and undisturbed, anonymous in the glimmer of a misty August morning in Budapest.

But this peaceful scene was all illusion. Hitler and his minions, millions of them, wanted her dead. She knew better than I what waited for her, invisible and in the middle distance, lurking outside the golden-tinted window.

Gisele stopped her rocking, and she tilted her head, her smile interrupting the armies marching in my head. "Ah, Magdalena, you've come back to me at last, and safe!" The cat meowed once, looked up, then settled back to sleep.

Without intending it, I had materialized enough for her to perceive me. I drew close to her, but not so close that she could pass her hand through my translucent form. "I've come back, yes and no."

Hot streaks of astral tears shot down my luminescent cheeks. I drew as close as I dared. "Gisi, I've come to say good-bye."

The breath caught in her throat, and a flush rose from her neck into her full cheeks. "But, you promised you'd come back, Magda."

"I know. I returned from the dead until I couldn't do it anymore. Our angel says I can do it again somehow, but I don't know how, really. There's none of me left to return to."

And I told her everything in a hushed half whisper, the train, the werewolves, the Staff, Capa and witches, Amsterdam and Paris. A guardian angel, a solemn oath sworn and forsworn, a madman possessed by a powerful demon.

"So, where is Raziel?" she asked.

"Here." His voice was warm as sunshine. And the angel manifested into human sight, where I had seen him waiting silent.

"Oh, you are beautiful. Thank you so for looking after Magda. I know you must have done your best." She sighed, and solemnly smoothed the tops of her cheeks with her fingertips. "So, we've failed. Nagymama witch was right after all."

I had no idea that heartache could cut a ghost so sharp. "I defeated the wizard. That's something. And freed the demonesses."

She nodded and smiled, a little too quickly. But we both knew my grand battles, victories though they were, had meant little, in the end. The prophecy would still be fulfilled, perhaps a few days later, perhaps not.

Raziel fully manifested, his body looking huge on the frizzled rug at Gisele's feet. "Do not fear."

Gisele's hands scratched at the sleeping old cat's ears. Her voice stayed steady and calm. "Magda's angel, I will try. Raziel, what should we do now?"

"Return to the Lord."

Gisele's face grew shadowed, and she flinched away from Raziel's words and my growing surprise. "No, angel. That can't be the answer. Me, maybe, but Magda! She's the one to live. I would trade for her in a minute."

The three of us faced each other, the points of a triangle that crackled with tension. I broke the silence, tried to still the tremble in my voice, failed. "That's not what you have in mind, is it, Raziel? One sister's life for another?"

The angel looked directly into my eyes. "No, Magda. Gisele could die for you and still it would change nothing. The wizard was right."

"So this is how all our striving and scheming ends? A ghost, and a girl left all alone with her old cat?"

"If you truly mean to return, you will. You must be willing to rise," Raziel said. "And if you insist on fighting, you must return. You cannot summon demons in spirit form. To work spells, to invoke your will, to sin—you must live."

I thought of Obizuth, a shadow flashing across the face of the moon and into the night. "Couldn't I do the job as a spirit of the air?"

"No," Raziel replied. "No matter what your lineage, you must live. You can fight as a vengeful spirit in death, and so you have, but your power can fully manifest only with life."

His expression filled with sadness. "You can still return to life. But the way is hard and narrow. You will suffer."

"I don't understand how I can return to life with no body to return to!"

"Wait!" Gisi's face shone triumphant, and she let the blanket slip from her shoulders to fall all around her fat little feet. "You are not all gone, my darling. Only . . ."

"Only what? What?" I sprang to her, almost passed through her in my anticipation.

She shivered and rubbed her arms. "Raziel's right. Oh, dear, this isn't going to be easy. My poor sweetheart. I'll do anything to help you. Even die. Anything."

I knelt at her feet, as on the day of her prophecies in this very room. "Don't die, Gisi, please. I don't see how two dead girls is any improvement over one."

Gisele played with the split ends of her long curls. I could see her fingers shaking. "I'm just a sentimental girl, Magda, you know that."

"No, that's earth-shattering news to me, Gisi." The teasing tone in my voice coaxed a smile onto her lips, but her eyes still looked remote and wild. She looked like a creature of the woods, a *vadleany* or a maenad on the verge of madness.

She blinked hard, nibbled at the frayed ends of her hair. "Do you remember when Mama died?"

"Are you kidding? Of course, silly." My astral fingers raked through the artifact of my own hair in my frustration— and the truth suddenly struck me like a stake through the heart.

My hair. After my mother had left this world, left me the head of the family, I had bobbed my hair, I guess to make it easier to pretend I was all grown up at sixteen. All brave artifice, but somehow I could pretend I was more in control of my fate with the short, rather daring bob, my first adult do.

When I looked again into Gisele's face, she had a crazy smile pasted on her lips like a cunning disguise. "And I of course kept your long locks. Safe, with my mementos."

Her expression made me laugh out loud. Gisele's memory box was filled with decrepit dolls, broken ballerina figurines, the feathers of eagles she had seen flying high overhead during summer vacations in the northern mountains. Out of such flotsam and jetsam of an ordinary life did my sister weave her magic of home. And out of such tschotskes I would have to somehow regenerate an entire body.

I shot Raziel an incredulous look. "But that's ridiculous. I can't come back alive through a lock of dead old hair!"

My sister turned on me, furious, looking like she wished she could punch me through the ether and knock some sense into me. "That's the way. The only way. You've had to do worse things already. And if you manage it, you'll have to go ahead and do much worse again."

She crossed her arms against me. "No princesses at this address."

I couldn't believe it. "Is this what you had in mind, Raziel?"

I never saw him go so pale. "It's going to hurt," was all he would say.

6

That night, at midnight, I found out just how much that return would cost me. The scene looked much as it had the night that I and the girls had once faced down the Witch of Ein Dor. Lace tablecloth, flickering candle. Except now a dull penknife and a hank of my old hair rested together on the table.

And this time, an angel of the Lord stood with us, his right hand resting on the hilt of an enormous sword.

Gisi and I exchanged glances. We knew what we had to do now, knew it was dead wrong. But we no longer had the luxury of being right.

Gisele covered her face in her hands, murmured a silent prayer so pure I could all but see the words floating up to Heaven. When her soft incantations had collected the three of us into a sacred circle, I began.

Slowly at first, then faster and faster, I began to declaim the words of the family spell of return. A cone of power rose like a waterspout over the table; Gisele drew forward and her fingers closed over the handle of the blade.

We looked at each other as she lifted the knife edge to her fingertip. Tears pooled in her enormous eyes. "I'm so sorry, Magduska."

She winced as the point of the knife pierced her skin. Blood welled at the tip of her finger, then dripped slowly, drop by drop, over my hair.

Her blood, we hoped, would animate my lifeless hair the way my blood had brought the fragment of *The Book of Raziel* back to life in Amsterdam. As I watched the droplets collect into a little puddle on the curling auburn lock of hair tied with a white ribbon, I prayed that Gisele's innocence could somehow carry me back to life.

The blood ran over the ribbon, staining it with pretty splashes of poppy red. I whispered the final words of the song of return, squeezed into a needle of light—

—and experienced the purest agony I have ever known. My ghost form struggled to melt into the bloody hair, and I screamed as I tried to fill out a human form that no longer existed.

My skin peeled, dead, dead, my senses were on fire underneath. I reached for Gisele's spark, frantically called her blood to me, and I almost died when I came into contact with the alien presence in her blood, a contagion.

My Gisele was not so pure as when I had left her. Her blood was not untouched. I detected, swimming like a living organism, the taint of Bathory's bite.

Oh, Gisele, what had you done while I was gone? How could I have lost you? The pain of knowing she had offered herself to Bathory tormented me more than the physical ordeal of regrowing bone, muscle, organs, from a dry, dead husk of hair. As I came together into a living form, my body and soul felt like they were being ripped apart.

After, my sister made me plates of egg noodles smothered in sour cream and sugar, pots of chamomile tea. She wrapped me in every blanket and knitted thing she had, and cried salty tears into my shoulders. But it changed nothing. Nothing, past or future, was changed; nothing that Gisele had done, nothing that I was still going to have to do.

I looked alive, sounded alive, acted alive. But I wasn't going to fool anybody.

✳ 28 ✳

Bathory's apartments reminded me of the Christians' "whited sepulchres." From the street, the champagne marble façade glowed in the moonlight, cool and milky like the moon herself. And once inside, his rooms were cavernous, with vaulted ceilings and curtains made of fabric that cost thousands of pengös a yard.

But threaded through this silky opulence was a humming undertone of rot. If you tore your attention away from the Louis XIV settee and the pair of magnificent Ming vases that framed the oversized entryway, you would see pathways of dirt tracking over the Persian silk carpets and polished parquet floors. The air, too, held a mausoleum mustiness trapped like cigarette smoke. Bathory's coffin rested atop a bed once owned by the Emperor Franz Josef, but he still needed a fresh supply of Transylvanian dirt to keep him in fine fettle.

Still, if one did not study the scene too closely, the public areas of Bathory's apartments dazzled like a rare, if somewhat musty, jewel. I sometimes expected to see a writhing knot of worms emerge through the silk fringes of his favorite horsehair-stuffed armchair, or a mischief of rats nesting in his enormous, dusty bookcases. But someone like Eva, or even Gisele, would be in grave danger should they dare to enter my master's deceptively luxurious lair.

I had been here before, but never of my own volition. When I rang the bell, Bathory, unlike himself, answered the door. He evinced no surprise at the sight of me standing, living, on his threshold. "Back at last," he said, his smile businesslike and cordial.

"Yes. After a fashion."

His smile faded as he drew closer, seeming to float along the ground. He squinted against the moonlight that filtered in behind me, backlighting my silhouette with shifting, restless night.

"Good heavens, Magda." He sounded put out, as if I had shown up to work sick, or drunk. "You haven't come back at all. Not at all."

"I am no ghost."

"Let's not play nicey, shall we? You are more undead than am I, little chicken."

His pet name drew a little chuff of laughter out of me, though laughing still hurt me all the way to the marrow.

He braved the moonlight to come out to the threshold where I stood, still unsteady on my feet. "So pale. Like the blood in you, a pale memory of life and youth."

He wore a crimson nobleman's pelisse, quilted by nuns no doubt sometime in the sixteenth century, patient hands long dead. It looked new and unsullied, just as he did. The count must have feasted on fresh human blood, and recently.

If only a long drink of blood could revive me. I would even have resorted to that, if it could strengthen me for the battle that was all but upon us now. "I didn't come to discuss my health, or the lack of it."

His thin, bony hand caressed the edge of my cheek, and slowly his long, manicured fingers withdrew. "Certainly not. Did Knox find you the Book?"

"Not hardly. The Book found me, more like."

His face lit up with the news. "Ah, the superweapon. That means a great deal of money for me from the carpet merchants, you know. Do you have it with you?" He tried to restrain himself, but the greed in his voice overshadowed his excellent manners for once.

"No. A wizard stole it from me, murdered me. And no less a personage than Hitler himself holds the power of it in his grasp."

"Ah." His shrewd, bloodshot eyes widened, and he turned and shuffled back into his magnificent mausoleum of a mansion. He seemed to age with every step, but I still had trouble keeping up with him as he retreated into the sanctuary of his sitting room.

He lit a cigarette, drew deeply on it, and reclined languorously on a tangle of Turkish silk pillows and wrappers thrown pell-mell over a huge leather couch. "Bad news for my revolutionary friends with the deep pockets. And for me."

My throat tightened as I thought how very bad the news was

for me and my kind. "Deep pockets" was the least of it, for us. "Why do the Azeris care, anyway?"

"Hitler will surely invade in the East now, in short order." He took a long, slow drag of smoke into his lungs, and it seemed to steady his nerves. "The Nazi-Soviet pact is the final toss of dirt on our graves. It is most unfortunate."

"The what?" I suddenly had run out of breath, and sat next to him with a thump; my unreliable, new limbs could not bear the weight of this sudden, shocking news.

"Did you not hear? Hitler and Stalin have signed a mutual non-aggression pact. Yesterday the Fascists and Communists were sworn blood enemies. Today, they toast one another and curse the Jewish plutocrats who force the world into war."

I reached for his smoldering cigarette, took a huge drag, and felt the reassuring burn of the smoke in my battered, new lungs. "So, my little book has done its work already. They would never have joined forces without it."

"I am not so sure, if that is any consolation. Most people think that wily old bear Stalin is only buying time until he attacks the Germans. Or maybe that is only a comforting fairy tale we all tell ourselves." He crushed the stub of the cigarette out in an enormous square glass ashtray overwhelming the rickety side table, and he leaned forward to stare intently into my face. "What shall you do now?"

I sat straighter among the slippery cushions. "As long as Hitler draws breath, I must fight him. To do less will guarantee he will kill us all. So that is why I have come to you now."

"Rest assured, I will not betray you. I am a Hungarian patriot, but Horthy is a useless pig. You are as Hungarian as I, and your fight is mine."

His protestations of loyalty made my head ache. "Is it, now? I, too, love Hungary, but let us face facts, Count Bathory. Beautiful, aristocratic Hungary doesn't love me back."

Bathory knew it as well as I did; there was no point in haggling over the truth. He shrugged, watched the cigarette smoke dwindle away into nothingness. "Love need not be returned, to be true."

"I have come to ask you to release me from your service."

His gaze stayed direct. "Why?"

I shrugged. "You know why. In any event, Hitler has my book, or some part of it, anyway. I have to stop him, or die trying, it's the end. Gisele was right."

"No."

I shook my head, my negative fiercer than his. "I will not accept no for an answer, Count Bathory."

"Yes, you will. I order you to stop Hitler, immediately. And because the job is so very odious and dangerous, I am doubling your salary." His thin pursed lips stretched in a sudden, genuine smile, and his fangs peeked out from under his whiskers, like pearls.

"By God, you *are* a patriot."

He laughed. "I always enjoyed your Budapest sarcasm, my dear. You know what motivates me. Those Azeris want that book, and you, on their side. They will pay cold cash, gold even, to get it, and you. They take you as part of the bargain, for they believe they can free themselves from Stalin with that book. Apparently they have their own seer and set of prophecies. We both know patriotism has nothing to do with this."

I could not bear our dance of courteous deception any longer. "I know about my sister."

He licked his lips, but otherwise became entirely still. As I watched his pupils dilate and his face go paper white, I almost pitied him.

Almost. It is dangerous to feel anything for a vampire, even a courtly, personable charmer like Bathory. Human as he looked, he was not. As I am now not. And though human beings had proven my bitterest enemies, a vampire scorned was no small adversary.

"You did not turn her, and for that I thank you. But when she came to you, in despair, desperate, you did not turn her away."

Silence.

"After I came back to the living, this last time, I could see the changes. Her spirit—untouched. Again, I thank you for that. But her body . . ."

My heart battered my ribs from the inside. "You drank from her, Bathory! Almost drained her dry."

"She did nothing a hundred starving artists haven't done to survive. She gave me what she wanted to give, and I let her keep the rest. I did more than that. I kept her alive and safe."

We both knew he had not betrayed my trust. He had only done what was in his nature to do; my fury and grief were all for Gisele, or that is to say, for the innocent, fragile creature I had created as an idol of the mind.

I picked at the hem of my skirt, which Gisele had expertly finished with her nimble little fingers. "I haven't figured out what to live for yet, Bathory, but I certainly have learned how to die."

"She came to me, Magda. I did not seek her out."

"You speak the truth. But you need to repay us for what you took. My sister's blood."

His spine stiffened with the insult: it was more than mere rudeness to refer directly to blood-drinking to a vampire's face. Bathory hissed softly under his breath.

Once I would have been afraid of his anger. But no more. "I mean what I say, count. Everything is ending now: the only choice is how we will end with it. Choose, vampire. You say you are a patriot. But this battle goes deeper than Hungary or the blasted Treaty of Trianon. Are you a man? Or a servant of evil?"

He gaped at me, and I stared back, unwavering. I was sixteen when I started my apprenticeship, the same age as Gisele now. I had always suspected he meant to turn me, when I had served him long enough to come willingly to him. But now . . .

The count bared his fangs at me, but it was an empty threat. I stared him down, and after a time he dropped his gaze.

I kept my voice quiet, respectful at least in tone. "I need you to write to your connections in Berlin. Hitler is occupied, willingly, by a demon named Asmodel. In my name, challenge the demon to a duel. Heroes' Square. Tomorrow night."

Bathory gasped. "You cannot rush a duel, Magda. You are completely mad—challenging Hitler to a duel!"

"Not Hitler. His demon. And you must." I left the threat unspoken, but he winced, because he knew I no longer had any compunctions worth appealing to, that I would compel him by spellcraft if he did not serve my cause willingly.

Bathory blinked hard and smoothed his brilliantined hair against his delicate skull. He removed another cigarette from the ornately carved wooden case, rolled it between his fingers like a silver bullet. "I am not your enemy. Wasting your fury on me is pointless."

My smile was sad; my words remained merciless. "I have no

time to debate niceties with you. Hitler is on the verge of invading Poland. The world is about to explode."

Bathory stared down at his cigarette, a tiny smile playing over his thin, delicate lips. Slowly, he rubbed his jaw against the stiff collar of his quilted pelisse, and for a moment's flash I could see the young nobleman he once had been, long ago in another vanished world.

"Please, Count Bathory."

The supplication in my voice was concession enough to satisfy his wounded pride. His smile became steadier. "Horthy will have my head for this."

"You said yourself he was a buffoon."

"Do not underestimate the old man. His motives are at least decent." Bathory sighed, lit the cigarette with a heavy brass lighter, sucked at the smoke like blood. "It means my head to write that letter. But I will do it. And not because you threaten me, little chicken."

He reached for the telephone, which rested inoffensively in its cradle on the side table next to the giant ashtray. Bathory, still reclined on the cushions, cleared his throat. "Janos, bring the car around. We must go to Café Istanbul, immediately."

He rose and stretched like a cat, walked for the door without looking back at me. "There is no way Asmodel will accept your challenge. He will simply have you arrested by the Gestapo and you will disappear."

"No. I am not the kind of ghost that fades away, dear Count Bathory."

My former employer stared at me through the smoke, and finally I fidgeted under his gaze when I realized I had won our battle of wills. He enjoyed his meaningless triumph over me. "You were supposed to be my prized possession, little chicken. What a presumptuous fool I am."

6

We rushed to Café Istanbul, Bathory, Janos, the gazellelike driver, and I. The place, all but empty, buzzed with the tension of impending war. Bathory swept upstairs to his balcony seat, settled in his chair in the corner. I took my accustomed seat at his right hand, and the driver joined Imre, the vampire's enforcer, at his place downstairs at the bar.

Without hesitation, the waiter swept up with the usual: a bottle of seltzer, two espressos, and a plate of rumballs. He arranged our refreshments with his usual flourish, and under his breath he murmured:

"A pleasure to see you again, sir. But be aware the Arrow Cross has been looking for you."

I suppressed a gasp: The Arrow Cross was the Nazi Party of Hungary, a pack of vicious, degenerate fascists at least as awful as the German variety.

"Of a certainty. They know where they can find me, eh?" He patted the waiter's hand, shifted his attentions to the rumballs.

When the waiter went away, Bathory removed his pen and stationery from the leather folio he had carried in under his slender arm. "Ah, how does one challenge a demon to a duel? What are the proper formalities?"

"He is a Biblical demon of old, if that helps you any. I think if you just write it in German that will be sufficient."

Bathory nibbled at his quill pen, and then he laughed, a huge roar that overwhelmed his wiry frame. "You are mad, little chicken."

"No, just desperate."

"I never said madness was any disadvantage. Sometimes madness will sustain you in battle, where good mental hygiene will only lead to despair." He sipped his espresso, patted at his whiskers with a linen napkin. "May I order you a full meal, my dear child? You look positively skeletal."

"No thank you, Count Bathory." I was beyond eating now.

He shrugged and reached for a rumball. "I have many a time thanked the Maker that as a vampire I may enjoy the fruit and vine of man." He studied me with a long, cool look. "Apparently you may not do the same."

I shrugged. "I don't care. As long as I complete my mission, nothing else matters."

"You're lying." But then Bathory reached for his papers and troubled me no more.

I watched the customers clustered at the tables below us, and listened to the scratching of Bathory's pen. A group of men walked in the front door together, and the people standing at the bar drew back. Imre made a hasty exit behind them, and the bartender wiping the bar with a rag paused, pointed up at the balcony, at me.

The Arrow Cross.

They marched in lockstep across the mosaic floor and to the enormous curving stairway leading to the balcony. They were not in uniform, but they did not need to be: they moved with a single mind, a sole intent.

Bathory did not look up until the half-dozen men stood

directly in front of us and their leader rapped rudely on the marble table.

The vampire took his sweet time, folded his missive into the thick envelope and addressed it before giving the small mob his full attention. "Good evening, gentlemen. How may I help you?"

"You come with us, you and your—girl here." He sneered at me, and I could all but hear his thoughts: your dirty Jewess, your filthy little Hebrew witch. I narrowed my eyes, whispered his true name under my breath.

He gasped and took a half step back, and his minions looked at him in surprise. I blinked hard, whispered his name louder, and he fell to his knees.

"You do not belong to the Horthy administration," Bathory continued, as if the Arrow Cross thug weren't suffocating to death at his feet. "You have no authority to order Hungarian citizens around in this brutish manner."

I released him, and the wretched man huddled on the floor, gasping for air, his eyes streaming with tears.

"Please, sir, get off the ground and stand up. Your pants will get all dusty on that filthy floor—I will tell the night manager to sweep."

The Arrow Cross man rose slowly, looked daggers at me. I smiled, leaned back in my chair, and took a sip of espresso, though I couldn't taste it. "You've come for me really, haven't you? Well, you can't have me."

The Arrow Cross bastard crossed his arms, and I savored his fear, enjoyed it as once I had the espresso. He tried to ignore me, but I smiled again, and watched him twitch as he waited for me to whisper his name.

One of the men standing behind him, fat and sweaty, fished

out a dirty handkerchief from his back pocket and mopped his face with it. With the remaining shreds of his menace, the Arrow Cross sergeant snapped each word like a cur. "Count Bathory, we come in the name of the Chief Vampire of Berlin. You are hereby summoned to the MittelEuropa Tribune of Nosferatii."

Bathory laughed again, a bray like a trumpet. "Oh, that's rich, my dear friend. Since when does the Chief Vampire have need of human minions to deliver his missives to his under-lings?"

"Since he became a member of the National Socialist Party and swore fealty to the glorious Adolf Hitler, that's when. He summons you in the name of the Reich."

Bathory said nothing. My poor count. "In fact, I have a letter for him here. Quite a coincidence. I suppose I will simply deliver it to him in person."

He rose, kissed my hand. "My lovely little chicken, I fly for Berlin. It is hardly past midnight, so I will reach my master be-fore daybreak."

"But, Count Bathory . . ."

"Do not worry about me. I will deliver your letter, and will take care of myself thereafter. You, clearly, have no more need of my protection." And he nodded at our mortal friend from the Arrow Cross, who had become quite the model of courtesy since I had almost choked his life out.

"Farewell, Magda Lazarus." He looked long and significantly at me. "Go in peace."

We both knew peace was not my destiny. I stood up, kissed his cheek. "Deliver that message for me, and I will be forever in your debt."

He bowed formally, kissed my hand again. "In that case, I go to Berlin gladly."

I remained standing as Bathory swept down the stairs and to the front door of the Café Istanbul, his mortal handlers following ineffectually in his wake. Regardless of the count's concerns, I knew Asmodel would certainly accept my challenge: the demon knew I had failed, and my very vulnerability would ensure his presence. Tempting a demon was not so difficult as tempting an angel, and I had managed that without wanting to.

The count disappeared, I feared forever. "Farewell, dear count," I whispered to his departing shadow.

✳ 29 ✳

We sat together in an apartment on Dohány Street, me, my little sister, and an angel of the Almighty who refused to go away and return to Heaven. Eva was gone. As she had never returned from Amsterdam, we all feared the worst, but we did not have the luxury of worrying about her now.

"Do you think Asmodel will actually answer the challenge?" I asked. The three of us sat over steaming hot crepes stuffed with poppy seed jam, Gisi's specialty, a veritable feast. But the crepes sat untouched on their plates.

Raziel played with a fork, balancing it on his fingers as if the implement were a wonder. "Asmodel will come. I know he will."

A sick feeling settled in my stomach. I pushed my plate of crepes away. "You don't think we can beat him, do you."

"I think you are our best chance."

"Why not you, Raziel? Can't an angel trump a demon every time? Isn't the Lord supreme over the Satan. His adversary?"

"Of course, of course, the Lord Almighty reigns over all," he said quickly, his voice warm and low. "But he reigns over the Satan too, and the Satan works His will. We must accept that it may not be destined for us to prevail." And he frowned fiercely down upon his plate; his eyes contradicted every word he had said.

"Poor angel," Gisele said. "Eat your crepes, you'll feel better. And look! I boiled you some eggs, too. Here, you peel off the shells like this. And then you shake the salt on, from the shaker, like so . . ."

What a feast Gisele had laid out for us. She had cooked every last bit of food she had. Poor Gisi. She didn't think we were coming back, either.

"We need our strength," she said, an edge of steel creeping into her voice.

Our strength? *We* needed it? "Oh, no, Gisi. You are not coming with us tonight. You stay here and wait for us."

"No, I will come. If only to see what happens, to be a witness. And if I die, so be it. Magda, all of us are going to die someday. This way is better than . . . the other."

I argued long and hard, but the girl who had been my sweet little mouse would not bend. She stayed gentle, but my Gisele would not budge.

"We don't have to do this, you know," I said, because someone at the table had to speak the Satan's case. "We could still run away.

"Survival is a victory," I continued. "We should do like Eva, leave, warn the others what is going to happen so that they can run too." Our food sat cold and unappetizing on our plates.

I looked at Raziel. "You told me once that I should accept the will of God. And yet, here you sit."

He shrugged, and placed his fork with exaggerated gentleness on the table alongside his plate. "Something happened in Berlin while you were imprisoned in the amulet, Magduska. Something so terrible that I could not see it from the second Heaven. We must battle against whatever it was that the Staff and Asmodel did."

The demon's name visibly pained him. I patted his hand as Gisele gave me a long, rather shocked-looking stare. "Could a demon like Asmodel use the Book, all restored?" I asked. "And give Hitler invincible power?"

"A demon can't, just like an angel can't. But a human being . . ."

"But Hitler has no magic," I protested, my voice a near whisper.

"Even if not, one of his wizards may well have enough magic to do it for him." Raziel hesitated, took a sip of Gisele's rich, perfect coffee. The hideous yellow flowered curtains in the alcove fluttered in the morning breeze at the open window. Somehow, the angel looked perfectly at home in our splintery and pockmarked kitchen.

With a sigh, I made a show of nibbling at the by-now cold crepes. I could not taste them, I could not taste anything since I had sort-of returned from the land of the dead. "So we stay and fight. It is decided."

I took a look around the little apartment, as if it were the last time. Gisele rose to wash her dishes, sniffling all the while, and

I spoke to her back as she scrubbed. "Gisele, I spoke to Bathory about what you did."

Her back stiffened, but she didn't say a word. I pressed on in my hardheaded, blundering style. "I just wanted you to know, sweetheart, you did what you had to do. No matter what happens now, there is no shame in surviving to fight another day, no matter how you do it."

She would not look at me. "Eat your eggs, please, Raziel," Gisele murmured. But I knew he needed eggs as little as did I.

Instead, he rose from the table, carrying his plate of eggs, and he came to where Gisele stood at the kitchen sink. She wiped her hand on a dish towel, then dabbed at her eyes, lips trembling. Raziel took her chubby little hand in his, her finger still scabbed over where she had sacrificed her blood to bring me back to life.

It was absurd, ridiculous, but I knew it to the bone: Asmodel would answer my summons. That night, at midnight.

And only one of us would walk away.

At dusk, the three of us walked in silence along the Danube. On the surface of my mind, I fretted about Bathory, in Berlin at his peril, and Eva, gone missing altogether. But underneath, in the depths of my spirit, a silent calm overspread everything I saw or touched.

Fantastical blazes of color striped the sky over the iron gray river and the lights of the old city began to sparkle far away on the hills of Buda. Night settled over the face of Budapest, and I whispered my good-bye.

One time, or three, I considered speaking aloud and breaking the spell of silence in which the three of us walked. But Lucretia de Merode had taught her wayward pupil well; I left Raziel and Gisele to the labyrinths of their own thoughts.

We paused by the enormous parliament building facing the Danube, and I stole a secret glance at Raziel's face. His heavy-lidded eyes looked across the gray river, to the sparkling far shore. The delicious summer breeze played over his thick black hair, and a half smile hovered on his lips.

✳ 30 ✳

At midnight, we stood in the middle of Heroes' Square. The huge, empty space echoed outward from where we stood, silently at the center, keeping watch.

I could stand the silence no longer. "Do you think . . ."

"Asmodel will come," Raziel said. He reached out, slowly stroked the side of my face with his fingers. "Magda . . ."

"Don't say it, my dear," I replied. "I couldn't bear it."

Gisele rubbed her arms with her palms, shivered though the late August heat had not broken in the night. "Is he hideous, Magda? The demon?"

"I only ever saw him inside the body of Adolf Hitler. From what I saw, he is hideous enough." My pulse pounded behind my eyes, and I squinted into the darkness.

Raziel looked into the sky, his face composed and peaceful

as always. I loved him, but I could not say it now, not in front of Gisele. And not in the shadow of death. "You're not the slightest bit afraid, are you?" I asked.

"I am here for the right reasons. I have nothing to fear."

I remembered what Capa had to say on the subject of goodness, and felt sick to my stomach.

High above our heads, a statue of the Angel Gabriel presided over our earthly travails from a lofty pedestal, while the non-Christian, forest-god worshiping prince Árpád stood at the base of the pillar, keeping watch over his thousand-year-old kingdom. The Millennium Monument was designed to provoke awe, to commemorate, but all I could think of, as I stared up at Gabriel trapped on high, was that long ago my beloved father had taught me how to ride my bicycle here, in a time when I was safe from harm.

Exactly at midnight, the bells of St. Stephen's Basilica began to peal in the darkness, as they usually did only at midnight on New Year's Eve.

"He comes," Raziel said, his voice mingling with the bells.

Black polished leather caught the dim reflection of starlight. First his boots, then his legs, then the full figure of the Great Führer materialized, standing all alone before us in the center of Heroes' Square.

I squinted and searched the sky, and inky black, hidden by night, the form of Adolf Hitler was framed by a moving tapestry of scaly, silent demons filling the sky from Earth to Heaven. We were, to put it mildly, outnumbered.

I said a little prayer under my breath, and braced for a blast of fire, a slash of fang, something supernaturally awful. Gisele trembled but held her ground. Raziel stood perfectly still, steadfast.

I contemplated Hitler's stern, unyielding face, uncertain. I expected Asmodel, a slavering, demonic monster, not this neat, energetic little general. I searched him with my witch's sight.

"You seek my true aspect," he said, in German of course, a small, knowing smile stretching his thin, chapped lips. "But what is truth, little Lazarus."

He smiled again, flickered for a moment into his demonic form before replacing the mask of Adolf Hitler, and he shrugged his shoulders almost apologetically. "You have seen what a page of the Book can do. My late lamented wizard Staff revived the entire Book, before you destroyed him. It is over."

"No, it isn't." I spoke a little too quickly.

His smile widened still further, and I could see the tips of his yellowed teeth under his funny Charlie Chaplin mustache. "We have more than enough to accomplish my objective. With the Soviets on our side, Poland is finished. Stalin knows his Red Slave Army is outnumbered by my demonic host, even now. I have told him so, demonstrated it if you will. All is in readiness."

"So what need do you have of me?"

Asmodel planted Hitler's hands on his hips; his laughter was a knife slashing into the sky. His fingers twitched inside their black leather gloves as they yanked a dusty little book from inside the breast pocket of his buff-colored general's jacket, with its black braid and shiny black belt at his waist.

I saw the cover of the little book clutched in his hands, and the strength drained out of me into the cold, unyielding earth.

"You know what I have here." He played with the Book,

opened it, riffled the pages, studying my face for my reaction. His smile got wider and wider, as if his face was going to split open and spill his brains out onto his boots.

My rickety heart had all but stopped; my fingers went numb. "How did you get my book?" My voice sounded dry and far away to my own ears, like I was again, and forevermore, speaking from beyond the grave. "How is it that a bound, modern book is in fact my book? *The Book of Raziel.*"

Because I had no doubt. He did not need to further taunt me with it, prove what I already knew to a certainty. *The Book of Raziel.* It called to me, and my fingers ached to touch it. But the Book was no longer mine; it was lost to me.

"You did me quite a good turn, fraulein. Rabdos was a cunning, clever sorcerer, but disloyal. You eliminated him for me before he became too troublesome. And with such brilliant timing. He restored the Book from the shards he had, breath by breath, sold his own oversold soul to retrieve it. And he bent it to my service in Berlin, before he came to Budapest to steal the Book's power for himself by using the amulet."

Asmodel's smile, pasted on Hitler's lips, turned surprisingly kind and genuine, a clean, joyful smile. "Angels are not Jews. Nor are demons. Germany will now arise from the ashes of the Great War, and angels and demons will take their welcome places in my Reich, unencumbered by the chains of your God."

I crossed my arms, took a long, steadying breath. "You know that book is worthless to you without a sorceror's magic."

He grinned, drew closer. "But I have an entire coven to choose from, my pet witches in Berchtesgaden."

My heart all but stopped. "Trudy," I whispered. Their safety in Bavaria had not even been a vivid illusion, more like a desperate wish. But I had wished for it, too.

"Don't listen to him," Gisele said, in the singsong voice she used in prophecy. "The Daughters of Arachne remain true, true to the death." A sob caught in her throat, and her voice stilled.

My heart pounded so hard I thought my body would perish from fear. But I thought of my own imprisonment inside the amulet, and kept my voice steady. "I know what it is like to be captured by mortal magic; and Hitler first captured you, yes, using the Staff's power the way Solomon employed the witch of Ein Dor. I have a simple proposition, Asmodel. Let's trade— the Book for your freedom. Release my book to me, and I will bend the Book's power to free you and every spirit of air, angel and demon alike, entrapped by human sorcery. I understand that vengeance moves you. But freedom is better than revenge. Leave Hitler to commit his own human evil."

I held my breath; hope is such a fragile thing, but it is very hard to kill. We all stood in the silence of the night, the marble pagan Árpád standing guard alongside us.

Asmodel, wearing Hitler's aspect like a costume, looked from me to Gisele, and then his gaze rested long on Raziel, his fingers nervously rubbing at his mustache.

I watched him as he considered my parley, as he imagined flying free, unencumbered by power or human desire, into the darkness. And then he growled again, his eyes glowing orange in the darkness like banked fires. "Silence, mortal."

Far, far above our heads I heard the shrieking of the airborne demons, and in the distance I heard the faint baying of wolves in the city center. My sister's fear quickened along my skin, sharp like a razor blade at the throat.

"Gisele will die first," he said.

I saw the movement out of the corner of my eye and reacted instantly, without thinking. I leaped back and sent a blast of witchfire scorching in a circle all around the three of us.

But the demons had been instructed to miss, I am sure. Like a cat, Asmodel toyed with me, enjoying the endgame. I drew a cone of protection around us in the air, and Raziel drew his sword.

"Raziel, what do we do?"

His face stilled in the flashing lights that surrounded us like fireworks. "We die like heroes, Magda."

It seemed a hard end, after all our adventures in the land of the living and the dead, after we had done so much to avert the harsh decree. I did not know if I could return from death again, not after what I had endured the last time. Gisele had not the gift. As for Raziel, I did not know that he could die at all.

"What are the rules of death for fallen angels, Raziel?"

He smiled then, a fierce warlike smile that filled me with determination. "I am about to find out."

Outside the cone, the demons swarmed like a cloud of black flies. Through the buzzing clot of darkness, I saw the Book glowing like a secret ember in Asmodel's black-gloved hands.

Through all my hunting, all my scheming, I had never dreamed the search would end this way. Never imagined that, like me, *The Book of Raziel* could be summoned back from the dead whole, entire, complete and yet not what it was before.

Asmodel's laugh, a screaming gale, slammed against my circle of protection. His human form melted away, and through the mass of demons he loomed huge over the square, a giant clot of evil blocking the starlight from earth. Huge ram's horns curled around his pointed ears; his fangs reached low enough to graze the sides of his massive neck.

"Now you die, your people die. And the rest of the world rejoices to see your kind die."

"No."

He laughed again, flickered in and out of Hitler's form in the midst of the demonstorm.

"Sh'ma!" I sang in reply, and he drew back with an enraged roar. The trembling in my body stilled, and I took a deep breath, summoned my power up through the soles of my feet, up from the living earth.

Asmodel roared again to drown out my voice and break the concentration I needed to unleash the spell. Gisele touched my shoulder, her presence strengthened my intention, and I heard the voice of Raziel calling to the Almighty Himself to augment the force of my spell. I sent my spell down, and the earth under our feet rumbled it in an echo.

"Now, Leopold," I called. His name ripped a hole in the sky, and my imp child led forth the host of demons born of my willfulness. They swarmed their demonic brothers, the host of Asmodel, and demon to demon they fought in the sky, a furious clash of darkness against darkness.

I stepped out of the circle of protection to face Asmodel. He towered over my head, but I held my ground.

"You are damned," he said. "You have cursed yourself and your kind for all eternity. You dare to work sorcery."

I knew Raziel stood at my back, and I was filled with a crazy courage, the courage of someone who is expert in the art of death. "Back to Hell, Asmodel! I come in the name of the Lord."

"You presume, Magda Lazarus," he said, in a mockery of Raziel's words. "You presume. So I fell, so Raziel falls. So you fall. Do you not know? Do you not know your lineage?"

I thought of Obizuth, and I did not falter. "Even the daughter of demons may serve the Lord."

He frowned. "And that is why you fail."

"Perhaps. But I choose to fail with glory. Do you not remember, Asmodel? Even you were made by the Most High, and no matter what you do, or how far you stray, you still serve His plan."

He roared in negation and threw a huge bolt of fire at my head. I blocked it and sent it back at him, and Asmodel screamed in agony. Like a wild beast, the demon lunged for me, but faster than the eye could follow, Raziel hurled himself between us. Gisele waited inside the circle of protection I had drawn, but it certainly would not hold out for long.

Demon and angel looked into each other's faces, in the middle of a scorched circle on the stones of Heroes' Square. Their profiles mirrored each other, brothers of the higher and lower realms.

I touched Raziel's shoulder, and he jerked roughly away from my hand. "Magda, stay back." His voice sounded calm and ordinary, the same as in the apartment on Dohány Street.

We both knew he could not vanquish Asmodel alone. And though my magic was not enough to save us, it was still something. He swept his sword in an arc, held it high above his head to keep Asmodel at bay. "He doesn't want me, Magda. The demon only needs you, a sorcerer to work his will. The Daughters of Arachne do not have your blood. Stay back!"

Raziel shot me a knowing glance. "Not long ago, we made a

pact, you and I. I was the one to stand aside, I was the one who could not be spared. It is the other way, now. You are the one we cannot afford to lose."

I drew inside my wards, my lungs burning with the black sulfurous smoke that now surrounded us. "No, Raziel, I cannot just stand by—"

"You must. Magduska, you must be free."

He didn't wait for my response, instead pressed forward to attack his demonic adversary.

"You make a fatal mistake, my brother," Raziel called. He no longer sounded furious, only resolved to fight, and the compassion in his voice pierced my heart. The witch of Amsterdam had taught me my strength lay in my vulnerability. Only now did I understand what she had meant.

A low growl ripped my attention back to Asmodel. He and my angel circled low as the battle raged all around us, in the air as well as on the ground of Heroes' Square.

"Brother, why do you throw your soul away?" To my surprise, it was Asmodel who spoke.

Raziel stopped circling, his sword at the ready. "Because I could no longer stand by and watch you pervert *The Book of Raziel* to suit your ends. The Lord has His ways, but Heaven stays neutral." He glanced back at me and smiled. "And I am no neutral."

Raziel made a dazzling feint with his sword, and Asmodel parried using his huge claws. "Yes, the Almighty did not send you," Asmodel growled. "And so you are mine."

And they fought so fiercely the limbs of demon and angel blurred together in a furious cloud of black smoke.

I stepped forward, to the very edge of the cone of protection

I had created, and I peered into the acrid darkness. I could not stand it, the zone of safety in which I stood. "Raziel, I'm coming—we can try to beat him together."

"That is what he wants! Get back, Magduska. Let me handle him alone. Keep Gisele safe, and stay clear."

"But Raziel—"

I saw his face, half consumed in smoke and flame. "At last you understand the frustration of angels. Be strong, Magduska." And he disappeared back into the fury of the battle, as I and Gisele stayed back, protected, safe and lost to him.

All of us die moment to moment. Each day slips away and it can never return again, no matter what our magic. In all my grim determination to master death and to avenge it, I had forgotten that what I fought for was love, the gift that passes through time and yet lasts forever.

Now, Raziel gave me that gift. The angel unfurled his wings in all their blinding, golden glory. In a brilliant flash, he assailed the demon, filled the darkness with his painful, white-hot light.

Asmodel screamed and belched bloodred and orange flames. Red hellfire consumed Raziel's wings, and smoke rose from him in billowing sheets. "Be strong, Magduska," he said again. Smoke enveloped him, and Raziel ascended to heaven in a white plume, like a gigantic feather reaching into the sky.

My soul seemed to follow his trajectory into the sky, and only Gisele restrained me to earth. "Magda," she cried, "bind him, stop him. Don't let him get away."

Asmodel could not sustain such a massive blow only to remain unscathed. Before Raziel ascended, he had blasted him with godlight, and it had shriveled Asmodel's thick, mailed skin; it hung, peeling, off the bloody muscles of his cabled body. Raziel had weakened him. I could not destroy him—if Raziel could not, no one could but the Almighty—but I could stop him, now.

Lucretia had taught me the ancient binding spell of Solomon, as recorded in his Testament. I stood with her, with Trudy, the Daughters of Arachne and the daughters of women. "I bind you with chains, with words, with clay and with blood. AS-MODEL, I bind you thus . . ."

Asmodel writhed within the cone of energy I held within my hands. I chained him fast, compressed him between my palms, and kept him wrapped tight like a sick, vicious cat caught in a blanket.

I searched for the Book upon Asmodel's person. But, alas, the Book he had held in his hands was no more than a sending, a projection of reality like the form of Hitler had been. Adolf Hitler, the mortal man, held the real Book in Berlin, or wherever he waited for the invasion of Poland to begin.

Asmodel snapped at my fingers and snarled, compressed now into a reduced form. With the sounds of his struggle, the demons all around us realized that the demon general was captured. Leopold's brothers screamed in hoarse triumph and they assailed Asmodel's children, harried them in the sky.

The battle drifted away like smoke into the night, and Gisele and I were alone except for the demon I had trapped in my spell. Asmodel snarled but said no more. I bound him tighter, so tight that he could not escape, as tightly as the Staff had once bound me.

A low howl in the distance rose to our ears and Gisele trembled. "The wolves . . ."

"After Asmodel, I am no longer afraid of the wolves." I held the demon fast, and took in the sight of the carnage left behind, the bodies of demons smoking all around us. Leopold had vanished: ascended, I was sure, as Raziel had ascended.

I looked in vain for the sight of Raziel's face, and my heart finally broke. It was true: he was gone.

The marble angel stood on his pedestal, unreachable, his blank eyes blind to the battle we had just fought. I never expected to see Raziel again.

✳ 31 ✳

We had failed most magnificently. As with the Staff, I had dispatched the supernatural threat, not the real one, the human one. The world braced for war: Hitler planned to invade Poland on September first, and he didn't need a resident demon to do it. If anything, by binding the demon, I had freed Hitler's *vril* to rule even more strongly on its own.

A day or two after I had captured Asmodel, I got word from Eva that she still lived. The doorbell rang at the flat on Dohány Street, and when I opened the front door, a little runner, a red-nosed little guttersnipe no older than eleven or twelve, handed me a wadded-up, filthy piece of paper, and he ran away before I could say a single word.

I uncrumpled the sheet of paper. In Eva's strikingly beautiful handwriting, she had written:

Little Star,
I am on the bridge, and the Horvath twins are
coming. Please bring the medicine; I am with Blue
Eyes.

Eva did not sign her name. She did not need to.

Blue Eyes was an ancient crone from Tokaj; we called her Blue
Eyes because she used to sing the old lullaby in a great, mournful
voice as she gathered her flowers up into tissue-wrapped, soggy
bundles to sell by the train station. Her florist's shop was on Fer-
enc körút, and once upon a time in a different universe, she had
been Eva's nursemaid. In an extended thank-you to Eva's own
long-dead mother, Blue Eyes had hired her to work in the flower
shop, though she could pay Eva only in posies, not even in roses.

As for the Horvath twins, they were among the bullies I had
tossed off the bridge long ago, as a schoolgirl and latent witch
back in Tokaj.

So: Eva was in trouble, but thank goodness she was alive. I
left Asmodel locked securely in his prison, an empty tin of
sweet paprika that made him sneeze red pepper dust out of the
sifting holes on the top. Gisele made the world's most gentle
and trustworthy jailer.

When I arrived at Blue Eyes's florist shop, the corrugated
metal grating was pulled down and padlocked, and the place
looked deserted. Why not? Who could eat flowers? But I
knocked on the metal grating anyway, in our old code: *tumbelah, tumbelah, tumbelah laika . . .*

The grating rolled up a foot, and Eva's face peeked out from
beneath. The plate to which the padlock was attached slid up
with the grating, detached from the wall. Eva reached out and

yanked me under the bottom of the grate and into the darkened store.

Blue Eyes was nowhere in evidence. Eva herself was as well dressed and as pretty as ever, as if she were unaware we met in the dingy shadows of a defunct florist shop. Instead of flowers, the place was now packed to the rafters with crates of guns, ski boots, and bullets—evidently the Zionists had taken her warnings to heart.

Eva struck a long wooden match and lit a gas lamp, and then lowered the flame as low as she could. To a casual observer she looked more beautiful than Marlene Dietrich, but to me . . . anyone who loved her could see the depths of Eva's trouble.

"Did you get the Book?" she asked, without bothering to say hello. Her fingers played nervously over the edge of the big wooden matchbox.

She caught me staring, and she put the matchbox on the brass cash register with a great show of restrained dignity.

I couldn't stand the silence for another minute. "Hitler has the Book."

The calmness in my voice finally cracked her reserved façade. "So why are you smiling? Have you completely lost your mind, Magdalena!"

My smile widened, and for once I let the tears fall freely, smoothing over my cheekbones, burning my lips where I tasted salt. "But I've always been crazy, silly goose. How do you think I've stayed alive and in rumballs for so long? It's a crazy world we're living in."

Eva exhaled loudly, as if she'd been holding her breath since before I'd arrived. "Ah. If crazy was royalty, you, my dear little star, would be the queen."

"Forget crazy. Even if we are doomed, we still have to fight. Win or lose."

She winked at me, but in the shadows Eva seemed more frightened than unflappable. "You know, sometimes the best way to win is to run away as fast as you can, save the fight for another day. Zanzibar still sounds pretty good."

Bless her, Eva made me laugh even now. "Nowhere for us to run, my darling. Not even Zanzibar."

The smile faded from her lips. "Palestine. We are getting at least the children of Budapest out, any way we can. Britain has blockaded the coasts, but as always, a smile and some hard cash can work magic. And Knox, of all people, is supplying us with money and connections." But she wasn't smiling; for once, Eva was dead serious.

"Don't despair. I swore I'd see you and Gisele through, and I haven't broken my vow yet. But we still have a long way to go."

Eva started pacing, ten steps one way, ten steps back. "Give me something I can use. You were always so good with gossip . . ."

"That's because I make everything up."

"Of course, we make everything up, every day we're alive. It's the only way anything gets done in this mad world."

I laughed again, and hugged her, hard. Fate may drive our steps in a certain direction, but we decide whether to shuffle or to dance as we go. Though my Raziel was gone, at least I hadn't lost Eva to death's dominion as I had once feared.

I reached for her hand, smiled when I found the little red-gold ring I'd given her still on her thumb. "Do you remember?" I half whispered into the curve of her neck, wiggling the ring. "Being good never will get you anywhere but dead."

Eva half cried, half laughed, and I pulled her even closer. I whispered into her ear: these were things I did not want the Zionists to know, and Eva would keep my secret if I asked her to. "Hitler has the Book, yes, but I'm too crazy to just give up now. I will summon a demonic army."

She tensed in my arms, and then hugged me even harder. "You just answered my fervent prayer. Hallelujah, Angel Magduska."

My eyes prickled with tears; nobody had ever called me an angel before. When I stayed silent, she poked me in the ribs, dug in until both of us laughed and laughed, peals of hard mirth that still ring in my ears.

"You'll never guess who bought us all these goodies," Eva said as she wiped at her eyes. "I am sitting on a pirate's treasure of explosives."

"The Hashomer, the Young Guard, right? Or wait, is it Knox?"

"No. You aren't going to believe it. Bathory's carpet merchants! They are convinced that if Poland somehow holds out, they can break away from Stalin. So they want to help us fight. In three days."

We looked at each other for a long minute in the sudden silence. "I have to get to the leader of the Hashomer, Eva. It's not just the Azeris who need us to hang on in Poland. If we can turn Hitler back, maybe Gisele's prophecy can be averted even now."

Eva looked and looked at me, as if she saw a ghost in her arms. "You feel solid as wood, little star, but you seem so far away, another galaxy."

"No, my darling, I'm here with you." I tried to smile, to hide my grief. But I longed for Raziel, ached to know where he had gone to from this world.

But I could not speak of it. Instead, chin up. "We've got to keep our spirits high."

She shrugged. "I'm all out of jokes, downright grim I am. I'll talk to my group leader and see if you could meet with the Budapest chief before we are deployed. But, Magda, I'm just a courier, a nobody. It's the Zionist faithful who run the show."

I shrugged back in reply. "Or so they think. You'd be amazed who really runs the world, my darling. Amazed."

I put my leather satchel on the floor and took out a white paper bag filled with almond horns. "From Gisele. She said you have to keep your dimples up."

That finally made Eva smile, for real this time. "Bless you, Magduska! If you need a girl without a drop of magic, I'll be here, fighting, win or lose . . ."

Ah, Eva. She was braver than the rest of us put together, magic or no magic. I kissed her cheeks, made sure she at least tasted the cookies Gisele had sent. And at the threshold, I turned and said in farewell, "Be strong, Evuska. Be strong."

I left her there, surrounded by tools of war. But not alone, never alone. Celestials are not the only angels; when the messengers of heaven must leave us, we can be angels to one another.

✳ 32 ✳

The Kozma Street Cemetery was the final resting place of ballerinas, engineers, and famous thieves. Swimmers and potentates, unbelievers and rabbis, their only commonality their Jewishness, their final neighborhood the ultimate ghetto. Tired-looking gray clouds drifted across the face of the flat summer sky, so pale blue it looked almost white.

The cinder path through the cemetery wound long and low through a row of weeping willows. All around me echoed the souls of my predecessors, brushing past me in silent benediction.

My parents' graves lay side by side, near the grave of the wonder rabbi Oppenheimer. The rabbi's gravestone was inundated with a veritable avalanche of pebbles left by supplicants, seekers, and sincere mourners; my parents' graves looked windblown and wild, and the long grass covered over their names on the single headstone.

I worked no magic; I swear it. I kneeled at my mother's grave, pressed my hands against the cool ashy marble of her marker, and I silently prayed for her and for myself. My cheek rested against the scratchy edge of the stone, and after my prayer was done, I dozed.

And in my mind's eye, my mother appeared, her soul mended and at peace, her fingers interlaced with my father's fingers. I could not see my father's face, but his loving presence brought the worn remnants of my own soul back to life.

"Go in peace, daughter," Mama said. "I lift my curse from you. Take your soul back, go back to life. Go, go."

I murmured my thanks, wept silent tears both in my dream and over my living face. And I watched as the Witch of Ein Dor rose up behind them, a shielding presence, not a curse.

I would have traded places with my mother, if she wanted to return and if it were possible. But the world does not work in this way, one life traded for another, except in moments of grace granted by the Almighty Himself.

My questions were all for my ancient grandmama, the Witch of Ein Dor. "Why didn't you come back when you could, at your will?"

"Simple, little star. We need to make room for you."

I looked over her shoulder. No guardian angel stood over the Witch of Ein Dor to protect her. No sheltering wings to canopy my brave family matriarch in glory: she no longer needed any protection.

The gift was too big. "I don't know if I can do what I am supposed to do."

The Witch of Ein Dor shrugged her bony shoulders. "Do what is right, and everything else will fall into place. The afterworld is a busy place. It is now your time for life, and we go to our place in the plan of the world. Never doubt that God made you, little star. You have the right to live, to sin. To love."

"But your curse?"

She laughed and shook her head. The three of them faded away, an ordinary dream, and they left me weeping in the silence of an August afternoon in Budapest.

When I awoke, the feeling had returned to the tips of my fingers, I could smell the peppery chrysanthemums planted in beds all along the pathway, and the mossy grass underneath the weeping willows.

I was alive. Time to leave my beloved parents to their peace, and time to return to Budapest, still fighting for her life. But words, magic itself, had failed me.

I knelt by my parents' headstone, my forehead resting against the cool marble. Loving fingers brushed against my shoulders, warm, living fingers, and I closed my eyes against their kindness. But I wiped my eyes, smoothed back my hair, and rose to face the gentle soul who stood with me in my grief. I hoped it was Gisele, suspected it was Eva.

But I was wrong. It was Raziel. He wore a charcoal gray suit and smart fedora, and he stood silent in the August heat.

I held my breath, unwilling to shatter the illusion with tears. Our eyes met, his hands reached for mine, and only after he drew me close did the realization hit me: his wings were gone. Folded out of sight, rendered invisible, or taken away.

Did I still dream? "My God, it's you," I whispered.

"Yes, I'm back. To stay, this time."

My heart fluttered like a little bird looking to escape, to fly free. It was true. Raziel lived. "You are an angel no more."

He smiled, inclined his head to look down at me. "No. But I am still in. And ready to fight."

I tilted my head back to look into his whiskey brown eyes, squinting into the sunlight, my mind full of doubt—

And Raziel's lips closed slowly over mine, answering all of my questions with a single, sublime, soul-shattering kiss.

✳ 33 ✳

August 30, 1939
Dohány Street, Budapest

And now it's war. I told Eva the truth—Hitler will indeed invade Poland on September 1, 1939. The day before, a small group of SS soldiers, disguised in Polish uniforms, will cross the border from Poland into Germany and seize the Gleiwitz radio station, in a false demonstration of Polish anti-German aggression. To add a note of realism to the counterfeit attack, the soldiers will execute a Polish sympathizer, dress him in the uniform of the provocateurs, and leave his body, riddled with bullet holes, at the station.

Thus the Nazis will ignite the war with lies. Hitler is the king of lies, and he wants to convince the world he was provoked to act, you see. A good Führer, he guards the honor and dignity of the Reich, protects her from unbearable provocation. Or so he likes the world to believe.

Asmodel told me all of this, knowing it was too late for me

to act upon his information and try again to change the war's destiny. Hitler met with his generals last week and said, "I shall give a propaganda reason for starting the war, whether it is plausible or not. The victor will not be asked whether he told the truth."

So it will be that the truth will die on September first. Hitler's host will roll into Poland, with tanks, his human armies, and with the power of *The Book of Raziel* investing the killers of the Reich with an infernal power.

But Hitler will not invade unopposed. The Polish Army, duly forewarned by the Young Guards, will be waiting, noble cavalrymen and infantry standing to fight against artillery and planes. Zionist guerillas will join them, as will an army of the demons and the dead.

And I? I will come from out of the shadows, and I will show no mercy when I appear. A girl with a talent will use it, win or lose, damned or saved. And if I die along with the truth, I will refuse to stay dead for long.

Every epoch has its magic, tales of the old country, tales of triumph and dream. *The Book of Raziel* was first offered in solace and passed from one loving soul to another when the world was young. Now the Book and all the world hover at the edge of destruction, and the truth of my tale is a fragile amulet indeed. Can anyone avert what is ordained? We know that we must: at least it will be said that we fought to stop it.

Now I ask you on the eve of war, because neither my story nor your own is fully told, because these are the questions that matter, hidden within the shadow of death:

Who do you love?
Do you seek the darkness or the light?

LADY LAZARUS by Michele Lang
BOOK CLUB QUESTIONS

1. How do places such as Budapest, Amsterdam, and Paris function as characters in *Lady Lazarus*? Do these settings change over the course of the story? How and why?

2. *Lady Lazarus* is a fantasy based on historical events. How would the world be different today if World War II had started at some point later than September 1939, or if Hitler had been stopped before the war ever broke out?

3. Does the presence of celestial and demonic creatures in *Lady Lazarus* imply that an Almighty being does exist in the world of *Lady Lazarus* and is involved in the world's affairs?

4. Can magic be a metaphor, and if so, for what—creativity, connection with a Creator, a destructive exercise of human will? How does magic interact with the reality of death in the world of *Lady Lazarus*?

5. Raziel is safe within his role as a divine messenger. Why does he struggle with his traditional role and his safety in the celestial realm, and how does he transcend that role?

6. Do you think the story of *Lady Lazarus* could have been told in any other historical setting? Why or why not? What lessons of 1939 are relevant to the world of today?

7. Do you think that Magda will survive the war? Gisele? Raziel? Why or why not?

ABOUT THE AUTHOR

Lady Lazarus is Michele Lang's first historical urban fantasy novel. Like her protagonist, she is of Hungarian-Jewish ancestry. Lang is the author of the science-fiction novel *Netherwood*. She and her family currently reside on the North Shore of Long Island, New York.